"You are all und... ...yne...

"you have not been out in this weather?"

"Aye," he murmured.

"But why?"

"To find a measure of peace."

Sorrow knifed through her, far more painful than what her body had just experienced. "Oh, Kayne," she murmured sadly, stroking strands of wet hair from his face. "'Tis all my fault. I am so deeply ashamed and sorry."

He shook his head. "You are not the one to blame, Sofia. It is my own sickness that makes me ill within. You are my only refuge from the misery of it. I need you, Sofia." Whispering the words this time, he said again, "I need you. But if you tell me to leave, I will go at once. Indeed, I should go. I have no right to ask anything of you."

Sofia swallowed heavily. "I want you to stay, Kayne. But I am afraid…!"

The Stolen Bride
Harlequin Historical #535—November 2000

DON'T MISS THESE OTHER
TITLES AVAILABLE NOW:

#536 SILK AND STEEL
Theresa Michaels

#537 THE LAW AND MISS HARDISSON
Lynna Banning

#538 MONTANA MAN
Jillian Hart

The Stolen Bride

Susan Spencer Paul

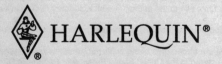

HARLEQUIN®

TORONTO • NEW YORK • LONDON
AMSTERDAM • PARIS • SYDNEY • HAMBURG
STOCKHOLM • ATHENS • TOKYO • MILAN • MADRID
PRAGUE • WARSAW • BUDAPEST • AUCKLAND

ISBN 0-373-29135-3

THE STOLEN BRIDE

Visit us at www.eHarlequin.com

Printed in U.S.A.

Available from Harlequin Historicals and
SUSAN SPENCER PAUL

Please address questions and book requests to:
Harlequin Reader Service
U.S.: 3010 Walden Ave., P.O. Box 1325, Buffalo, NY 14269
Canadian: P.O. Box 609, Fort Erie, Ont. L2A 5X3

To my beautiful daughter, Carolyn,
who came up with the title for this book,
and who fills each day of my life with joy.

Chapter One

"Nay, Father, I tell you I will have none of him. And I'll not see him. Sir Griel must suffer the disappointment, I fear."

With this, Sofia returned her attention to the needlework in her lap. She was perfectly calm.

Her father, however, stood in his place near the door, sweating profusely and wringing his hands.

"Sofia, you must come and speak with him," Sir Malcolm pleaded. "You know what it means to overset Sir Griel. I beg you, daughter, only speak to him, show him a measure of sweetness, such as you alone can do. That will be enough to sate him for a time."

Sofia was unmoved by this.

"Sir Griel is a violent, evil, untoward man, Father, and I've no wish to sate him in any way. What I desire is that he leave us in peace, for I vow I shall never wed him." The thought made her visibly shudder. "Nothing could induce me to it."

"God's mercy," her father said, shaking his head. "He's brought twelve men. *Twelve,* Sofia, and all fully armed. They're standing with him now in the great room below, awaiting your arrival. If you don't go to him, he'll wreak havoc. I know he will.''

''He only means to intimidate you, Father,'' she said soothingly. ''If you refuse to be thus cowed, he'll leave you be, in time.''

''Nay, he'll not leave at all, until you've come to speak to him,'' her father insisted. ''He has said so, and I've no desire to put such a challenge to the test.''

Sofia sighed loudly.

''Sofia, please,'' Sir Malcolm begged.

She set her needlework aside and stood.

''Very well.''

''There,'' he said with relief. ''That's a good daughter you are, Sofia. A very good daughter. Make certain to tell Sir Griel that—''

''I shall bid him to the devil, my lord,'' she stated, striding out of the room, ''as I do every time I see him.''

Sir Griel Wallace was a dark, ominous man, short but muscular, with hair, beard and eyes as black as coal. He was standing near the large hearth in the great room as Sofia descended the stairs, and turned to watch with open appreciation as she approached. Just as her father had said, a dozen of Sir Griel's fighting men were with him, standing on either side of the room, looking very much as if they had prepared for a battle.

Sofia could scarce blame her father for being so distressed at the sight of them. Sir Griel had clearly brought them with the intent of intimidating the entire household—herself included. The last time he'd come to visit her, she'd treated him to a rigidly polite manner of behavior which forced a certain formality from him in turn, but she'd found it impossible not to scoff at his few crude attempts at lovemaking. His pride had not withstood such a rebuff, no mat-

ter how intelligently or elegantly given, and he'd left Ahlgren Manor red with anger.

With this visit, he clearly meant to make himself better
understood, if not through sweet speeches, then through a
show of force.

As Sofia moved across the room, Sir Griel gave a signal,
causing all his men to straighten to attention. Sofia lifted
her chin and ignored them.

"Mistress Sofia," Sir Griel said. "Your beauty, as always, is a welcome sight. I pray I have not come at an
unseasonable time?"

He held a hairy, burly hand out, palm open, in what was
obviously meant to be a grand gesture. Sofia set her teeth
and strove to appear gracious as she laid her own in it. He
was abnormally hairy, and was covered down to his fingertips with thick black hair which made him look far more
like a heavily furred animal than a man. The idea of having
to receive such a man's intimate caresses made Sofia feel
exceedingly ill. Just touching him now caused her stomach
to churn nauseatingly.

"My lord, Sir Griel," she said in proper reply, making
a curtsey and deftly sliding her hand free all in one smooth
movement, "I am sorry to say that you have. I am used to
making my visit to the village at this time of day, and was
nearly ready to depart."

He made a bow. "Forgive me, mistress. I was not aware
that you kept such steady habits. I would be greatly honored
if you would allow me to accompany you throughout the
village as you pursue your duties."

"You are kind," Sofia said with a thin smile, "but I
require no such escort. I am very happy to go with but my
maid and a few menservants to fetch and carry, and you
are far too busy a lord to waste such time upon anything

so foolish. And this could not be your purpose in honoring us with your presence, I think.''

"Nay, 'twas not," he admitted, frowning. "I had thought to spend some time in your company, however, and so I told your father. I believe you realize my purpose."

Sofia gazed at him, all innocence. "Do I, my lord?"

His already dark face darkened even more, and his brow furrowed. "If not, I shall tell you plainly. I mean to court you, Mistress Sofia, and to that purpose I have come and will continue to do so until you agree to be my wife."

Sofia regarded him steadily, taking in his fine, rich manner of dress, his strong and muscular body, his intensity of expression and temper. She supposed that there were many women who would be grateful to become the wife of Sir Griel Wallace. He was titled and well favored by the king's regents. His estate, Maltane, was among the finest in Sussex, and he was powerful both in the strength of the small army of knights and soldiers he kept at his castle and the enormity of his wealth.

But she could not rejoice at the idea of such a match. Sir Griel was a cruel man. There was not the least bit of sway or softness in him, and he must ever have his way or no way at all. She'd witnessed his implacable nature first-hand in his dealings with the merchants and craftsmen in the village, all of whom lived in dread of Sir Griel's random visits. Once he'd whipped a villager simply because the man had walked in front of his horse, and Sofia had heard rumors of far worse beatings that were regularly dealt out to any of his castle servants who happened to displease him.

Standing firm against such a man was not so easy a matter as Sofia wished it might be. Everyone in and around the village of Wirth was afraid of Sir Griel, most especially her father. And she knew very well that if he'd determined to have her for his wife, he wouldn't take her refusal easily.

But Sofia would not be cowed by the man, though she found him both fearsome and physically repulsive.

"I believe I understand your meaning, my lord," she said calmly. "You do me great honor. I am perfectly aware of how much so, and thank you for such kind consideration. However, I fear that you would do better to look elsewhere for a bride. I do not intend to marry."

Sir Griel's eyes widened. "Not marry?" he repeated. "Mistress Sofia Ahlgren not marry? 'Tis an impossibility, I vow. 'Twould be a grave sin to let such beauty as you possess go without its proper tribute, my lady. But, nay," he said, laughing now, "you mean to tease me. I nearly took your word for truth. What a clever female you are, mistress. And how very much," he added with a more meaningful look, "I shall enjoy taming you."

Sofia drew herself up full height—almost as tall as he was—and looked at him directly.

"My lord," she said clearly and distinctly, "pray let us have an understanding. I will not be your wife, and you would do well to look elsewhere. This is my final word on the matter, and now, I beg that you will take your men and leave. Good day to you."

She turned to walk away from him, but felt his steely hand close over her shoulder, daring to fall where her skin was bare above the neckline of her surcoat, roughly pulling her back. His face, she saw as he jerked her about, was taut with anger.

"We will indeed have an understanding, Mistress Sofia, and one that you will accept. I *will* have you for my wife. You, and no other woman."

Sofia was trembling horribly, and knew he could feel it, but with every bit of strength she possessed she held his deadly gaze. "You cannot force me to it, my lord, and you will not. My father will not accept your suit, and even if you should manage to terrify him to such cowardice, I would petition the crown to grant me the freedom of my own authority. In but four months I will attain the age of twenty, and inherit all that comes to me through my mother's will.''

''Before that day comes,'' he vowed, ''you will be Lady Wallace, and all that you inherit dowered to whatever children you give me.''

Sofia struggled to be free, but Sir Griel cruelly dug his nails into her bare flesh to keep her captive, drawing long, deep gashes of blood along her skin as Sofia panicked and wrenched away.

Gasping, she reached up a hand to touch the raw, stinging wounds, and gaped at him in shock. Sir Griel looked at the blood he'd drawn with a satisfied smile, and nodded.

''My first mark upon you, Sofia. The first of many, if you continue to displease me.''

Blood seeped through Sofia's fingers, trickling across the back of her hand and downward in streams to seep into the cloth of her surcoat. She was nearly too shocked to speak, but uttered, ''Nay.''

He reached out again, this time to grasp her chin with tight, punishing fingers.

''Aye, mistress.'' His voice was low and as dark as he was. ''But you've time to learn. Four months' time. Before the day that your twentieth year arrives, you'll beg me to take you as wife. On your knees, yet. Aye, I shall have the satisfaction of seeing you there, to repay the insult you've given me not only on this day, but so many others.''

''No,'' she murmured, shutting her eyes, striving to turn out of his grasp. *''No.''*

''And once you're my wife,'' he went on, ''you will learn to please me very, very well. 'Tis a promise I give you, Sofia. A promise—and I do not make such as those lightly, as you will discover. Heed me well, mistress,'' he warned, leaning very close. His strong finger squeezed the fine bones of her chin, bringing tears to Sofia's eyes. "Heed me well," he repeated more softly, then released her at last.

Sofia reeled back with relief.

Sir Griel held his hand out, his black eyes snapping with command.

"Give me your hand, Sofia."

She was too frightened now to refuse, and instinctively held out the one that did not yet clutch at her bleeding wounds.

He shook his head once. "Nay, the other. Give it."

She did as he said, and placed her bloodied hand in his own. He smiled down at it and then lifted it to his lips, seeming to relish kissing her trembling fingers through the blood that covered them. Afterward, he licked his lips of the droplets that remained. Sofia's stomach lurched at the sight. Free of his touch, she backed away and stared at him with horror. She had thought him merely violent and cruel, but now she knew him for a madman.

Sir Griel made a slight bow.

"I will bid you good day, Mistress Sofia, and pray to visit with you again soon, with a far happier greeting."

Sofia was painfully aware of the dozen men who had stood silently throughout their lord's brutal attack. They must all of them be knights, and yet not a one of them had stepped forward to keep a lady from injury. Such was the measure of power that Sir Griel held over them.

Her shoulder burned as with fire, and her surcoat was bloodied. Sofia was ashamed to stand before such an assembly of strangers—with none of her own people, not even a servant to give her company—so completely vanquished. She strove to regain as much dignity as she could by drawing herself up, lifting her hand to cover her wounds once more, and saying, coldly, "Good day, my lord."

He walked out of Ahlgren Manor with his men at his heels, and Sofia sank into a chair near the fire, yet holding her hand against her shoulder. Slowly, after the sound of Sir Griel's many horses faded away, the servants began to come into the room. They showed an immediate concern for their lady's bloody wounds, but she turned them away, and accepted no aid, not even from her father, who entered the great room last of all.

"You *must* accept him, Sofia," he said, desperation in his tone. "He'll kill us all—aye, even you—if he does not get his way. Here, daughter, let me send for the leech to bind your wounds. You cannot go about untended."

Sofia shook her head and rose from her chair.

"Nay, Father. I'll tend it myself, as I have tended many such small hurts before. Have no fear. None of the villagers will know what has happened here, if all remain loyal in their silence." She cast her gaze over the servants, who nodded their agreement.

"But, Sofia," Sir Malcolm protested, "you cannot go into the village today. You must rest and recover, and think of what you will say when Sir Griel visits us next, for you know it will be soon."

"There is too much to tend," Sofia told him stonily, weary and stunned by all that had occurred. "None of it can be put off. I will change my clothes and go, and rest after. As to Sir Griel," she said as she moved slowly toward the stairs, "I believe he means to give me a measure of time to think upon the folly and danger of refusing him yet again—and you may be assured, Father, that I will use that time wisely, in finding the way to avoid him forevermore."

Chapter Two

"There," said Anne the baker's wife to the women who were gathered near the warmth of her husband's great ovens. "He's coming, just as I said he would. Every day, he comes. At noon, and never later."

The women, as one, leaned to peer out of the baker's windows at the tall figure walking through the village, drawing ever nearer. Kayne the Unknown was indeed a man worth looking at, and so they all agreed, young and old alike. He was surely the handsomest man ever to set foot in the village of Wirth, as well as the strangest and quietest.

He'd arrived one afternoon a year ago, a stunning figure riding atop a large, black destrier such as only a knight of the realm might possess, tall and powerfully built with hair so blond it was almost white. All the people had come out of their doors to stare at him, wondering how such a man had come to visit their small village. He had gone straight to the abode of their only blacksmith and, upon learning that Old Reed wished to quit his work, bought his home and smithy for so great an amount of money that all who'd heard of it had been amazed. On such a fortune, Old Reed would be well able to spend the remainder of his days in the finest luxury.

But then Kayne the Unknown had done something even more surprising. He had given Old Reed his home and smithy back, freely, in exchange for the promise that the older man would remain in Wirth and help the newcomer set up his own shop, and on those occasions where his skill might prove lacking, impart whatever knowledge might be required.

He'd left Wirth for some few days following that, and those who had applied to Old Reed for every detail had been gravely disappointed. The old man smiled and nodded, but said nothing, save to say that the stranger's name was Kayne, and that he'd refused to give any other. Shortly after he'd gone, rumors began to fly that the stranger had bought the finest piece of land to be had in Wirth, three full acres that Sir Malcolm Ahlgren had always refused to part with—until now, when enough money had been offered. But where would a mere blacksmith find such money? And why, having it, would he continue to labor at such a trade?

Long before his return the villagers had begun to call him Kayne the Unknown, and to whisper that he wasn't quite right and therefore not to be trusted. Only a madman—or worse—would labor when he had no cause to, or spend his money in a village so poor and lacking as Wirth. Nay, something was far wrong with Kayne the Unknown. He'd assuredly bring evil and ill-doing to Wirth with his strange ways, and it was decided among the villagers that those of them who were true and Godly folk would stay far clear of such a man.

Kayne the Unknown had returned with several men—carpenters and masons—and built the finest dwelling that anyone in the village had ever seen, apart from Sir Ahlgren's manor home. It had wooden floors instead of plain earth, and real glass windows like those to be had in the richest castles in England, and a stairway leading to the upper floor, rather than a ladder. Next to the dwelling a large barn had been built, part of it to stable horses, and part to hold a new, and very fine, smithy.

He lived with Old Reed while all was being built, but he made no attempt to introduce himself to the village, or anyone in it. When he went to buy his bread and eggs and other goods, he spoke quietly and briefly, giving but the least return to any greeting or question, and was on his way again before one could do more than attempt the simplest exchange of courtesies.

Two months after he'd first ridden into Wirth, Kayne the Unknown had opened his gate for custom, and on the very same day Old Reed shut his. But no one in the village took their smithing needs to the newcomer, not for many weeks, preferring instead to make the journey to nearby Wellsby to make use of the blacksmith there.

But one night, five months and more after Kayne the Unknown's arrival, a fire had started in Harold Avendale's dwelling, and become so quickly fierce that no one dared rush in to save the family—no one, save Kayne the Unknown. He'd burst the door wide with a mighty thrust of his powerful body and gone charging in past the smoke and heat to bring out not only Harold and his wife and children, but even a table and three chairs that had not yet caught fire. And he'd remained, after all this, his blond hair singed nearly black and his face and hands angrily red with many burns, and helped to douse the cottage with water from the village well.

When it had all been over, the damage great but enough left to rebuild, Harold had sought to give Kayne the Unknown his thanks—though it would be impossible to impart enough gratitude for such gifts as the lives of his family. But Kayne the Unknown had disappeared, and could not be found.

For many days afterward, the gate to his smithy had remained shut, and he'd made no visits to the village. Harold and his wife had taken him two loaves of bread and a pail of fresh milk one morn, not daring to enter his dwelling, but leaving the offerings of gratitude at his door. Otherwise, the only person who'd had the courage to visit Kayne the Unknown had been their own good lady, Sir Malcolm's daughter, Mistress Sofia, who had been seen entering his dwelling each morning and evening following the fire, always with her maid and always with a basket of her medicinal treatments. She had looked very grave the first two days, both coming and going, but by the third day had regained her usual calm manner. By the fourth day, she had declared herself—when asked about Kayne the Unknown's progress—well pleased.

One month later, Kayne the Unknown had opened his gate again, and the villagers had come, one by one, to seek his services. Before the noon hour there had been a line ten deep until Kayne the Unknown, his burnt hair cut short by Mistress Sofia and one of his hands yet bandaged, had at last asked those remaining to return the following week, for he had more than enough to keep him busy until then.

His bravery in the fire had not been enough to make Kayne the Unknown completely acceptable to the village, but it had been sufficient to make him acceptable as their blacksmith. And a grand blacksmith he was, at that, as able as Old Reed had been, if not moreso. If Kayne the Unknown was yet content to keep his own company and remain quiet and apart, no one complained of it so much anymore.

But they did continue to whisper. And with good reason,

for he was a man possessed of strange habits, who went out riding late at night on his great destrier, its hooves making a loud, eerie sound as he rode through the village in the dark chill of both night and early morning.

No one in Wirth, save Mistress Sofia and her maid, had been allowed into Kayne the Unknown's dwelling, but there were rumors that he had many rare and extraordinary possessions. A locked chest filled with a treasure of precious jewels, and books—which surely he must be able to read, if he had them—and many strange weapons which no mortal man had ever before seen or been known to use.

And some of the villagers vowed that they had seen Kayne the Unknown meeting with frightening strangers during his nighttime wanderings. Men dressed in armor, on horseback, like ghostly warriors come out of battle.

Aye, there was much that was odd and fearsome about Kayne the Unknown, and the villagers of Wirth spent a great deal of time trying to discover all there was to know of him. Especially the women, who could scarce understand why a man so handsome and moneyed should not also have a wife. There was many a pleasing maiden in the village, and the mother of each would have happily seen her daughter wed to Kayne the Unknown—aye, despite his strange and quiet ways.

"Now, watch," Anne said, nodding out the window. "He'll stop and buy eggs from Mistress Jenna. Only half a dozen or so. Always wants them fresh, he does, every day."

"He needs laying hens, so he does," one of the women said. "A wife would fetch him fresh eggs every morn, and see that his bread was baked."

"Aye," said another. "A man like that needs a good wife to care for him."

"Ah, look. He's coming," Anne said. "Hush, all."

Having carefully arranged his recently purchased eggs in the basket he carried, Kayne the Unknown was indeed at last approaching the bakery. His white-blond hair had regained it's length after the fire, and though his face still bore some few faint scars from his burns, these only made his handsome, finely boned features more notable. He was a tall, muscular man, with a powerful stride and solemn manner. His blue eyes seldom sparked with emotion; his shapely mouth seldom smiled. His manner, though ever respectful and polite, was constantly reserved and cool. In all, it would have been hard to find a more attractive or less attainable man than Kayne the Unknown.

Anne hurried to greet him at the bakery's long, open window, where he stood as the lone customer.

"Have you my bread ready, Mistress Anne?"

"Aye, Master Kayne." She handed him the two fine loaves that she'd only just set aside. "Out of the oven but half an hour past, and still warm." He took them, set them in his basket, and handed Mistress Anne two coins.

It was the same exchange as occurred each day, in the same manner, with the same words and actions. Giving a nod of his head, Kayne the Unknown turned and continued his course through the village, on his way back to his own dwelling, leaving the women in the bakery gazing out the window after him.

Kayne recognized at once the two servants who were standing outside his smithy gate, and his heart reacted accordingly, giving an almost painful thump. His step faltered, and he nearly came to a halt, but at the last moment he made his feet continue their steady course.

Mistress Sofia's maid and one of the young menservants from Ahlgren Manor were far too interested in their private conversation to take much note of Kayne. He'd almost walked past them and into his smithy before the maid curt-seyed and said, "Mistress Sofia is waiting inside for you, Master Kayne."

"Very well," he murmured, and pushed his gate wide to walk through, out of the heat of the summer sun.

It was blessedly cool and shaded inside the large build-ing, save for the far corner where the forge glowed red with its constant fire. Mistress Sofia Ahlgren was sitting on a long bench at the opposite end, in the coolest, darkest area where the horses were stabled. She seemed not to have heard him either opening or closing the gate, for her head was lowered and she made no movement to raise it in greet-ing. Indeed, she made no movement at all, but sat very still, head bowed, hands clutched together in her lap, almost as if she were at prayer.

Kayne made no special attempt to be silent as he neared her, and his steed, Tristan, whinnied in loud welcome at his approach. She surely knew that he was there, yet she gave no sign of it. He set his basket aside on a worktable and stopped at Tristan's stall to scratch the horse's soft black nose, not far from where Mistress Sofia sat. He waited for her to look up and acknowledge him, but she remained silent and still, and Kayne stayed where he was, gazing down at her forlorn figure.

He remembered the first few times he'd seen the lady of Wirth, just after he'd come to the village, going about each afternoon in pursuit of her daily chores. He had readily admired her beauty—as surely any man would—but had given little thought to her, otherwise. He'd known many beautiful women in his day, and had long since learned that they were best kept at a distance. Apart from that, he knew too well the condition of his soul, and of his heart, that they could no longer be touched as when he'd been a youth. War and death had put them beyond reach.

And, yet, Sofia Ahlgren had touched him in a singular way. Kayne wasn't quite certain just how it had come about, but the knowledge unsettled him no small measure. She had nursed him tenderly—and mercilessly—after he'd been wounded by the fire at Harold Avendale's cottage. He had come awake in an agony of pain to find her beside him, insistent upon caring for him regardless how firmly he told her to go away and leave him in peace. She'd ignored him completely and done exactly as she pleased, bathing his wounds and covering them with a soothing balm that relieved him greatly, and then forcing a foul tasting potion down his throat which made him sleep.

It had been much the same on the following days, and Kayne had finally put aside both modesty and his intense desire for privacy to let her care for him. The fact that Mistress Sofia had been so forthright about being in such intimate confine with a half-naked man, lying upon his own bed, made it somewhat easier for Kayne to accept the same. There had certainly been nothing unseemly in her care of him. She'd hardly even spoken to him, save to ask how he felt and to warn him of what she was about to do.

He'd begun to look forward to her twice daily visits while he was so ill. She was so very pleasing to the senses—especially when a man was wretched with life, physically, mentally and in every other way. Just to look at her…a woman of such quiet beauty…was soothing.

When he spoke, Kayne made his voice calm and even.

"You are deep in thought, Mistress Sofia. Is aught amiss?"

She lifted her head, gazing at him fully. He was struck anew by her pure beauty. Her features were perfectly formed, delicate, yet as strong as she herself was, and framed by golden-brown hair that danced and sparkled beneath sunlight. Her lips were full and inviting—surely the most sensual part of her face, though perhaps those deep-blue eyes, wide and tilting slightly upward, might arguably be her most alluring feature.

But now, Kayne saw, her delicate face was marred by a troubled frown, and her lovely blue eyes, shadowed by the small light of his shop, were further darkened by some unknown cause. Seeing this, Kayne paused, checking the concern that rose up within and the stronger need to take on whatever it was that held her in such obvious misery.

"No," she murmured. "I'm merely weary, I thank you, Master Kayne." She glanced to where a large iron pot sat on the ground near her feet. "I've brought this for repair. There's a crack near the bottom. I pray you'll be able to mend it."

Kayne moved forward and knelt to examine the great black pot, tilting it up on one side and running a callused finger along the crack she'd spoken of.

"Aye, it can be done." He glanced up at her. "Tomorrow, by midday? Will that be soon enough?"

"Yes. Thank you."

She spoke so sadly, gazing at him with an equal sorrow, almost as if she might begin weeping any moment.

"You should not have come out in this heat," he told her, rising to his feet. "I think you must be unwell, mistress."

"Nay, I am quite well, Master Kayne."

She set a hand to her shoulder, placing it carefully over the silk cloth loosely draped there, and slowly rose to her feet.

"I'll take no more of your time," she murmured.

"Allow me to convey you back to the manor house, milady," Kayne said. "I like not the paleness of your skin." He reached out to touch her arm. "'Tis easy to see that you are not well, even in this darkness."

She flinched at his touch, making a sound of distress, and stepped back.

"My lady?"

"'Tis naught." She pressed her hand against her shoulder as if to press a measure of pain away. "Forgive me, I must go."

Head down, she tried to walk past him. Kayne stood in front of her to bar her way.

"Be still," he commanded in a low tone.

He lifted a hand to pull away the delicate cloth draped over her shoulders, and she protested, "Nay, don't!" and put her own hand up to grab his.

"Mistress Sofia," Kayne said patiently, gently prying her fingers free. "I learned from you how to manage an unwilling patient."

She looked away as he plucked the square of cloth aside.

Kayne was silent as he gazed at the brutal red scratches that marred her lovely skin, fighting hard against the fury that rose up at whoever had dared to do this vile thing.

"These are fresh wounds," he said at last. "Perhaps made no more than an hour past. And you've not yet tended them."

She would not look at him, almost as if she were ashamed. "I've had no time," she whispered. He could hear the tears she'd refused to shed heavy in her voice.

"Nay, of course you have not," Kayne said more gently. "You, who tends all the ill in Wirth almost before they've begun to sneeze. Come."

He was careful to take hold of her other arm this time, but she resisted when he tried to pull her toward the nearby door that led from the smithy into his dwelling.

"I cannot," she said. "My servants are waiting...."

Kayne refused to let her go, and firmly, though carefully, guided her toward the door. "They will continue to wait, pleased as they are with each other's company. They'll not worry over their mistress for a few spare moments—mistress, I beg you will not struggle so. I mean you no harm, and I've no intention of giving you insult, unless I must."

She continued to struggle. Kayne bent and picked her up in his arms, easily carrying her past the door and into his home. He set her on the nearest chair he could find, next to a small table upon which an elegantly bound book of verses lay.

"If you run away," he told her as he stood, his expression severe, "I will follow you to the manor house and demand of your father who it was visited this vile act upon you. And then I will go and deal with the man." When she opened her mouth to protest, he added, "I give you my word of honor upon it, mistress, and I have never given it without keeping it."

She shut her mouth and glared at him. Kayne moved away to open a chest near his eating table. As he began to dig through it, Sofia said, "You've no right to keep me here."

"Just as you had no right to force me to your ministrations, when I had no want of them."

"Is this some manner of revenge, then?"

"Nay, not in the least." He lifted a small pewter jar from the chest before closing the lid. "'Tis merely thankful repayment. Like for like."

Rising to his feet, Kayne fetched a bowl and filled it with a small measure of water, then found a clean cloth and tossed it over his shoulder and returned to kneel before her.

"Sit still," he commanded. He leaned closer to examine her wounds more carefully, then lightly fingered her sleeve. "Pull this down a little."

"There's no need," she told him, frowning.

He gave a light shrug and began to wet the cloth in the

basin. "As it pleases you, mistress. The wounds will seep for a time, and your surcoat will be bloodied." Gently, he began to bathe the long, red marks. "You've already lost another surcoat to these grievous wounds, I would wager."

"Aye," she admitted unwillingly. "'Tis soaking now, to remove the stains." She sighed and began to unlace her gown. "Wait," she said. He obeyed, and she loosened the top of the garment enough to pull the sleeve partly down. Her cheeks heated with embarrassment as the cloth revealed her shoulder and arm.

Kayne took note of her distress and kept his gaze impersonal as he continued to press the cloth against her skin.

"'Tis worse along the back of your shoulder," he said. "Whoever did this possesses strong fingers. He dug deeply, intending to draw blood."

"How do you know?" she asked, searching his face. "Could it not have been accidentally done?"

He lifted the cloth away, looking her full in the eye. "Was it?"

She was silent, as if she would not answer, but at last replied, softly, "No."

Kayne expelled a slow breath, mastering himself. It was on his tongue to demand who the culprit was, but he knew that Sofia Ahlgren would never reveal such information. She was far too proud to speak of her private troubles. But Kayne had an idea who had committed the crime. Sir Griel Wallace, the lord of Maltane, had made his intentions to wed Mistress Sofia so clear that even a man who never heard the village gossip, as Kayne did not, would know of it. Kayne had met such men as Sir Griel before, and had no doubt that he was capable of every manner of cruelty, even to the woman he desired for a wife.

He reached to open the pewter box that he'd dug from out of the chest, dipped two fingers inside, and withdrew a small amount of a pale, white ointment. It smelled lightly of mint and honey.

"What is that?" Sofia asked as he began to apply it to the first angry stripe on her shoulder.

"Do you not recognize your own healing potion? You used it often enough on my burns, when I suffered them."

"Oh, of course. How foolish of me."

"You are quick to take care of all others, mistress, but not yourself. 'Tis clear that you stopped the bleeding and changed your bloodied clothes, but nothing more."

"I've already told you that I had no time. There was so much to take care of in the village. So many chores."

"Aye," Kayne agreed. "I understand very well. It is easier, in such times, to push every thought and remembrance aside. To be done with it and go on."

She lowered her head once more. "Yes, that is the way of it. I want never to think of it again. 'Tis foolish, I know, but it is my prayer, all the same, to forget entirely."

Kayne smoothed the ointment with a delicate touch over each separate wound, making certain to cover them well.

"You'll not forget. 'Tis an impossibility. But, in time, you may come to know that the fault was none of your own, and this will ease the memory."

"I do not know that I will ever be able to do so," she said. "I was headstrong, as I ever am. A grave sin and weakness, just as the priest has so often told me. I brought this affliction upon myself. That is the truth of it, and it cannot be forgiven."

At this, Kayne ceased what he was doing and set his other hand beneath her chin, lifting her eyes to meet his own.

"It is hardest, often, to accept and forgive our own frailties. But harder still to claim ourselves as prey to another. You are indeed strong of will, Mistress Sofia, but sin or not, such as that does not give another just cause to inflict harm upon you. In *this* matter, you are fully innocent."

He returned to his ministrations. Sofia remained silent.

When Kayne was done, he laid a thin, clean square of soft linen over the wounds, then carefully pulled Sofia's sleeve back up. When she began to lace the top of her surcoat, he rose and busied himself with putting everything away.

"Thank you, Master Kayne," she said, standing. "I cannot properly repay you for such kindness."

Kayne closed the lid on the chest and stood full height, turning to look at her.

"There is no need. It was small service in exchange for all you did for me following the fire at Harold Avendale's."

"Nay, 'twas far more than that." Lifting a hand, she gingerly touched the shoulder that he'd cared for, her beautiful face filling with indefinable emotion. He wondered if anyone had ever performed so simple a service for her before. Mistress Sofia was always the first one called upon when others were in need, always so strong and capable, even caring for matters that should have fallen upon her father's shoulders. But perhaps no one ever thought that she might welcome help once in a great while, too.

"Thank you," she said again, and abruptly turned and departed.

Kayne watched through the door that fell open upon her leaving as she made her way through the shadowed stable, her skirts swaying gently back and forth as she walked in her usual steadfast and upright way—the lady of Wirth again, and no one seeing her would ever notice that aught was amiss.

Chapter Three

A week passed before Sofia returned to the blacksmith's shop, striding alone through the village in the late morning with a basket swinging on her arm.

She had dressed with particular care, glad to see the long, red streaks that Sir Griel had placed upon her finally beginning to fade. But she no longer looked at them with the same measure of fear and rage that had possessed her after Sir Griel's unwelcome visit. Nay, not since that afternoon, when Kayne the Unknown had so kindly—and tenderly—cared for her, had Sofia looked upon the wounds in such a manner. Now, when she saw them, or ran her fingers across the healing scars, she did not even think of Sir Griel, but only of the blacksmith, his handsome face so close to her own as he bent over her shoulder, his warm breath caressing her skin, his white-blond hair falling forward over her brow…and, most of all, the sure, steady touch of his hands on her bare flesh.

Sofia knew herself too well to deny the truth of what she felt. She had begun to fall in love with Kayne the Unknown almost from the start, when she'd cared for him following the fire. She, who had seldom in her life even admired men—*any* of them—had found herself helplessly, and certainly unwillingly, drawn to the quiet, solemn, soft-spoken blacksmith. A man who was a mystery to one and all, who kept to himself and befriended no one, who was completely unsuitable in every way. Not that it mattered, for she knew that he felt nothing for her, nor for any of the village women who threw themselves so openly in his path. His kindness to her a week past had been only that—kindness, and perhaps a small measure of pity. He seemed to realize, when no one else did, how lonely and difficult her life in Wirth was.

It wasn't that Sofia was unhappy with the lot that had fallen her way, but she did often wish that her father was possessed of a larger measure of courage, and a greater desire to care for his vassals and the people of the village. Sir Griel, being the most powerful lord for many miles, should have been the one to take a hand in caring for the local citizens, but he cared for no one save himself, least of all his own people or any of the villagers.

Since the age of ten and three, Sofia had been the only one to worry for the people of Wirth. She had gone to the nuns in the abbey and learned all that they knew of medicines and healing, she'd spent countless days beneath the instruction of her father's steward, learning how the estate was managed, how the crops were grown, how the harvest was prepared and sent to market, and she'd relentlessly harried her tutors, all of whom she'd forced her father to hire, to teach her what a man must know in order to be a good lord. They'd not wanted to impart the knowledge to a mere female, thinking it far better that she should possess only those skills that a lady might require for the managing of a manor house, but Sofia had pressed until they'd all given way. She'd discovered, very quickly, what it was to fight and strive for every bit of knowledge she required.

But for all that she'd learned during the years that had

passed between her thirteenth and nineteenth birthdays, Sofia had never known what it was to have soft, womanly feelings...until she'd met Kayne the Unknown.

They were strange and distressing, these emotions he wrought, making Sofia forget who she was and what her responsibilities were, and causing her to dream of things which could never be. She struggled to set such foolishness aside, to harden herself, but it was not so simple a task. Her mind obeyed, but her heart...ah, it was traitorous in every respect, and refused to believe that the impossible could not be overcome.

Still, Sofia was careful not to give it too much free rein, for love, she had found, could be far more painful than sweet. Seeing Kayne, being close to him, was painful indeed. He felt nothing for her beyond the quiet friendship that had grown between them during the weeks that she had cared for him, and even if he had, a woman of her birth and stature would never be allowed to wed a common tradesman, even one so skilled and unusual as Kayne the Unknown.

Sofia heard the sharp, distinct sound of metal striking metal as she neared the smithy, and stopped at the half gate to peer into the darkness toward that part of the building which housed Kayne's working area. His tall, muscular figure was shadowed against the heat and light of the furnace as he bent over his anvil. Through the shadows, she could clearly see only his blond head moving up and down in rhythm with the hammer blows he dealt.

He was far too occupied to notice Sofia as she slowly and carefully opened the gate and stepped inside. Tristan, from his stall at the other end of the building, whinnied in greeting, and she cast a glance back at the magnificent black stallion. His presence was but the first of so many mysteries surrounding Kayne the Unknown. Only a knight or famous soldier would have need of such a horse, one trained in the ways of war or tournaments. Otherwise, such a beast was of little use—especially for a tradesman who would do far better to own a workhorse. Of course, Kayne the Unknown possessed other fine horses for different purposes, but a destrier like Tristan was expensive to feed and care for, and why a mere blacksmith should desire to spend good money on such an animal largely useless to him was beyond comprehension.

But that led to yet another mystery. Kayne was clearly possessed of greater wealth than he earned—or ever could have earned—at his trade. Sofia had seen for herself the manner of house he possessed, as fine as that of a minor nobleman with its wooden floors, Italian carpets and fireplaces with polished hearths. He had fine furniture, as well, which rivaled that of Ahlgren Manor. Hand-carved chairs and beautiful tables made of gleaming rosewood filled the dwelling's lower room, and in his bedchamber abovestairs French clothing chests and a beautiful, tall bed with an expensive feather mattress graced the room.

Most intriguing of all, Kayne the Unknown possessed books. A book of common verse, a Book of Psalms, and a beautifully illustrated Book of Hours. They were the kinds of books that any wealthy person might have—Sofia's own father possessed similar volumes. But far more amazing was what their presence revealed—that Kayne, a blacksmith, a mere tradesman, could read. And if he could read, then he had somehow been educated, and young men, even those learning a valuable trade, were seldom educated unless they came from a noble or wealthy family who could afford to hire tutors or buy their son a life in the Church. Boys apprenticed in a trade required only enough knowledge of reading and writing to sign their names. They would have little pleasure time for reading, and far less use for it. Kayne the Unknown, however, made great use of his rare skill. During the days while she'd cared for him, Sofia had often caught him reading, whiling away his confinement in bed.

She turned back to where Kayne yet labored over his anvil, his rhythm the same as it had been all the while since she'd first heard it, strong and steady. Hefting the basket she held a bit higher, Sofia made her way toward him.

Now that her eyes had become accustomed to the darkness of the stable, she could see that he was naked from the waist up, save for the heavy leather apron which hung from his neck and was loosely tied about his hips. It was much hotter on this side of the building. Intense heat emanated from the forge, fanning over Sofia like a hot wind as she drew nearer. Kayne was covered in sweat, his muscular chest and shoulders glistening with it and long strands of his blond hair sticking to his face and neck because of it.

He was a magnificent sight, so handsome and strong and fully masculine; a creature of power and beauty, just as his steed Tristan was, and impossible not to admire. Sofia remembered the days she'd spent tending him after the fire, of touching him and feeling the strength in the muscles that lay beneath his flesh. She had wanted so badly to run her hands over him for the sheer pleasure of it, but had refused to give way to such wanton, sinful desires. Kayne would have been repulsed by anything more than the most impersonal touch, and Sofia had already had a difficult time as it was in simply being allowed to tend the stubborn man.

As if sensing her approach, Kayne glanced up when Sofia was but a few steps away. The rhythm of his hammering came to an abrupt halt, hand midair, and he stared at her for a long, silent moment. Then, with a brief nod that acknowledged her presence, he returned to his work.

It didn't take long. A few more strokes with the great hammer and he was done. Straightening, Kayne lifted a partly formed ax-head from the anvil with a pair of tongs, examined it, then carefully placed it in a nearby tub of water. The water sizzled and steamed, and then fell still. Kayne put the tongs and his hammer aside and, without looking at Sofia, walked to a worktable nearby where another basin sat. Dipping his fingers in, he scooped up several handfuls of water and splashed his hair, face and neck, shaking his head until water flew in every direction and coursed in small rivers down his chest. He took up a towel and dried himself. Then, at last, he turned to Sofia.

"Mistress," he greeted in his usual solemn manner.

"Master Kayne." Sofia gave a slight nod in turn. "I hope I do not disturb you in too important a matter? I meant only to render my thanks for the kindness you showed me some days past."

He glanced at the basket on her arm.

"There is no need, just as I told you."

She smiled. "I realize you desire no measure of gratitude, but I wish to thank you even in this small way." She walked to the table and set the basket upon it, pulling away the cloth that covered the goods inside. "You see? 'Tis only a few sweet cakes and some tarts with pears and apples that our cook made yesterday. Nothing more sinister, I vow."

"And this?" He tapped one long finger against the lid of a small pewter jar. Another similarly lidded jar sat beside it.

"Almond cream," she said, distracted by the sight of his hand. "And currant jelly." Those same strong fingers had touched her bare flesh, and so carefully soothed her pain. But on that day she'd been too mired in her own misery to care that his wounds were not yet fully healed. Now, she could plainly see that the burn scars were cracked and reddened from such harsh work.

"Kayne," she murmured, reaching out to take his hand when he would have pulled it away. "You shouldn't be laboring in this harsh manner so soon. Look at your hands. Merciful God." She bent to take his other hand and lifted it up to examine. "Oh, Kayne," she said unhappily. "'Tis bleeding here." She gently touched one of the severest scars. "'Twill never heal properly if you do not take greater care." Still holding his hands, she looked up at him, but the rest of the tirade set upon her lips died away.

She hadn't realized how closely they stood together. So close that their bodies were almost touching. His face was but inches from her own, and his blue eyes were gazing down at her in a manner that made her heart leap within her chest. She had seen that look before on the faces of other men, most especially on Sir Griel's, but never before had it produced such an effect on her. Instead of disgust, Sofia felt something altogether different, and far more alarming. Flustered, she released his hands and stepped away.

"Forgive me," she murmured, busying herself with covering the basket once more. "'Tis none of my concern, though I dislike seeing my handiwork gone to naught."

"As do I," he said. "You seem much improved today. Your wounds are healing?"

"Yes, thank you, Master Kayne. Very much so. But I have not continued to neglect my wounds as you have done. You chided me for such only a week past."

Kayne looked at his hands, flexing and unflexing the fingers. Then he gave a shake of his head and moved back toward the tub where he'd left his work cooling. "I do not have the luxury of being able to coddle myself," he told her, using his tongs to fish the ax-head from the water, "nor have I ever done so. The scars will be with me all of my life, and both they and I must learn to live with this manner of labor."

"You have many scars," she murmured, watching him thoughtfully. She had seen the number of the wounds he bore while she'd cared for him. "Were you ever a soldier, Master Kayne?"

He glanced at her over his shoulder. "Aye, I was once. I fought in France for a time."

Ah, Sofia thought with satisfaction. A small part of the mystery unfolded. He had been a soldier, and bore a soldier's scars. But he must have seen many a battle indeed to be so heavily marked.

"Is that how you come to have Tristan?" she asked, then wished she hadn't. He was a solitary man, and would not want to be plagued with such questions. Kayne the Unknown had made it clear since he'd come to Wirth that he valued his privacy above all else.

But he replied readily enough. "Tristan was given to me as a gift by a very great man…a knight of the realm."

Sofia was astonished. "'Tis a fine gift, indeed. Did you save his life during battle?"

He was standing to the side, turned nearly away from her, but Sofia thought that she could see a slight smile on his lips.

"Nay, he saved mine." He glanced at her again before lifting the ax-head higher into the firelight to examine it more closely. "The pot I mended for you has not cracked again?" He clearly wished to speak of himself no more.

"Your mending has held," she said, "and will, I think, until the pot can no longer be used. 'Tis better than new, I vow."

He uttered a laugh. "Nay, that it is not. I am not so skilled a blacksmith."

"You are the finest blacksmith in all of Sussex," she said chidingly, "and well you know it."

Now he smiled—truly smiled—at her, looking so handsome and beguiling that Sofia found it necessary to draw in a deep breath.

"If you insist, Mistress Sofia," he said. "'Twould be useless to argue with you o'er the matter, even at the risk of embracing false pride, for I've well learned that you will have your own way or none at all."

Sofia smiled, too. "I have learned much the same of you, Master Kayne. But you've naught to fear in the matter of false pride. I have not overstated the matter of your excellence."

He had returned to the working table and laid the axhead upon it, beside an array of smithing tools. "You are very kind," he said. "I shall pray to meet all your expectations."

"Not mine, nay," she replied at once. "You already labor far too long and hard." She took a few steps about the large, airy building, admiring its cleanliness and purity of form. How different it was from what such places usually were—dark, foul-smelling and filthy. But both this building and Kayne the Unknown's dwelling were open, spacious and inviting, always clean and in perfect order. "You are ever here in your smithy. Do you never have a day for rest and pleasure?"

"I need none."

She turned to watch as he deftly prepared the ax-head for further work.

"You have lived in Wirth for fully a year now, yet you have never attended any of the fairs or celebrations. Tomorrow is Midsummer Day, and there will be much to do." She took a step toward him, suddenly bold. "Come to the feast tomorrow and be merry for a few hours. Will you?"

Intent upon his work, he gave a shake of his head. "Nay, I've too much to do."

"But you'll have no custom brought to your door tomorrow," she said persistently. "All the villagers will be there, dancing and feasting. 'Twill be a fine and pleasant day, I vow."

"And you will dance around every bonfire once darkness falls, no doubt," he said, still turned away.

The words—and what they implied—made Sofia blush hotly. A young woman seeking a husband would be married within a year if she but danced around seven bonfires on a Midsummer Night, or so it was believed. Sofia had ever scorned such tales, but Kayne's speaking of it seemed to reveal some unspoken truth hidden away in her heart— one that she could not admit, even to herself.

"Nay," she said firmly, pushing such foolishness aside. "I have no desire to wed."

He put his work down and turned to look at her, surprise written on his handsome face.

"Never?"

She shook her head. "My father has too much need of me, as do the people of Wirth."

His expression darkened. "You are unjustly burdened, Mistress Sofia. A woman such as you should wed and seek her own happiness."

"It is not so easy a thing, Master Kayne," she said with a weary smile. "But I am happy as I am. And content, in my own way."

He was clearly dissatisfied by her answer. "What of Sir Griel?" he asked. "He has made it known to one and all that he will have you for a wife before the year has gone."

Sofia tensed with anger. "I will *never* be wedded to such a man," she vowed. "No matter what he may do to me, or how he may strive to terrify my father."

Kayne drew nearer, searching her eyes.

"He's the one who did this to you, is he not?" He lightly touched her shoulder, where her flesh had been scratched.

Sofia moved away, unable to tell him the truth of what had happened. No one outside of Ahlgren Manor knew the fullness of her shame, for her servants had remained loyal in saying little. But she knew that rumors were being whispered among the villagers, and feared that it would not be long before everyone knew Sir Griel had given her such grave insult. And once the truth was known, the citizens of Wirth would fear him even more than they already did. Sofia would have no one to turn to for help and protection.

"I have kept you from your work for too long, Master Kayne. Forgive me."

"Sofia." His hand curled around her arm, gently, holding her still. "I give you my word of honor that you can trust me, even if you can trust no one else. If Sir Griel has threatened you—"

"I'm not afraid of Sir Griel," Sofia told him tautly, "or of any man."

"You should be," Kayne said. "He is a man of great cruelty, and therefore a man to fear. If he dares to set a hand to you again, come to me and I will deal with him, for your father will never do so."

Sofia pulled free. "You are kind, Master Kayne, but I would not ask that of you. 'Tis too much, and you owe me naught."

"For all you did for me after the fire," he said, "I can never fully repay you. But it is not for that alone. I will not stand aside and watch any man bring harm to a woman. I have sworn before God that I would always defend—" He fell suddenly silent. "Only tell me if he should trouble you, mistress. Promise me that."

Sofia touched her arm over the place where his fingers

had curled, holding her in so careful a grasp. How strange
he was! Had he sworn, as a knight did, to protect and defend women? But he had been a mere soldier. He'd just
told her so.

"I will give you my promise," she said slowly, "if you
will promise to attend the Midsummer Day feast. And to
dance with me."

"I do not make merry," he told her stonily.

Sofia gave a curt nod. "Then I will likewise make no
promises. Good day to you, Master Kayne."

"Good day," he murmured, adding, before she could
leave, "I will return the basket to you on the morrow."

"I will be busy on the morrow. Dancing and feasting
and having a fine day. And you will be here alone, as
ever."

He made a sound of aggravation. "Then I will return it
the day following."

"As it pleases you, Master Kayne," she said, and turned
to walk away.

Chapter Four

It was nearly midnight when Kayne rode out of Wirth, cloaked in a heavy black cape and riding atop Tristan. He knew that the destrier's heavy hooves made a great deal of noise, but the pleasure he experienced at riding his magnificent steed far overtook his fear of unsettling the villagers.

A powerful mount, Tristan readily bore Kayne's muscled weight, moving with a speed and grace that made it seem as if he carried nothing at all. Once clear of the village, he gave the horse full rein, bending low over the animal's neck as it lengthened its strides, galloping for several long minutes with clear enjoyment.

When they neared the forest, Kayne at last reined the majestic beast in, slowing his pace by degrees. Just as he had been during their years together in France, Tristan was instantly obedient to his master's will. Without such obedience, Kayne knew, he'd have been long dead. More times than he could recall it had been Tristan's perfectly honed skills as a warhorse that had kept them both alive.

It was an easy matter to find the place where he needed to turn in, though it was not always so in the midst of those nights when he journeyed to the forest. Tonight, however, the moon was nearly full, giving plenty of light for such late wanderings. Tomorrow night, Kayne thought, glancing upward, 'twould be even brighter, and all those celebrating Midsummer Night would rejoice to have their dancing and feasting made that much more pleasant.

Sofia, especially, would enjoy herself. She had a gift for happiness; one that he envied greatly. He could almost envision her now, with her long golden hair unbound and flowing free, crowned with a circlet of flowers and swaying like the finest silk cloth as she danced about the bonfires. She'd have no lack of partners. Nay, she'd suffer quite a different trouble by having far too many vying for her hand, both young and old alike.

It wasn't far to the clearing which was his destination. Senet and John were there before him, waiting.

"Where is Aric?" Kayne asked as he brought Tristan to a halt. He dismounted with ease as the other men approached, and held out a hand in greeting.

"His wife, Magan, is heavy with child," Senet Gaillard, the lord of Lomas, replied, clasping Kayne's arm in the manner of long friendship, "and he will not leave her for fear that the babe might come with him gone. 'Tis good to see you again, Kayne. You are well?"

"Most well, as you see," he assured him before turning to greet the other man. "John, well met."

John Baldwin, who had recently become the lord of Capwell, shook his hand warmly.

"Aye, indeed, Kayne. I was sorry not to come when Senet and Aric last met you here, and so had to come this time. Clarise sends her warmest love."

"Give her my thanks, and send my own affections in return. She is well and happy? But I think she must be, now that you are wed."

John smiled and nodded. "Most happy, we are, the both

of us. But what of you? Your burns are much healed from what I saw many months ago.''

''He has the lady of Wirth to thank for it,'' Senet said, grinning at Kayne. ''A very beautiful lady, from what is told of her, and most attentive to our Kayne. Mistress Sofia Ahlgren is her name, but to hear the words fall from his lips, you would think her named 'Loveliest Angel,' instead.''

Kayne scowled at him. ''You are pleased to make jest, yet there is nothing more to Mistress Sofia's kindness than mere Christian duty, and nothing more to my speaking of her than gratitude. But you did not ride so far in the dark of night to speak of such things. Something is amiss if you come to meet with me again, so soon after our last parting, and only a day before Midsummer Night. You'll wish to be home with your wives on the morrow, and not here with me. Though I am not sorry to see you, of course.''

''Nay, of course not,'' Senet replied with a raised eyebrow. ''But it may seem so, as you refuse to let us come to your home, as friends might expect to do.''

''You know why it must be so,'' Kayne said quietly, grieved in his heart to treat his dearest friends—men who were as his own brothers—in such a manner. They had been inseparable during the ten years they'd spent together fighting in France, and nothing save death could have parted them. But once they'd returned to England, Senet, Aric and John had taken wives and set up their own estates within miles of each other. They had begged Kayne to do likewise, and take the fortune he'd amassed during his years at war and become master of his own land and manor house. But his soul had been too darkened to carry on a life of planting fields and overseeing servants and vassals and pretending that all was well. Too much of him had died during the war to let him live in that manner.

He had craved solitude and peace, and above all, namelessness—to put his old self away forever and never embrace it again. But becoming unknown had required great sacrifice. He could leave Wirth to visit his friends, but he could not receive their visits in his home. If any of the villagers saw Senet or John or Aric, they would know at once who Kayne was, and what he had once been, and the small measure of peace he'd striven so hard to gain would be lost. He would have to leave Wirth...and Sofia...and begin all over in a new place. If he could find one.

It had taken months of hard searching to find Wirth, and he'd been especially glad of it for it kept him so close to his friends. Only twenty miles separated him from Senet and Aric, and another ten from John. He did not like to think of being farther away, in case they should ever need him, and because of this, he stood firmly in his determination to keep his friendship with such noblemen—famed warriors all—a secret.

"Aye, we know," Senet said more kindly. "My prayer is yet that you will one day come to yourself again, and cease such solitude. If you had gone into a monastery and taken vows, you could be no less cloistered than you are now."

It was true. Kayne had even considered taking such vows when he'd first begun to seek peace. He might have done so, if not for the vow of celibacy. He was not a man given to much dallying with women, but neither was he a man to forever deny himself the company of females. Even if he'd been able to conquer outright lust, desire was something he knew he would never vanquish.

"Kayne," Senet said, the timbre of his voice changing, growing sober and serious, "there is indeed a certain task that causes us to come to you this night. I've had a missive from your father."

Kayne looked sharply at his friend. "From my sire, you mean. I have no father, though I might name Sir Justin such, as he was a father to us all when we were boys."

"Aye, Sir Justin was truly a father to the fatherless," John agreed, "but you were more fortunate than the rest of us, Kayne. You knew your parents—both mother and father, even if your father never claimed you as he should have done."

"Neither my mother, may God assoil her, or me," Kayne said tightly, hot anger seeping through every pore. "I've tried not to hate the man, but the truth cannot be denied. He used her for his pleasure—a simple serving maid who knew no better than to love her lord—and when she found herself with child, he sent her away with naught but what she could carry."

Senet stepped forward. "I know you're full angered with the man, Kayne, but you must realize that he did the best he could for her. He could have turned her out and left the both of you to suffer, but he sent her to Briarstone, where both she and you could be safe, and he sent money every quarter...."

"Don't speak of it!" Kayne shouted furiously, turning away from them. "Money to buy her silence. And to keep the truth of who my father was a secret from one and all."

"Nay, that is not why. Even your mother never thought that was so," John argued gently, speaking with great care. "And when she died, Lord Renfrow sent for you, to bring you back to live with him at Vellaux. He did not want you to be alone, once she was gone. 'Twas your own stubbornness that kept you from going."

"I never would have put myself in his grasp," Kayne muttered with a shake of his head. "By then he was only desperate for an heir. The wife he'd taken after sending my mother away never gave him a child—nor did any of his other women. I only became of import to him when he began to fear that he'd die without a child of his loins to inherit his grand titles and estates. If God had blessed him with other sons—legitimate sons—he would have forgotten me entirely.''

Senet gave a long, weary sigh. ''You are one of the best men on God's earth, Kayne,'' he said. ''It grieves me to hear you speak so bitterly, when I know that your heart is above all things gentle and kind—except for the man who gave you life.''

Kayne rounded on him. ''He made my mother a whore, and then abandoned her. She spent her remaining days longing for him—for a man who cared nothing for either her or me.''

''None of us can claim perfection, Kayne,'' John argued. ''Has he not tried to make amends? He is ill. He may be dying.''

The argument on Kayne's tongue fell away at this. He gazed first at John, then at Senet.

''Dying? Is this true?''

Senet nodded. ''His physicians have given little hope that he'll live another twelve months—and will be fortunate to survive but six. His one desire before he greets death is to see you, Kayne.''

Kayne closed his eyes briefly, staring at the ground when he opened them again. He shook his head. ''I cannot.''

''You must,'' Senet pressed, ''else you face God's punishment for letting sinful pride overtake righteous compassion. You've never even met the man to judge him so harshly.''

''And I'll not meet him,'' Kayne said stubbornly. ''By the age of ten, I'd known enough of my mother's tears to vow that I would never crawl to that bastard—for any reason.''

Senet held out a beseeching hand. "Kayne..."

"If he'd wanted a son by his side," Kayne cried, cutting him off, "then he should never have sent my mother away in favor of another."

"He may regret that he did so," John said quietly. "Indeed, I think it must be the greatest regret of his life. But you'll not know unless you go to him." John hesitated, clearly considering what he was about to say. "I want to tell you something, Kayne—something I've wished to tell you for many years now."

Kayne turned his gaze to the smaller man. When he'd been a boy, John had ever spoken first and thought last, the greatest chatterer among them. But as a man, he'd become quieter, more considering, and when he spoke, it was a good thing to attend him. Kayne did so now, asking, "What is it, John?"

"When we were boys at Briarstone," John said, "before Sir Justin had taken us to Talwar to train in the ways of battle, I used to watch you with your mother—you and Aric and all the others. 'Tis true that they were all women who'd suffered a great deal, and almost all of them bearing children out of wedlock, but they were alive and loving—and I was tormented with a jealousy that you cannot begin to know. I had neither mother nor father nor any kin to claim me. To have had only a mother, such as you had, would have meant everything in the world. I would have gladly given my life to know but a week of such joy."

"I know that, John," Kayne said with heartfelt sorrow. John had been abandoned as a newborn babe, left to die in a filthy ditch on a dark London night. He'd been rescued by the owner of a nearby tavern, and spent his earliest days living on London's streets more like an animal than a human. If Sir Justin hadn't discovered him and brought him to Briarstone—a place of refuge for all the unwanted—he'd surely have died long before reaching his tenth year. "But you did have a family at Briarstone. All of us were kin to one another there."

"Aye, and a blessed thing it was, too," John agreed. "And, yet, for all that I knew of goodness there, I was jealous. Of you more than any other, for you had not only a mother, but also a father who was faithful to send money and goods and even gifts at Christmastide, and who made certain that you and your mother were comfortable and well-kept." John moved nearer, holding Kayne's gaze. "If there is a man on this earth who would step forward this very day to reveal himself as my father, and who was full sorrowed at having lost me and pleaded, as your father has done, that I come to him, I vow by God above that I would move mountains to see him just once. Just once. Kayne," he said, setting a hand on Kayne's arm, "you don't know what you have—what someone like me has dreamt of all my life. Don't throw it away as if it were naught."

Kayne was stricken to his soul. He said nothing, but only continued to gaze into John's set face.

"Go to see him," John pressed. "Speak to him. Give him a chance, Kayne. I beg it of you not for his sake, but for mine, if you bear me any love at all."

"You know I do," Kayne said. "You are as my own brother. All of you."

"Then I ask it of you as a brother," John said somberly. "I cannot tell you how it will grieve me if you turn so precious a gift aside."

Kayne's resolve crumbled. John had never asked anything of him before, not even during the many years when they'd all been together, fighting in France.

"Aye," he murmured, setting his fingers over the hand that John yet held on his arm. "For you, my brother, I will go. If it will ease your mind, you may come with me."

"Surely you didn't think we'd let you go alone?" Senet said from where he stood, leaning against a tree, his arms folded over his chest in a relaxed manner. "You're a brave fool, Kayne, but even you will admit to dreading such a first encounter. We know you too well to think that it would be otherwise."

Kayne smiled at his friend's teasing tone. "Aye, you knave, I admit it. Any man would feel the same, I vow. 'Twill be much like going into battle. But I have done that many a time before, and can do so once more. You need not go with me, to coddle me as if I were a child."

Senet sighed and pushed himself upright. "Nevertheless, we will. Why do you not come with us now, back to Lomas? We'll spend Midsummer Day there and begin for Vellaux the following morn. I'll send your father, Lord Renfrow, a missive telling him of our coming."

"Nay, do not," Kayne said with a shake of his head. "'Twould be easier to meet him without formality. He must take me as I am, when I come to him. Give me a week to prepare and close my shop. I will meet you at Lomas on the seventh day."

"Are you certain?" John asked. "Can you not come with us now?"

"Nay," Kayne said. "There is something of import that I must do tomorrow—on Midsummer Day. Someone I must meet."

Both Senet and John looked at him with open interest.

"Someone?" Senet repeated with a grin.

"Aye, someone," Kayne said testily, "and you may keep your thoughts to yourself, my lord. You've no need to fear that I will be delayed in coming to Lomas. I'll meet you there at the end of next week, and we can begin for Vellaux. On my word of honor, we will."

Chapter Five

The dancing began at midday, even before the feasting had taken place. Sofia refused the first few requests to join in the merriment when the music filled the air, hoping yet that Kayne would change his stubborn mind and arrive. She knew that he would be reserved—if he came—and would feel an outsider to the other villagers. It was her intention to stay by his side every moment, bearing him company to make his time as pleasing as possible. If he could but see that there was naught to fear from knowing and communing with his neighbors, mayhap 'twould be easier to lure him to such festivities in future.

It was a perfect day. The sun was bright overhead, but not too hot, and a cool breeze carried the many delicious scents of the faire across the fields where the festivities were taking place, down to the banks of the river, where children were already making small boats out of leaves and twigs, and even into the forest, where young couples sought the shelter of the trees to share stolen kisses or begin searching for the fern blossoms which became imbued with great power in the coming darkness of this most magical of nights.

Sellers had set out their wares—jewelry, flowers, toys,

herbs, medicines, crafts of every kind and a variety of foods. Great mounds of wood were being set out for the bonfires that would later be lit, and many smaller fires were already being used to roast whole pigs and haunches of venison and beef.

All the village maidens, Sofia included, had twined ribbons in their hair and adorned themselves with circlets of flowers, and were brazenly teasing and dallying with the young men. The young men, apart from admiring the maidens, were waiting for the contests to begin in order to prove their strength and prowess in such skills as archery, running and wrestling. There were prizes for the winners of each contest, all to be awarded with great ceremony by Sofia's father, Sir Malcolm, who was already strolling amongst the feasters, merrily jesting and laughing and drinking far too much ale and wine. When the dancing began, Sofia noted, her father was one of the first to take a pretty maiden by the hand and draw her in among the other dancers.

"Will you not dance, Mistress Sofia?" Olvan, the cobbler's handsome eldest son, cried out as three maidens laughingly pulled him toward the music.

Sofia smiled and shook her head—then laughed along with the maidens as Olvan stumbled at their urgent tugging and quickly righted himself, flushed with pleasure at being so sought after by the fairer sex. Everyone, it seemed, was smiling and laughing, and Sofia suddenly twirled about with her arms wide, uncaring of who saw. She felt gladsome and free and happy beyond measure. Could anything be better—or rarer—than a day of ease and pleasure?

She stopped spinning and closed her eyes, feeling the warmth of the sun upon her upturned face, thinking of what was to come. The feasting and games and contests, the sailing of wishes, and then, as night fell, the bonfires and music and merriment throughout. Oh, how she wished

Kayne would put his stubbornness aside and come. He would enjoy himself so very much—

"Sofia."

A cruel hand closed over her arm, pulling her about. Sofia's eyes flew open to see the man who's voice she'd already recognized.

Sir Griel.

He was dressed, as he always was, in black, and surrounded by a half-dozen of his fighting men. They were the only men present who were fully armed, as if for battle, and silence began to fall over the assembly as their daunting presence was noted.

Sofia drew herself up full height, refusing to let anyone see the fear that welled up at the memory of her last meeting with Sir Griel. His fingers gripped her in the same steely manner as he had done then. Sofia made one effort to wrench herself free, saw his amused smile, and fell still.

"My lord," she greeted coldly.

"Mistress," he replied, still smiling. "You are very beautiful this afternoon. But this, to my partial view, is as you ever are."

Sofia gave no answer to this, sickened by the way his gaze moved over her in so brazen and lecherous a manner.

"You have come to make merry for St. John's Day?" she asked, calling the day by its church-given name, rather than what it had been known by since time began. "You have not honored us with your presence on such occasions before. I'm certain the people of Wirth are most pleased to have you attend their festivities."

"But not you, Sofia?"

She lifted her chin.

"I have come," he said, "but only to celebrate the day with my lovely betrothed. To bear you company both the day and night long, as Midsummer is surely among the most romantic times of the year. A day for maids to discover who their husbands might be. But you've no need of such as that, Sofia—'' his tone grew softer ''—for you already know who that man is. Do you wish to dance?'' His grip tightened and he moved as if to draw her toward that place where the other dancers had fallen still, watching them.

''Nay, the music has stopped,'' she told him, struggling in vain as he dragged her along. ''There is no more dancing.''

''There will be music, presently,'' he promised. ''Where is your father? We will make him useful—though he is seldom so.''

The crowds melted away at Sir Griel's approach, and Sofia could see her father, standing in the midst of the now still dancers, clutching his partner's hand and gaping at Sir Griel in open fear.

Suddenly their way was blocked by a tall, muscular figure. Sir Griel actually ran into the man, so sudden and unexpected was his appearance, pulling Sofia into the same collision.

''Mistress Sofia.''

She looked up at the sound of Kayne's voice, almost afraid to believe that it was truly him. But it was, and he stood before Sir Griel like a strong, immovable mountain, completely unafraid.

''Master Kayne,'' she whispered. She was so glad to see him.

He held out his hand, holding her gaze, not even looking at Sir Griel.

''I'm sorry to be so late. We had arranged to meet much earlier. Come and teach me to dance, as you promised.''

She gratefully set her free hand in his, smiling up at him.

''Yes,'' she began, just as Sir Griel, yet holding her other

hand, tugged so hard that she slipped free of Kayne's reassuring grasp and fell against her captor.

"You overstep, blacksmith, to address Mistress Sofia in
so forward a manner," Sir Griel warned in a low voice.
"Move out of our way."

Kayne stood where he was, still ignoring Sir Griel. He
reached out to take Sofia's hand once more, and, with a
violent motion, Sir Griel shoved at him, unsuccessfully trying to push him aside.

"Move now!" Sir Griel shouted furiously. His men, as
one, drew their swords and stepped nearer. Except for the
sound of the river running nearby and the wind rustling in
the trees, the silence from those attending the festival was
complete.

Kayne gazed into Sofia's eyes with what seemed to her
an ineffable sadness, then he sighed and, at last, looked at
Sir Griel.

"I do not wish to make trouble, neither do I desire a
fight," he stated calmly. "I carry neither sword nor dagger." He held his arms out from his sides to prove the truth
of the words. "But I will not move until you have released
Mistress Sofia and let her make a free choice of who she
will go with."

Sir Griel looked at Kayne as if were a madman seeking
certain death.

"Mistress Sofia is my betrothed," he said with ill-
concealed fury. "She has no free choice in *any* matter, and
will do my bidding."

Kayne was clearly unperturbed by this.

"No banns have been read to proclaim your coming
union," he said, "and Mistress Sofia wears no betrothal
ring marking your possession of her. She herself has openly
denied any such betrothal, to which many who are present

can readily bear witness. By what right or law, my lord, do you make such a claim?''

Sir Griel's face had turned red. "By my own law and none other!'' he shouted. "Fool! I'll see you dead for such insult!''

The biggest of Sir Griel's fighting men lifted his sword and moved as if to strike Kayne. Sofia cried out with dismay, but Kayne moved so quickly that the other man never had a chance to so much as touch him. With an easy, fluid movement, Kayne bent, avoiding the blow of the gleaming sword, and picked the big man up. Just as easily he tossed him in a wide arc to the ground, where he landed with a loud thump.

Before Sir Griel's other soldiers could fall upon him, Kayne had snatched up the fallen man's sword and turned to face them. The first two were dispatched as quickly as the first, without an exchange of swordplay, and the other three stood back, holding their swords aloft and staring at Kayne warily, clearly unnerved by his calm and confident manner.

"Why do you wait?'' Sir Griel shouted. "He is but a village blacksmith! Take him!''

One of the remaining men made the attempt, running at Kayne in a furious charge. Kayne didn't move until his opponent's sword was nearly at his chest, then with a flick of his own sword pushed the sharp blade aside and, using his fist, struck the man soundly on the head so that he crumpled to the ground beside his groaning comrades.

The remaining two men stood their ground. One was shaking his head and staring at Kayne with disbelief.

"He is no common blacksmith, my lord,'' he told Sir Griel.

"Nay,'' Sir Griel muttered, eyeing Kayne with a thoughtful frown. "That he is not. But we will see what he is.'' He shoved Sofia away so abruptly that she stumbled and nearly fell to the ground. Keeping his sword at the ready and his eyes on his opponents, Kayne reached out a hand to pull her near, and Sofia gladly went. The warmth and strength of his body were a comfort beyond measure.

She was as shocked as everyone else present at the deftness Kayne the Unknown had displayed in dealing with Sir Griel's seasoned fighters. It had been almost too simple a matter, as if they'd offered him not the least cause for trouble or worry. And the way in which he held the heavy sword in his hand—as if it weighed less than a feather—was even more amazing. She knew that Kayne had been a soldier once, but he fought like a much greater man.

Sir Griel rubbed a heavily gloved hand over his dark beard and considered Kayne thoughtfully. At last, with a nod of satisfaction, he spoke.

"It was once the custom on Midsummer Day for two men to take up the separate halves of the Sun King—his dark and light sides—and battle for the favor of a lady. I challenge you to such a battle."

"That is a pagan custom," Kayne replied, "and not countenanced by the Church. I will not fight you without just cause."

Sir Griel's shaggy eyebrows rose. "You fought my men." He swept a hand at the pile of groggy men who, with the help of their two unwounded friends, were finally beginning to come back to their senses.

"Nay," Kayne replied, shaking his head. "I defended myself, as well as Mistress Sofia. I will fight no man for game or pleasure. It is a vow I have taken."

Sir Griel's eyes widened with amazement, and then, after a short silence, he began to laugh, loud and lustily, as if he'd never heard anything so amusing in his life.

"A vow?" Sir Griel repeated after some minutes, still

chuckling. "N-not to fight? But you jest, blacksmith. Surely you do."

"I do not," Kayne stated. "I will not fight you."

Sir Griel's black eyes still glittered with amusement. "I did not intend to attempt the task myself. There is one whose fealty I own—a knight of great renown—who I meant for the contest."

"You would send another to take your place?" Kayne tilted his head to one side as if this amazed him. "But surely you, being also of the knighthood, are not afeared?"

Anger possessed Sir Griel's features once again, and he replied tightly, "I'm afeared of no man, blacksmith, and far less of you. But I'll not make a contest of what is already mine, as Mistress Sofia is." He cast a threatening glance at Sofia that made her tremble. Kayne's strong hand steadied her. "And I'd never lower myself to fight a knave such as you are. I was knighted by the hand of the king's own regent, and have fought more battles than you could ever begin to dream upon, blacksmith."

Kayne smiled at this, though very grimly. Standing so close beside him, Sofia could feel his body tensing at Sir Griel's words.

"Mistress Sofia is her own," he said in a low voice, "and no one else's, until she decides otherwise. Take your sword and go in peace." He held the weapon out to one of Sir Griel's men, all of whom were now standing once more.

"I will go," Sir Griel said, "but I will return with my warrior. And then we shall see whether you will fight."

Kayne held his gaze. "If your man attacks me, even though I am unarmed, I will defend myself. If you should threaten harm to Mistress Sofia or any innocent person, I will stop you. And any man who will accost or bring harm to a woman, be she child, maid, mother or grandmother, him I will justly punish and not know a moment's sorrow. These are promises I give you, my lord. You would do well to heed them.''

Sir Griel's expression was as hard as stone. ''I heed no man save the king, and such insolence as you possess invites challenging. I begin to think my man is right. You are no common blacksmith.'' He stepped closer. ''Why do they call you Kayne the Unknown?''

''That is for you to decide,'' Kayne said. ''I will bid you good day, my lord, and wish you a pleasant Midsummer Day.''

''Wish it to me later—if you are still alive to do so.'' With one last glare at Sofia, Sir Griel turned and strode away, his men fast on his heels.

Slowly the crowd began to murmur, but once Sir Griel and his men had ridden away the murmuring turned into a loud chorus of voices, most of them filled with awe. Kayne turned to Sofia and opened his mouth to speak, but before he could utter a single word he was surrounded by dozens of onlookers, slapping him on the shoulder and heartily congratulating him.

Sofia watched with a measure of amusement as Kayne nodded and thanked his sudden admirers. He tried to maintain his usual stoic, somber manner in the wake of such much good cheer, but his cheeks were pinkened and he looked fully discomfited by so much attention.

When the well-wishers moved away, he looked down at Sofia and asked, ''Are you well?'' He released the hand he'd yet been holding and gingerly touched her arm where Sir Griel had gripped it. ''Sir Griel gave you no harm?''

''Nay, I am fine,'' she assured him, ''though only because of your great bravery. I am in your debt again. Thank you.''

His clear blue eyes regarded her steadily, as if he didn't

quite believe her. "You're still shaking. Come and sit in the shade." He lightly grasped her elbow and led her toward the river. As they walked, he looked about and said, somewhat grimly, "Your father disappeared almost as soon as Sir Griel and his men arrived."

"He's not very brave," Sofia admitted.

"Nay, he is not," Kayne agreed. "Not even for the sake of his own daughter—his only child."

Large oak trees grew along the riverbank, and their shade was much sought after by the feasters. But as Kayne and Sofia approached, all those near the river stood aside, making way for them with broad smiles and knowing winks. Kayne scowled and ignored them, choosing a private place to sit a bit farther from the water, beneath a tree where a small patch of grass made a more comfortable place to sit.

Sofia gave a sigh of relief as she tucked the skirt of her surcoat about her legs. "It began as such a wonderful day," she said. She looked up to where Kayne was standing, leaning against the tree with his arms folded across his chest. "You came," she said, as if she'd only just realized it.

"I came," he replied, "and now that I am here, you will do as you said and make me your promise."

Sofia didn't know what he meant at first, but finally she remembered. "You are good to have helped me today— and also before, but I cannot ask you to rescue me every time Sir Griel behaves in such a manner. I am already afraid that he will do what he can to kill you for what you have done this day alone."

"Sir Griel is a knave to be wary of, just as I told you," he said, "but I am a careful man."

Sofia gave a slight shake of her head. "You have just told him that you will not fight, save to defend yourself and others. 'Tis a powerful advantage you've given him."

"Mayhap," he said with a slight shrug. "But mayhap I have taken an advantage, as well."

"I do not understand you, Kayne the Unknown. I dislike sharing any belief with Sir Griel, but he spoke aright when he said that you are not a common man. And not a common soldier. You fight like no other I have seen."

"And you have seen many battles, then?" he asked, a smile tilting his lips.

"Nay," she said, frowning, "but I have attended tournaments in plenty. Not even the most seasoned knights had such skill as you showed this afternoon."

"Then they never served in France. Even common soldiers learn how to fight well—very well—when enough battle makes it necessary. If they do not, they die."

Two young women approached them, one carrying two tankards of ale and the other a basket brimming with choice bits of roasted meats, chunks of bread and cheese, and a variety of the many sweets being offered at the faire. They were gifts from many of the sellers, in gratitude for what Kayne had done in keeping Sir Griel from ruining the day.

"Thank you," Sofia said, accepting the basket and setting it on the ground. The young women blushed and smiled at Kayne as he held out his hands to receive the tankards. When he murmured his own thanks, they giggled behind their hands and then curtseyed and hurried away. Kayne gave a shake of his head, watching them depart, and Sofia laughed.

"You will have every maid in Wirth in love with you," she told him, "and every man jealous of you."

Kayne sat beside her, handing her one of the tankards. "I will pray it is not so. Women destroy a man's peace more easily than swords and arrows. Especially women in love."

Sofia smiled to cover the pain the words wrought in her,

and said, a little too merrily, "Are you hungry, Master Kayne?"

"Aye. It is one of the reasons I came. To eat and dance and…and to make merry." He sounded as if he were embarrassed by the words. Before she could reply he added, in a firmer tone, "You have not yet given me your promise, Sofia."

"Please, let us not speak of Sir Griel now," she said, handing him a linen napkin filled with the choicest bits of meat. "Let us eat and dance and prepare our boats for making wishes."

He looked stubborn, as if he would press the matter, but Sofia touched his hand and murmured, "Please, Kayne. Only let us enjoy the day. I will give you my promise when 'tis done, I vow."

"Very well," he agreed reluctantly, "I will wait. But only 'til dark falls. Then I will have your promise regarding Sir Griel."

"Aye," Sofia agreed demurely, "you will have it then."

Chapter Six

Sofia found reason upon reason long after dark had fallen to put off making her promise—there was dancing to be taught, more feasting to be done, and they most certainly had to watch all of the contests and games—until Kayne began to wonder why so simple a matter troubled her so. But those moments that he did think of it were fleeting. Sofia had a talent for making him forget everything…save her.

He had dallied with pretty maids before, especially at Briarstone and while he was in France. He knew the pleasure of a woman's smile, of holding a soft, feminine body close to his own as they twirled about in a dance—despite his great clumsiness and lack of skill. But what he had experienced before was as nothing compared to receiving Sofia's smiles, or of holding her as closely as he dared before so many watchful and interested eyes.

He had never seen her like this before. Today, she wasn't the lady of Wirth, ever concerned with the welfare of those beneath her care. Today she was all laughter and gaiety, so carefree and open and free of spirit that he couldn't think of words to describe it, and so beautiful—God's mercy, she was so very beautiful. He could look at her forever and never grow weary, regardless of what time would do to age her. Sofia's beauty was far beyond the physical, though heaven knew that she was passing all pleasure to gaze upon. It was something that shone out from within, from her beguiling blue eyes and that bewitching smile. And that was just what he felt she had done—cast some spell to captivate him so entirely. It was a feeling Kayne didn't like in the least, but knew himself as being helpless against.

Teaching him to dance properly was the first task Sofia set herself to once they'd finished their afternoon repast. Kayne was terrible at such a fine skill, and knew it. More times than he could remember he'd made the attempt to learn the simplest steps, but it had ever proved impossible. In the end, he'd merely moved about as best he could and tried not to knock anyone over. He had noticed, with a measure of relief, that he wasn't alone in his clumsy attempts, and that others dancing near him had seldom taken offense at his lack of grace.

It was much the same in the waning afternoon of Midsummer Day as Sofia tried to teach him to dance, but a far greater pleasure than any previous attempt Kayne had made. She held his hands and made him watch her movements—this he did willingly and with much interest—and physically turned him about in time to the music. To be so exposed to the curious eyes of the villagers would have been a torment to him before, but Sofia's joy-filled smiles and bright laughter held him too enchanted to think of how badly he might be humiliating himself. Indeed, after but a few moments she had him laughing, too, most especially at his many missteps and mistakes. Being clumsy had never been so great a pleasure.

They danced for what seemed like hours, laughing, twirling, gasping for breath until Kayne had to cry for mercy. Sofia shook her head and called him a very poor creature, but took his hand and led him to a nearby booth where ale was being sold. Bearing their tankards in their hands, Sofia next drew him to the shade of a tree where they sat and watched the contest of archery. At first, Kayne's years of warring came back to him and he began to think of the hundreds of archers who'd fought beside him in the king's army, but the contest soon became so close between two of the men that he forgot the war altogether, and watched intensely as each of the archers strove to best the other.

"Do you know how to shoot?" Sofia asked.

"Aye," Kayne answered absently, fixed upon the archers.

"Did you shoot often during the war?"

"Not often. I was not so exact as others were. The sword is where my skill lies."

"That I well believe, Master Kayne," she said, gazing at him with a teasing smile, "having seen the proof with my own eyes. Will you like to see the wrestling contest that follows this? Or perhaps one of the races?"

"Whichever pleases you best," he replied, though he hoped she'd choose the wrestling. She did.

As darkness began to fall the bonfires were lit with great ceremony, and there was a great deal more feasting. Sir Malcolm had finally returned and greeted Kayne in his cheerful, lordly manner. He gave Sofia permission to bring Kayne to eat at the manorial table, where Sir Malcolm and several of his favorite ladies sat, and there they enjoyed the choicest victuals to be had at the faire.

Sir Malcolm toasted Kayne's earlier valor as if he'd actually been present to see it, in such a loud, boisterous manner that Kayne began to wish he could find a way to escape. When Sofia suggested that they join many of the other festival goers in search of St. John's fern in the forest, he happily agreed.

Kayne had never believed the rumors that told of St. John's fern being graced with magical powers on Midsummer Night, but Sofia clearly did. She pulled Kayne into the darkest part of the forest in an effort to leave the other searchers behind. With only the light of the moon to guide them, it was very dark, indeed.

"'Twill be impossible to find any of the fern without a lantern," Kayne told her, to be hushed by Sofia.

"Shhh, else the others hear us and know where we search. Look for the fern's yellow blossom. It should be easy enough to see, for tonight it will shine like gold."

Kayne uttered a sigh, but dutifully began to peer through the darkness at the bases of trees and shrubs in search of a golden blossom. He tried to keep his thoughts on his task, but he couldn't seem to stop himself from glancing time to time at where Sofia was searching, her long, unbound hair falling forward as she bent over, inspecting promising spots. The light-blue surcoat she wore was luminous in the dark, turning her elegant form into that of a ghostly spirit.

He felt again the strength of the pull she held for him, and was unsettled by it. 'Twas well enough to dally with a lady such as Sofia on a night like this—aye, and even expected, for dallying was a large part of merrymaking days—but this one indulgence was all that he could allow. On the morrow, he must put aside every thought of Mistress Sofia Ahlgren save that which was most noble—to protect her from the cruelties of Sir Griel. Apart from that, there could be nothing else between them.

A loud cheering in another part of the forest revealed that someone else had found the first blossom of Saint John's fern and, hearing it, Sofia straightened and made a sound of great unhappiness.

"By the Rood!" she muttered. "They've won the greatest measure of magic, but there will still be plenty for the rest of us. Hurry, Kayne! We must find one before 'tis time to set our wishes to sail in the river!''

"Before that time comes," he said, setting his fingers about her arm to gently pull her to face him, "there is another matter you must tend to. You have not yet given me your promise regarding Sir Griel."

Sofia was silent, her face turned up to him, and then she sighed and pulled free. She leaned against the nearest tree, still looking at him.

"'Tis hard for me to put myself in the care of a man. Any man," she said in a soft tone. "I have never done so since I passed my childhood, and the thought of it…makes me afeared. I have seen how other women suffered, even my own mother."

"Oh, Sofia," Kayne murmured, drawing near. "You have naught to fear from me."

"You do not know what it is like to have to depend upon the whims of a man. To be beneath his hand just as his vassals and hounds and cattle are. I have taken care of myself and those people within my father's boundaries, and have been blessed to do so. I know that you mean only good for me, to protect me from Sir Griel, but if I do not face him myself and find the way to turn him aside, then I lose part of what is most dear to me. My very freedom."

"It would not be so," Kayne vowed. "I know more than you think of what a woman's life may be like when the man whom she has put her trust in betrays her. Upon my honor, I will take naught from you. None will ever know of it if I should be called upon to take Sir Griel to task for his misdeeds. But you must give me your promise, Sofia, for if he should harm you—when you have no champion to turn to—what good will your freedom do you? If he should force you to become his wife, you may be certain he will keep you well beneath his hand, and that hand will be heavy and harsh.''

She shuddered at the words and looked away. When she spoke again, her voice was filled with unshed tears.

''It is not only for myself that I fear, Kayne. If I give you this promise, mayhap you will kill Sir Griel, for now that you have humiliated him he will relentlessly push at you with all his power and might, and you know what would happen if you, a common man, should so much as raise a hand to a knight of the realm. You would be hanged without question...and I could never let that happen.'' Her voice fell to a whisper. ''I would rather suffer the torment of becoming his wife than to ever see you harmed.''

The words made Kayne's heart beat more rapidly. He felt strange and warm—and deeply stirred. Something within him responded to her sweet declaration with the same strong emotion, like for like.

Gliding his fingers along the silken skin of her cheek, he whispered her name and lifted her face, meeting her mouth with his own. Gently, tenderly he kissed her, sliding his fingers into her unbound hair, enticing her to draw closer. She did, and met his kiss with an ardent murmur. He felt her slender fingers, trembling, come to rest upon his shoulder, and somehow she turned so that she pressed up against him fully. Kayne's other hand found the curve of her waist, and the feeling of her, so feminine and soft, nearly undid him. He pulled away before he lost control altogether and did something that would surely shock and offend her.

''Forgive me,'' he murmured, pressing her away with the hand at her waist, dropping the other hand free of her hair. ''I should not have done that.''

''Not?'' she whispered. ''Why? 'Tis Midsummer Night, and a man may kiss any maid who is willing.''

''This is so, but you are not any village maid.'' He swept

a few stray strands of hair from her forehead with a careful finger. "You are a born lady, and I naught but a commoner—far more than you can begin to know. Your father would rightly have my head did he learn that I'd taken such liberty with his daughter." With the same finger, he lifted her chin up a bit higher. "Give me your promise, Sofia, regarding Sir Griel."

"Kiss me again first," she said, going up on her toes to find his lips.

Kayne firmly pushed her back down. "Nay, I have told you that I should not have done so. And I cannot trust myself to kiss you again. 'Tis because you are so innocent that you do not understand what follows such embraces. But each man has his boundaries, and I've nearly reached mine."

This, rather than alarming her, as he had meant it to, only seemed to awaken her interest.

"In truth?" she asked, all amazement. "I have never been kissed before in such a way—so that it was a pleasure and not a torment. But even beyond that, 'twas very different for me than what you describe. I felt as if there was so much more to know...so much more to discover. 'Twas most exciting, Kayne, and I did not want it to end."

He tried to push her even farther away. "Do not speak in such a manner," he begged. "I am no saint to resist such words. Nay, I will not kiss you again, Sofia—cease—oh, very well." He gave way as she continually strove to press nearer, and leaned down to press a firm, brief kiss upon her lips. "Now, cease climbing all about me and give me your promise, else we leave the forest this very moment."

She subsided, and gave a wistful sigh. "Aye, Kayne, I give you my promise. If Sir Griel should offend me in any manner, I will come to you, and let you be my champion. Will you promise me, likewise, that you'll not harm him?''

''Nay,'' he replied truthfully. ''I cannot do so, for I have no assurance that he will not dare his worst, for that is the manner of man he is. But I will bring him no fatal harm if it can be at all costs avoided. This I do promise, upon my honor.''

''Thank you,'' she said, relief evident in her tone. She suddenly grasped his hands. ''The fern blossoms! We've not yet found one, and soon 'twill be time to set our wishes upon the river. Hurry!''

Ten minutes of searching followed before Sofia at last cried out that she'd found one of the precious blossoms. By the time Kayne caught up to her, she had already knelt upon the ground and spread out a delicate white linen cloth to catch the small golden flower as she pinched it from the stem.

''Now I've captured some of the night's magic,'' she said with satisfaction as she carefully folded the napkin and tucked it into the neckline of her surcoat. She accepted Kayne's hand as he helped her rise to her feet.

''You will put it beneath your pillow, doubtless,'' he said, then wished he hadn't. Young maids used the supposed magic of such blossoms to bring forth dreams of the man they would one day wed—a thought Kayne didn't enjoy thinking of when Sofia was involved.

She smiled up at him through the darkness. ''Indeed, I will, Master Kayne. The magic will fade away too quickly, otherwise. But come!'' She took his hand and began to tug him toward the open fields, in the direction of the river. ''We must hurry to make our boats!''

A crowd had already formed along the riverbanks, and the feverish construction of small vessels made out of leaves and twigs was underway. Tiny candles were fixed in the middle of each, then lit by its owner, wished upon, and set adrift in the river. If the boat floated across the river with the candle yet burning, that particular wish would come true. If the candle went out, the sender must wait until the following year to float another wish across the water.

Some of the village children came running up as Kayne and Sofia approached, pressing crudely crafted boats into their hands and then running away. Kayne gazed at his with some dismay, wondering if it wouldn't sink the moment it touched water, but Sofia exclaimed with delight, "'Tis perfect! Now we needn't build our own, and can set our wishes afloat at once."

They knelt beside the river and waited to make use of one of the many candles being passed among the festival goers. Kayne watched as Sofia lit her candle, then, holding her little boat high, closed her eyes and made her wish. When she was done she smiled, opened her eyes, and carefully set the vessel adrift. Then she offered the candle to Kayne.

"What did you wish for, that it makes you smile so?" he asked, lighting his own candle.

"I cannot tell you, and you must not speak aloud your wish, either. 'Twill not come true, else."

Kayne didn't believe in floating wishes any more than he believed in magic flower blossoms, but he very much wanted his wish to come true. So he didn't tell Sofia that his wish was for the strong attraction he felt for her to fade, and silently lit his candle and set his leafy boat into the water.

Sofia's candle floated safely to the other side of the riverbank. Kayne's sank before it reached midway. When he dared to look at her, it was to find that she was still smiling.

They sat for a few silent moments, gazing out over the water at the small lighted boats as they floated away, turning the river into a beautiful spectacle of shimmering light.

"Hey, come to the bonfires!" someone shouted. "Tom the miller's son has already jumped over three of them!"

The crowd moved almost as one back toward the bonfires, where the young men of the village were challenging one another's mettle by seeing who could leap over the most bonfires unscorched, and where the young maidens were performing the yearly ritual of dancing about seven bonfires in the hope of gaining a husband. It was the most jovial part of the entire festival, which would come to an end at midnight. The musicians played loudly and merrily, and other feasters drank more ale and cheered the leapers and dancers onward. Kayne thought Sofia might leave him to join the maidens in their dancing, but she was content to remain by his side, laughing and shouting encouragement as the young people followed their different pursuits.

"You do not want to jump the bonfires?" she shouted up at him through the loud din.

He shook his head. "Nay, I've had enough of fire for many years to come."

"Oh, indeed," she replied with feeling. "You need no more scars to prove that it is so, Master Kayne."

The noise of the festivities began to grow quiet by slow degrees, just as it had done earlier in the day, beginning at the edges of the crowd and working its way forward. Kayne, hearing it, sensed that Sir Griel had returned, as he had promised. He had hoped that it would not be so, but knew that a man like Sir Griel did not make such vows lightly—most especially not when he'd been so openly humiliated. Since he and his men had left, Kayne had been waiting for the promised return, and could only wonder that Sir Griel had chosen this late moment to make it.

It took a long time for the musicians to halt their playing, and for the young men and maidens to cease their amusements. By the time all had grown quiet, Sir Griel was standing in the midst of them, surrounded by his men. He searched the crowd slowly for Kayne, who was standing with Sofia in the shadow of a tall tree, away from the light of the bonfires.

"Kayne," Sofia murmured, gripping his arm with both hands, "slip away now, before he finds you."

Kayne set one of his own hands over hers and pressed reassuringly. He didn't cherish the idea of the coming conflict, but if he did not make Sir Griel know that Sofia had a champion who would stand for her against every combatant, then the man would not leave either of them in peace.

"Wait for me here, Sofia," he told her. "I will escort you home when this is done."

He stepped forward, the light of the bonfires behind him, so that his face was yet in shadows.

"I am here, Sir Griel."

The short, dark man's gaze fell upon Kayne, and his heavily bearded lips drew into an unpleasant smile.

"You did not turn craven and run, despite my warnings," he said. "I told you that I would return, and my promises are as honorable as your own."

"You choose the dark of night to fight your battles—or to have others fight them for you." Kayne's gaze flickered past Sir Griel to the men standing behind him. "These are the marks of a coward, and I say it plainly to your face and before all those assembled, Sir Griel."

It was difficult to tell in the dim firelight what Sir Griel's reaction to this was. The crowds surrounding them murmured in some amazement at Kayne's boldness.

"You mistake the matter, blacksmith," Sir Griel replied. "I returned at the end of the festivities so as not to disturb the people of Wirth in their pleasure. But now, 'tis time for the merriment to be at an end. This is my man, who has come to play his part in our Midsummer Night battle." At the lifting of one of Sir Griel's fingers, a tall man dressed in full armor stepped forward. He was swathed in the black-and-red tunic that all of Sir Griel's men wore, and appeared the more ominous for it. Kayne could see at once by the way the man held his sword that he was a skilled fighter, and that there was strength in both his hand and arm—all of which would make him a difficult opponent to best. "Do you still say that you will not fight?" Sir Griel asked.

Slowly, Kayne shook his head. "I will only defend myself, if I am made to do so."

"Then you will be made to do so," Sir Griel told him. "I would offer you my sword, if you will take it."

"I will not."

"So be it."

Sir Griel stepped back, and the surrounding crowds did the same. Kayne stayed where he was, wanting to keep the flames behind him to both aid his sight and force his opponent to fight with the brightness burning in his eyes, distracting and blinding him. Each moment in such a fight was precious. Kayne's life now depended upon making every one count in his favor.

His armored opponent began to approach Kayne at once, though slowly, his sword at the ready, clearly taking Kayne's measure. He moved with care, not rushing into his attack as Sir Griel's soldiers had done earlier, and Kayne

could but admire and approve the tactic. Whoever had
trained the man had done well.

His opponent circled to one side, trying to force Kayne
to circle as well so that their positions would be reversed
and Kayne would be the one to suffer the fire's blinding
glare, but Kayne merely continued to step before him, foil-
ing the plan. Next the well-armored knight attempted to
push Kayne back into the fire by making his approach more
direct, but to this Kayne merely held his ground, inviting
a charge that could be easily sidestepped.

After a few minutes of this, Sir Griel's man clearly began
to realize the difficulty of trying to engage an opponent
who would not fight. The only option left to him, just as
Kayne meant it to be, was to charge, and this he finally
did. Sword held aloft, he ran toward Kayne at an angle—
a wise decision, Kayne thought, as he had no choice but to
leap forward, away from the fire, to avoid being cut in half.
He whirled about at once in an attempt to regain the advantage, but his opponent had already divined his purpose
and charged again, driving Kayne farther from the fire and
into the shadows.

Several frantic minutes followed as Kayne both avoided
and tried to disarm his attacker, though with little success.
The man was an admirable opponent. And more than that,
there was something familiar in his manner, in the way he
moved, with such care and skill. Kayne wondered if perhaps he had known this man in France, if they'd fought
side by side during one of the many battles.

Of a sudden, his opponent stopped, straightened and uttered angrily, ''Enough of this!'' He tossed his sword aside
and withdrew the long, sharp dagger at his waist.

It was exactly what Kayne would have done in a like
situation, for 'twas the only manner in which his attacker

could now come close enough to keep Kayne from leaping aside.

Kayne twisted as the other man charged, jumping just in time back toward the fire. But he had misjudged his opponent's quickness. Less than the beating of a heart passed before the gap between them closed. Hard fingers closed on Kayne's shoulder, and the gleaming blade of the knife flashed as it was thrust toward his heart. Kayne's own hands shot out to halt its progress, gripping his attacker by both arm and wrist to toss him to the ground. He was a heavy man, made heavier by his armor, and landed upon his back with a loud thud.

Kayne was upon him at once, taking hold of the hand that bore the dagger and squeezing the wrist and fingers with all the strength he possessed. The other man tried to throw him off, bucking and striking Kayne about the head and neck with fisted blows of his gauntleted hand. Gritting his teeth against the pain of each strike, Kayne continued to squeeze until at last the hand under his grip gave way, releasing the dagger so that it slid to the ground.

The man beneath him made a furious roar of noise, and with one mighty shove tossed Kayne off and over onto the ground. Kayne could feel the knife beneath him, and the other man's heavy body as he straddled his waist, one hand holding Kayne down by the throat and the other frantically searching the dirt for the fallen weapon.

"Now we'll have an end of it," the attacker vowed tautly, breathing harshly from the contest. "Even if I must kill you with my bare hands." Not finding the knife, he put deed to word and set his other hand at Kayne's neck, leaning down to gaze into his face. "I vow I'll—" His voice died away and, just as Kayne had prepared to strike him with both fists, he released him and sat up. The next moment he had pushed off of Kayne altogether, saying, "It can't be!"

Kayne took no time to wonder what his opponent was about. He reached beneath him and took hold of the knife, then leapt from the ground and tossed the weapon into the flames of the fire.

"Do you give way, then?" he asked, biting the words out against the burning pain in his lungs, for the other man simply continued to sit and stare at him. "Or do we go on with this farce?"

His opponent shook his head, and then he whispered, in a voice filled with disbelief, "Captain."

Kayne knew that voice—knew it well. But it was impossible. He swiped the hair from his face with one hand and gazed at the man more intently.

The soldier slowly rose to his feet, only to kneel before Kayne.

"My lord, Sir Kayne," he said reverently, removing his helmet to reveal a swath of dark, sweaty hair which fell about his shoulders, and even darker eyes which gazed now at Kayne, wide and hopeful. "Sir Kayne…Captain…can it truly be you? But my eyes do not deceive me. May God be praised!"

Kayne was too stunned to stop the younger man from taking hold of one of his hands and kissing it.

"I thought never to see you again, Captain. None of us did." The dark eyes blinked up at him in the firelight. Around them, the crowd began to chatter in confusion. "We tried to discover what had happened—where you had gone so suddenly, without even a word—until Sir John Fastolf himself rebuked us and we gave way at last. But we never would have done so, my lord, if any lesser man had forbade us the search of you."

"Gwillym," Kayne murmured softly, gently pulling his hand free and laying it upon the other man's head, touching the dark head as if he were setting a blessing upon it. "Gwillym, what are you doing here? How came you to be here?" He could hear Sir Griel's voice now, loud above the din of the crowd, and prayed that none had heard their exchange. It would be strange enough that Gwillym had recognized and knelt before him; Kayne could allow nothing more.

"Rise, quickly," he commanded, keeping his tone low so that only Gwillym could hear it. "Say nothing to anyone of who I am—for the loyalty you bear me, I ask this of you. I want none in this village to know more of me save that I am their blacksmith."

"But, Captain," Gwillym protested as he rose to his feet, "how can this be? Sir Griel told me…"

"Say nothing," Kayne repeated curtly. Sir Griel was approaching at the quickest stride his short, stocky legs could manage, utter fury written on his hairy face. "I will explain all to you later, when I have you safe at my dwelling. You must surely stay there with me after this, for Sir Griel will not have you in his service now."

"Nay," said Gwillym, thoroughly dazed. "He told me that you had gravely insulted his betrothed, and therefore I must kill you. I did not know 'twould be you, Captain, else I never would have dared…"

"Hush, lad," Kayne said. He held his gaze on Sir Griel, but from the corner of his eye he saw Sofia pushing out of the crowd to move toward him, her lovely face filled with concern. "I understand the full of it. Trust me, now, as you did in France. Do not call me 'captain' before any other, and say naught of what you know of me. I'll speak to Sir Griel."

"You will have to," Gwillym said, standing beside Kayne and watching as Sir Griel and his remaining soldiers approached. The crowds began to move closer, as well. "I know not how I could explain what has happened this night. 'Tis all so strange."

"More than you know, Gwillym, my lad," Kayne agreed, casting him a brief, reassuring smile, "but have faith. We will come out of it in one piece, I vow, just as we did from many a battle. Now be still, and follow what I say. We are about to become distant cousins."

Chapter Seven

"Your champion is my cousin, but did not know me until we came close enough to the fire and he saw my face. This is why he refuses the fight, Sir Griel. There is no other cause, and 'tis known by all that such relation forbids the shedding of blood. It is decreed thus by both the Church and the Crown."

Sofia had only just stumbled near enough in her rush to reach Kayne to hear the explanation he was giving a furious Sir Griel. The raptly curious crowd had formed an immediate and thick circle about the men, and she had to shove hard to get through.

"Kayne," she said as she at last reached him.

His gaze flickered toward her, and he held out a hand to draw her near. "I am well," he said before returning his attention to Sir Griel. "Unless you wish to set another of your men upon me, the contest is over."

She could scarce believe that Kayne put such a suggestion before Sir Griel, to allow another of his men the chance to kill him. This man who'd just fought him—his own cousin, thank a merciful God—had nearly succeeded in doing the deed, and Sofia had suffered agonies beyond all she had known in watching the confrontation. If the matter hadn't ended as miraculously as it had, she couldn't have said who would come away the winner.

Sir Griel's fury was evident on his face, and barely contained. "You lie, blacksmith. Sir Gwillym Raithman is no cousin of yours. He told me he has no family in Sussex. Is that not so, Gwillym?"

"I spoke wrongly, my lord," Gwillym replied. "I did not know then that my cousin had set up his smithy in the village of Wirth. We are distantly related, but indeed we are cousins, and therefore I will not fight him."

"Then you will leave my service, as well!" Sir Griel thundered.

"As you will, my lord." Gwillym made a courteous bow.

"And I'll make certain none will have your allegiance. You'll find no other lord to take your service."

"If that is your desire, my lord."

"As to you, blacksmith," Sir Griel said, turning his wrath upon Kayne, "we are far from finished in this matter." He looked at Sofia, who stood beside Kayne. "Think well on that, mistress, and on the great displeasure you've given me."

Sofia understood what he meant. She would suffer for the insults and humiliation he'd been dealt this night. She and Kayne both.

Kayne stepped forward, despite Sofia's efforts to hold him back.

"And you would do well, my lord," he said in a low tone, towering over the smaller man, "before you make such threats, to think upon the promises I gave you this afternoon. I bid you good eve."

Sir Griel said nothing more, but turned about and strode away, his men following.

"We must hurry and be quit of this place," Kayne said,

watching as Sir Griel and his soldiers mounted their horses and spurred away at a furious pace. "The sooner I have you safe to your dwelling, mistress, the better. Where is your mount, Gwillym? Quickly, fetch your sword and let us be on our way before the crowds refuse to let us go."

"Kayne," Sofia said, but he shook his head and pulled her forward, against the tide of villagers who desired to congratulate him a second time.

"We will speak later," he promised. "For now, let us find your father to tell him that I will take you home, lest he worry o'er your sudden absence—if worry he would."

Sir Malcolm was, after all the festivities, too drunk and sleepy to worry about much of anything—including Sir Griel. He patted Kayne on the shoulder and called him a "good lad," kissed his daughter, and sent them on their way with the promise that he would make his own way to Ahlgren Manor as soon as he'd shared one last tankard of ale with his particular friends.

"He'll not only be ill come the morn," Sofia predicted as Kayne led her from the field where the festival had taken place in the direction of the manor, "but also terrified of whether Sir Griel will visit him again."

"Aye," Kayne agreed, "but more than this, he'll remember that the village blacksmith dared to escort his daughter home, and will be unhappy at the thought. Rightly so, for tongues will be wagging for many days, and there'll be no stopping them. We must take all care, Sofia, to give the gossips no further cause for such talking."

"'Tis far too late for that, Kayne. They will talk a great deal, but not about me." With her hand on his arm, she pulled him to a stop, gazing up at him through the darkness. "I heard him call you 'captain,' Kayne, and so did many others."

His face was stern, set. "That means naught."

She shook her head. "'Tis a title of great respect, and spoken by him with great respect. He kissed your hand with reverence." She raised her eyebrows in a questioning look. "Do you tell me that means naught?"

He frowned darkly. "I tell you nothing at all, mistress. 'Tis none of your concern what any man calls me. Come." He began to pull her along again.

"He is not your cousin," Sofia stated after they'd walked a short distance. "You only told Sir Griel that to keep him from forcing his man to fight you. 'Twas the only honorable way out for a knight who has given his vow of fealty."

"If this is what you believe, then I pray you will keep such thoughts to yourself. Unless you wish to cause Gwillym great difficulty."

"Of a certainty I'll not speak of it," Sofia said with a measure of offense, pulling him to a halt again. "I should never bring any man harm apurpose—and certainly not to the benefit of Sir Griel. But if he is not your cousin, then who is he?"

"A friend," Kayne replied. "And that is all I can say of the matter. Here is Gwillym now." He nodded toward where the armored knight approached on his steed. "Speak no more of it this night, I beg of you, Sofia."

"Very well," she said. "But on the morrow, you must tell me the truth."

He smiled, giving a shake of his head, and ran the backs of his fingers across her cheek in a gentle sweep.

"On the morrow, you will be too weary to move out of your bed. You must stay there and rest, with your precious fern blossom beneath your pillow, and dream. I vow I will do likewise, for I am as weary after this day as I ever was from battling in France."

Sofia could not keep from smiling as well, despite her unhappiness at Kayne's evasive tactics. "You have fought today as if in battle—twice.'' The smile died away. '''Twas terrible to watch, Kayne. I thought, at moments, that you might come to grave harm.'' Lifting a hand, she touched his face. ''I could not bear to see such as that come to pass for my sake. I told you how it is for me.''

He took her hand and placed a kiss upon her palm. ''I will take care in all things, most especially with Sir Griel. Have no fears, Sofia. Now, come. Gwillym waits for us by the road, and Midsummer Night is done.''

Sofia discovered, the next afternoon, that Kayne had spoken truly. She was far too weary to bestir herself to dress formally enough for going out of doors, and instead spent the day in lazy self-indulgence. After sleeping until well past noon, she rose and called for her maid, Mariah, to prepare a bath. While it was being readied, Sofia broke her fast with warm sweet buns spread with fresh butter and a mug of hot, steaming cider.

She sent a message to her father asking after his health, and received a reply from his manservant saying that the lord of Ahlgren Manor was sick from drink and would spend the day in bed. Hearing this, Sofia immediately dug through her collection of medicines to find the herbal potion that had soothed her father many a time before when he'd suffered from such excess, and sent it to the manservant with directions for its use. Normally, she would have tended to her father, but today Sofia had decided to pamper herself—something she'd never done before.

When her bath was ready, she scented the water with oil of roses, then climbed into the large wooden tub and leaned back with a sigh, closing her eyes and enjoying a long, pleasurable soak. Half an hour or more later, she allowed her maid to wash her hair, then sat by the fire as the great length of it was carefully combed out for drying. With a happy sigh, Sofia closed her eyes and submitted with sleepy contentment to her maid's ministrations.

"Did the flower work its magic last night, mistress?" Mariah asked in a teasing voice, almost as Sofia had dozed off. "Did you dream of the man who will be your husband?"

Sofia smiled. She had dreamt of Kayne, but that was not to be surprised at. She dreamt of him almost every night.

"It matters not," she murmured. "'Tis unlikely that I shall ever wed, Mariah."

Aye, even though her wish had floated all the way across the river last night, Sofia knew that she spoke the truth. She had told Kayne the same thing only a few days past, and neither wishes nor magic could change what would be. But she might yet cherish such dreams, just as she would ever cherish her memories of the Midsummer Day she'd spent with Kayne.

It was wonderful to be clean and fresh, to smell of sweet roses and leave her hair unbound and flowing. Sofia dressed in her most comfortable chemise and spent the remainder of the day curled up in a pillowed chair, writing missives that had long needed writing and tending to small, pleasant chores that had been put off for too many months, such as rearranging the cupboards and chests that held her collection of herbs and medicines, making small repairs to her favorite surcoats, and mixing a new batch of her favorite scented oil to wear—all selfish tasks that benefited her alone. But Sofia could not feel guilty. Tomorrow she would be busy with her various duties again. For one special day she would do as she pleased.

The next morning, when she rose, feeling much the better and fully refreshed, Sofia dressed and ate and set about her work. She first inspected the servants and the manor itself, gave orders for cleaning and mending and meal preparation, and then sat down in the study behind her father's table to work on the estate's ledgers.

At noon, she went to visit with her father, who never woke before then, and who, though much improved, had decided that he should spend another day resting. He was sitting in his large paneled bed with the wooden doors pulled back, breaking his fast with a large quantity of food set upon a tray and two tankards of ale at the ready.

"If, by any chance, we should receive visitors today, Sofia," he said, clearly meaning Sir Griel, "tell them that I cannot speak to anyone for another week—at the very least."

"You cannot avoid him forever, Father," Sofia chided. "If you would simply tell Sir Griel that you refuse his suit, he might begin to leave us in peace."

Sir Malcolm looked truly ill. "He would more likely take his sword to my head, and that you know as well as I, my dear. And now this business with the blacksmith—I cannot like it, Sofia. Sir Griel will kill us all if he doesn't get his way. Oh, I wish the blacksmith hadn't overset him so, besting all his men. 'Tis sure to have done far more harm than good."

Sofia looked at her father with a measure of surprise. "But you were openly proud of Master Kayne when he won both encounters. You congratulated him long and loudly."

Sir Malcolm groaned and put his face in his hands. "Don't speak of it, Sofia. I was too drunk to know what I did, God save me. Sir Griel will hear of it and slice the ears from my head, I vow. Oh, Heaven's mercy, what shall we do?" He dropped his hands. "You must keep away from Master Kayne from this day on, Sofia. Never go to his smithy again—never even approach his gate. And certainly don't speak to him if you should meet in the village."

"Father, that's but foolishness," Sofia told him.

"Nay, nay, that is the way it must be, lest we call Sir Griel's wrath even more greatly upon our heads. Have one of the servants speak to the blacksmith if we have any custom for him, but you must keep far away from him."

"I cannot," Sofia protested. "I speak to each of the villagers, one and all, in the same manner and with the same courtesy. 'Twould be wrong to treat Master Kayne differently."

Her father gave her a hard look. "But you already treat him differently. Do you think me blind, Sofia, or believe that I've not noticed the preference you have toward the man? Spending Midsummer Day with him. Kayne the Unknown? Bah!" He threw down the linen napkin he'd used for wiping his lips. "I'll not have it, a daughter of mine dallying with a commoner—and a lowly blacksmith at that!"

"That lowly blacksmith," she said with care, striving to contain her anger, "saved you from humiliation at the hands of Sir Griel yesterday, for God alone knows you'd never have been able to protect me from that man's unwanted advances."

"Sofia!"

She set her hands on her hips and glared at him. "And Kayne the Unknown saved me, as well—*twice*—from the attentions of a man whom I utterly loathe. If you would repay such as that with insults, so be it. I will certainly not do so." She turned to leave the chamber.

"Sofia!" Sir Malcolm shouted after her. "Sofia, you'll do as I say!"

She whirled about to face him. "Only when I am no longer required to be the master of this estate. Do you wish to take over the duties, Father? Shall I bring you the ledgers and lists, and allow you to direct the servants and speak to your vassals and answer every missive? Will you collect the rents and tithes and pay the same that you owe to the Crown? Only tell me and I will gladly turn it—all of it—over to you now.''

Sir Malcolm had turned red in the face with anger, but after a few moments of blustering he uttered, ''You're a wicked, disrespectful girl, Sofia Ahlgren! I should take a whip to you for speaking to your own father in such an untoward manner.''

''Aye, do,'' Sofia dared. ''Then I would be the one taken to my bed, and you'd have to turn Sir Griel away when he comes to our door. I vow I'd much rather be bloodied for disrespect than ever see his face again. Give me your leave, Father, and I shall also fetch your whip, along with everything else.''

Sir Malcolm blustered a while more, then at last began to calm. ''Foolish girl,'' he muttered. ''Of course I should never raise a hand to you. Have I ever done so? But, by the Rood, you do press me so with such stubbornness. Befriend the blacksmith, then, if you must.'' He gave a wave of his hand. ''Ruin yourself and all the rest of us with you. But know this, girl. I'd agree to let Sir Griel have you before I'd ever see you wed to a commoner, and that I swear by God above. My mind is fixed upon it, and shall not be changed.''

Sofia gave him no reply, for this, at last, was something she could not dispute, though heaven alone knew how she wished she could. She quit the room and went directly to the kitchen, where she ignored the complaints of the cook and packed a basket with a loaf of bread and a variety of cheeses and cold meats. To this she added a skin of good red wine and two goblets. Then, taking up her cloak, she left the manor with basket in hand, heading for the black-smith's shop.

It was a beautiful day, warm and bright, with a soft breeze blowing, and Sofia felt her spirits rising as she walked toward the village. The fields near the river where the Midsummer festival had been held were cleared of every last sign of the many activities that had taken place two days past. It was almost hard to believe that so much merrymaking had occurred at all in such placid pastures.

Beyond the fields was the forest, and Sofia thought of the kisses Kayne had given her there. Such wonderful kisses—sweeter than anything she had ever known. If she hadn't already realized that she was in love with Kayne, she surely would have had no doubts after sharing such tender intimacy with him. What she was going to do about loving a common—though not so common—blacksmith was a matter she'd not yet discerned. Indeed, she seemed constantly to be pushing all good sense aside when it came to Kayne—even at the very moment, going to see him simply because her father had upset her so, when she knew very well that naught could ever come of it.

But that was how it was for her. She was in love with a man wholly unsuitable, who she could never wed but longed to be with every moment of both night and day, and who filled her dreams with such strength that she could not find a like strength to fight them—if she'd even desired to fight. Nay, it was beyond her own power to stop what she felt for Kayne the Unknown. If she would be kept from him then it must be done by the hand of another—her father, if he dared, or Sir Griel, if he found a way to stop her physically. Otherwise, she was captive to a force beyond her control, and glad to be so.

When Sofia at last arrived at the smithy, she found the gate closed but not bolted. Casting her gaze up and down the village lane to see whether anyone watched what she did, Sofia carefully pulled the latch and crept into the coolness of the great building.

The soft whinnying of horses greeted her, but little else. It was very much as it had been when she'd first visited Kayne, dark and quiet, with no coals ablaze in the furnace and none of the ringing, clanking sounds of smithy work. A moment of dread possessed her—could Kayne be hurt, as he'd been then, or perhaps even ill? Had Sir Griel somehow managed to visit some terrible harm upon him? The thought sent her striding in the direction of the door that led from the large barn to Kayne's dwelling, and she entered his home without so much as a knock upon the door.

"Kayne?" she called out, setting her basket down just inside the door. "Kayne, are you here?" She moved slowly into the center of the clean, spare room that comprised the bottom half of the house. Looking upward, toward the stairs, she added, rather foolishly, "'Tis Sofia...come to see if you're well."

Nothing. No reply, no sound. She looked about her and saw that he must have earlier been in the lower room, for the remnants of a small fire yet glowed in the hearth, and a black kettle that contained the scrapings of boiled oats yet hung near the flames. On the finely crafted table Kayne used for eating his meals were the clear signs of a meal partaken of only hours before, which had not yet been cleared away. The sight of two pewter bowls and plates— apart from being an unusual find in the house of a blacksmith, for only the very rich could afford to eat from actual plates—reminded Sofia that Kayne had brought a guest to his home two nights before.

"Sir Gwillym?" she called, turning about. "Is anyone here?"

Still no reply, save answering neighs and whinnies from the horses in the barn.

"Where could they have gone?" she murmured aloud, pondering the question. Out riding, perhaps? She'd not looked to see if Tristan was in his stall. But surely not. Kayne's habits had ever been to rise early and open his gate for custom. The villagers depended upon his skills so greatly, and neither weather nor illness—nor the painful burns he'd suffered in saving Harold Avendale and his family—could keep him from attending to his work. Sofia well remembered how she had argued with him regarding the care of the wounds she'd tended after the fire, telling him openly that he was a fool to go back to his smithy too soon, but he'd not listened to her. The farmers of Wirth could not till their fields unless they had a blacksmith to repair their plows and scythes or to shoe their cattle, and the women of Wirth could not keep their families whole if there was no blacksmith to mend their pots and kettles.

If such painful burns as he'd had then could not keep him from his labors, very little else could. Sofia cast another glance upstairs, and without thinking too much upon what she did, began to climb them. She was well familiar with Kayne's bedchamber, having spent a great deal of time in it during the weeks following the fire. But during those tense days, when he might so easily have become ill from his wounds and died, she'd paid little attention to the room's actual character. Now, as she walked into it, she took note of all that made it so unusual.

Like the rest of Kayne's dwelling, it was large and airy and filled with as much natural light as any room she'd ever before known. Four glass-paned windows—the cost of which Sofia couldn't begin to measure—were covered only by the finest and thinnest of white linen cloth, and these Kayne kept drawn back by hooks upon each of the room's four walls, so that both sunlight and moonlight streamed freely in and the music of rain and wind could be readily heard.

She had thought that winter's biting chill would seep into the dwelling through such windows, and yet it had ever seemed most pleasant and comfortable during the cold weeks in which she'd tended Kayne. She had learned that one reason why was that the hearths and chimneys had been built using the latest knowledge, so that they drew cleanly and put out a greater amount of heat.

Kayne's bed was a thing of beauty, simply but finely built, as all of his furniture was, but very large so that a man as big as he was might move about comfortably, and fitted with a feather mattress that was both firm enough to hold him and yet soft enough to seem most inviting. He had spurned the idea of wooden panels as foolish—so he had told her once during the long hours of her care of him—and had instead decided upon curtains. These, just like those that hung over the windows, had ever been tied back upon the bedposts whenever Sofia had occasion to see them.

But what a strange thing that was, she thought as she moved farther into the quiet, comfortable room, that she should be so intimately acquainted with not only a man's private chamber, but also with his bed, knowing whether its curtains were seldom tied back or not.

Lifting a hand, she touched one of the curtains, feeling the fine cloth beneath her fingertips. The bed was made and the chamber itself was neat and clean and uncluttered—just as Kayne himself was, a purely simple man.

Sofia gave a sigh and, using both hands, pushed herself up to sit upon the high mattress. She hooked the low heels of her soft boots against the bed rail in a comfortable pose and sat in thoughtful silence.

There was something about Kayne's house, even more about his bedchamber, that invited peace of mind. He had clearly intended that it be thus, for every inch of the house proclaimed the monkish life he'd sought—at no small cost—in Wirth. A part of it was the cleanness and simpleness, even to the lines of the furniture, but another was that the chambers were paneled almost entirely in wood, rather than brick or mortar. And not the dark, rough wood that might be seen in a tavern, but a light, smooth, polished wood that gleamed from the light given by both sun and hearth. Sofia had never seen the like before, or known anything more beautiful and pleasing to the senses.

Oh, where could Kayne be?

Sofia didn't know whether she should be more distressed by Kayne's absence, or by the grave disappointment she felt at that absence. She was in a sad way, indeed, if such as that could bring her low.

With another sigh, she pushed from the bed to stand upon her feet, knowing that she must not allow herself the luxury of thinking that she might intrude upon his privacy in so ready a manner. She was not his wife, nor even his betrothed, and had no right to sit upon his bed and wish for him—nor even to enter his home as she had done, unannounced and uninvited, as if she were naught but a thief.

Nay, she would not intrude upon him so, loving him as she did and wishing to protect all that was of value to him. She would return to Ahlgren Manor and take up her many duties, and then, later, she would make her round of the village to see if there were any who required her aid in some...

"What is this?" she murmured softly, seeing for the first time the door which fell open from the midst of one wall—a door that, unless it were open, would have gone entirely unseen. She had spent many an hour in the chamber, yet had never known it was there, so closely did it blend in with the golden panels that lined the wall. There was not even a latch that Sofia could see as she moved to inspect the door, touching it with careful fingers and letting curiosity get the better of her as she at last swung it wide to reveal the closet beyond.

"God's mercy," Sofia whispered at what she saw before her, and the next moment went down on her knees to inspect more closely the gleaming suit of armor that hung in the secret compartment. With reverent care, she brushed her fingertips over the leg guard, shaking her head with disbelief. This was a knight's armor—but, nay, even more than that. It was armor such as only a very great and noble knight would wear, bright silver trimmed with gold, polished to such a blinding brilliance that Sofia was almost dazed by it, and yet so heavily dented that there could be no question of the many battles it had seen. Staring up at the face plate, she could almost see Kayne's blue eyes peering from beneath the visor.

But there was more. Beneath the armor, swathed in heavy velvet, lay a great, many-jeweled sword.

"So it's true," she said. "The rumor. How could anyone have known?" She touched one of the jewels in the hilt, a large square ruby. Even she hadn't known—she, who'd been in Kayne's dwelling far more often than anyone else in Wirth. This secret closet had been too well concealed to be so easily discovered. "Next I'll find a treasure chest filled with gold and jewels," she muttered, sitting back on her heels and letting her gaze wander all about the closet. There were other articles of war hidden within. A large shield that matched the armor, though even more dented, emblazoned with the King's own colors, two fine bows and a quiver filled with arrows, a crossbow, several shorter swords and half a dozen daggers in a variety of lengths.

Finally, hanging upon wooden pegs in the farthest corner of the closet, there were several sets of courtly clothes, all made of fine cloth and beautifully ornamented with gold, silver, and more precious jewels. There were garments made of pure white silk to drape over the suit of armor, whenever it was worn before the King, and soft-footed boots such as noblemen wore.

"Kayne," Sofia said softly, feeling a measure of distress and wonderment, "what can this mean? Who can you be, to possess such things?"

"He is a very great man, Mistress Sofia," someone said from the chamber door, "but you did not need to see such hidden treasures to know that."

Sofia turned with a gasp to see Sir Gwillym leaning against the doorway, his arms folded indolently across his chest and a smile on his handsome face. He was far improved from what she had seen of him two nights before, clean and dressed in some of Kayne's clothes, which she recognized.

"Sir Gwillym...I...did not mean to..." She couldn't think of what to tell him, being caught in so obvious an act of spying.

"Nay, of course you did not," he replied easily, pushing from the door to stroll a few steps forward. "The fault is my lord, Sir Kayne's. He left rather quickly this morn, and so did not take his usual care to properly close all his closets."

"All?" Sofia repeated, gazing about the room. "You mean to say there are others?"

"Two others that he showed me this morn, as I helped him to pack for his journey. They are well concealed in the paneling, but here—" he reached out to touch a certain wooden panel "—is a prayer closet, and beside it—here, you see?—is another closet filled with clothing chests. If I knew the secret to opening them, I would prove that I speak the truth, but he did not show me how 'tis done, and as there are no latches, you must simply believe what I say. 'Tis quite extraordinary, is it not, how 'twas all built to look so plain and innocent? But, then, my lord, Sir Kayne, is a man uncommon in all things, and ever has been, since the day I first knew him.''

Sofia pushed slowly to her feet. "Kayne has gone away?''

Sir Gwillym gave a curt nod. "Aye, and will not return for several days—perhaps a fortnight or more. He has left me here to guard over you, mistress, and keep you safe from my former master, Sir Griel. I admit that I did not expect the task to be so simple—for here I find you beneath my hand, and not, as I had thought, out and about where I must follow your every step.''

Sofia flushed at the meaning in his tone. She knew how damning it was that he should find her here, in Kayne's bedchamber, going through his personal belongings.

"I came in search of Master Kayne," she said, "and grew worried when he gave no reply to my calls. I nursed him once when he was very ill," she told him with a measure of some insistence, as if he would not believe her, "and thought mayhap he might be abed and in need of...of..." Her voice died away as she thought of what her explanation seemed like. Just to speak of Kayne being in his bed was beyond all that could be allowed an innocent maid.

Sir Gwillym's expression was filled with interest. "Of more nursing?" he finished for her, his appreciative gaze wandering the length of Sofia's figure until she burned with even greater embarrassment. "I should think any man would be pleased for such as that. I must pray to fall very ill before my lord makes his return.''

"You misunderstand me!" she retorted. "I only meant to see if he was ill, and in need of care. When I saw that he was not here, I surely should have left at once, but the door was ajar, and—I fully admit my sin in looking where I had no right."

"I do not condemn you," he said, lifting his hands up in a shrug. "Sir Kayne told me what manner of woman you are, and warned that I must not expect any meek, mild maiden who keeps to her own path. He also told me that you would come today, asking questions and demanding replies."

"Did he?" Sofia said, suddenly angry. "I did not realize he held me in such contempt as that."

Sir Gwillym's frowned slightly. "'Twas so far from contempt when he spoke of you that I can but wonder how you would think it. He said these things with all admiration, mistress, and—perhaps I should not admit the truth of this—with more even than that."

The insult Sofia had felt died, to be replaced by hopefulness and wonder. "I see," she said softly. "Well—" she turned away to hide her smile "—I will close this door and Kayne's secrets may be hidden again. I am glad that he warned you of my curious nature, for I do intend to ask you many questions." She turned back to face him. "Will you answer them?"

"My lord gave me permission to speak of certain matters to you, but only if I can first gain your solemn vow never to tell anyone what you hear."

Sofia nodded. "I so vow, by God above, that I will tell no one."

"Then mayhap you will be so good as to come belowstairs and offer me some of the food I saw in the basket you left?" Sir Gwillym stepped back and swept his arm toward the door, making an elegant bow as he did. "I am sorry if you meant it for Sir Kayne and not for me, but 'twould be a sin to let it go wasting, when here you have a man both glad and willing to sate his hunger with it.''

"Of course I shall be pleased to feed you," Sofia said as she moved past him and toward the door, adding, "in exchange for the tale of how you came to know Master Kayne, and what you know of him." A thought occurred to her, and she stopped to look at him. "Did you not think an intruder had come into the dwelling, when you saw the door opened and the basket on the floor? A dangerous thief?"

"Nay," Sir Gwillym said with a laugh, taking Sofia's elbow to guide her to the stairs. "I was afeared of no such thing. Thieves do not usually smell of sweet roses, my lady."

Chapter Eight

"**Y**ou are not truly cousins, are you?" was Sofia's first question as she cleared the table of the dirty plates.

Sir Gwillym shook his head. "Nay. 'Tis the first lie I have ever heard my lord speak, though he did not utter it to save himself, but me, and there was little else to be done."

Sofia carefully laid out two linen cloths, one before Sir Gwillym and one for her own use. "You call him your lord," she said as she began to lay food upon each cloth. "Is he, in truth, a nobleman? For I know he is of the knighthood—all in the secret closet abovestairs proved the truth of that. But then why would he come to Wirth to live in such a manner? To be a common blacksmith?"

"Please, mistress, I beg of you," Sir Gwillym said, holding up a staying hand, "give me time to make answers to all of these. Much of it I do not know, but that which I do, I will tell."

He accepted the goblet of wine she gave him, and began to speak.

"I first met Sir Kayne seven years ago in France, where I had gone with my older brothers to fight in the king's army. We are Welsh, loyal to England, and my father the baron of a large estate in Caermarthen. My brothers had already gained the knighthood, but I, being but ten and seven then, was only their squire.

"We joined Sir John Fastolf in Normandy to receive his orders as to whose command he desired us to follow, and to our very great fortune, 'twas to Sir Kayne's service we were given. He was captain over five hundred men, well-loved by all."

"That's why you called him captain," Sofia murmured. "I heard you say it on Midsummer Night."

"Aye, that is why. 'Tis far too old a habit for me to be broken of it. He was my captain and I thank God for it, for Sir Kayne kept me alive while I fought beneath his command—me and both my brothers, as well—and because of him I attained the knighthood. Sir John Fastolf himself dubbed me, because Sir Kayne asked it of him, and now I am one of the few men to have attained that great honor. But Sir John would do such as that for my lord, for Sir Kayne was among his own most honored warriors. Sir Kayne," said Gwillym, lifting his goblet, "is known to be one of the greatest knights in the king's service."

Sofia watched him as he drank deeply from the cup. When he set it aside, she asked, "But how can this be? How has he come down to such as this? To be a mere blacksmith?"

"I do not know the full answer to give you, mistress," Gwillym told her, "but I know why he left France, and a little of why he left the knighthood.

"You see, there were four of them who went to France, seeking their fortunes—four friends, of whom Sir Kayne was one. Each was a great warrior and proved himself on the field of battle, and each was knighted and received great boons for their brave deeds, save one. They were Sir Kayne, Sir Senet Gaillard, Sir Aric, and a man who was

only ever called, within my hearing, John Ipris. Each of
them, save John Ipris, were given command of several hundred men, and for the friendship they bore one another,
their troops were kept closely together, so that those of us
beneath Sir Kayne's hand fought beside Sir Senet's men,
and also Sir Aric's. John Ipris fought bravely upon the battlefield as well, but he performed other duties for Sir John
Fastolf which were secret even to his friends. Often he
would disappear for many days, and then suddenly reap-
pear, with no explanation, to rejoin Sir Kayne and the others.

"In time, John Ipris and his wanderings began to take
us—those of us who were beneath Sir Kayne's hand, and
Sir Senet's and Sir Aric's—away from the main battles to
more dangerous tasks, and most especially our troops, for
Sir Kayne's command often led the others. We scouted
villages and searched for traitors, or, worse, the enemy, and
destroyed those places that harbored spies. When trouble
came, we were the first to find and fight it, and Sir Kayne,
being by no means a coward, never let his men do what he
would not do first. I tell you, mistress, that you have never
seen a man fight as our captain could do."

"You speak the truth," she murmured. "Two nights
past, I saw him fight against you, and never saw the like."

Sir Gwillym made a scoffing sound. "That was as naught
compared to how he fought in France. He but defended
himself two nights past, but in France he both defended
and attacked. He fought, mistress, like one of God's mighty
angels, come down from the heavens. And all I know of
such fighting I learned from him, else how could I have
even hoped to match him as I did on Midsummer Night?"

"A lesser man would have been felled far more
quickly," Sofia agreed. "He bested several others earlier
in the day with great ease."

"Aye, that is how he is," Sir Gwillym said with pride. "A great knight. A *true* knight. Not a man without honor or skill such as Sir Griel, who purchased the knighthood for a great deal of gold. I was proud indeed, and yet proud, to have served under Sir Kayne's command. And, yet—" he sighed and gave a shake of his head "—in time, it began to be hard for him. We could all see it, the great despair he would feel after each battle was done, though he had fought well and bravely throughout. 'Twas the killing—the endless killing, month after month."

Sofia leaned forward. "He killed many?"

Gwillym nodded. "Hundreds—hundreds upon hundreds of soldiers and fighting men. It did not seem to bother Sir Senet or Sir Aric, but for Sir Kayne and John Ipris, 'twas a hard thing. They were in France ten years, mistress, serving the king upon the battleground."

"God's mercy," she whispered with horror. "Ten years. Almost from his youth, then…"

"Aye, and his life for each of those years was spent killing—and having little in return for it. Sir Kayne grew rich in time, for he received many boons from the crown for his brave deeds, but the fight itself—the cause of England—never went forward. 'Twas all but useless foolishness, and naught was gained for all the blood that was spilt upon the soil of France."

"This, then, is why he left France, and the knighthood?" she asked.

"In part, I think. Another part, perhaps, is what he began to be called by many of his men and some of the other captains. 'Twas done by them as a matter of pride, for proud they were, indeed, of Sir Kayne's abilities upon the battlefield. But he hated the name—nay, even more than that, he full despised it, my lady—and each time he heard it I saw the darkness that already filled his eyes grow darker yet." Sir Gwillym gave a dismal shake of his head. "By the time he left France, Sir Kayne had become as hard and cold as any living man might do, and yet still be called living."

Sofia was almost afraid to ask the question, but she did. "What did they call him?"

Sir Gwillym lifted his gaze to meet her own. "Kayne the Bloody. Kayne the Destroyer."

"How could they have named him such?" she murmured with horror. "So kind and gentle a man as he is?"

"'Twas a badge of honor, just as I have told you, and any other man might have seen it so and accepted such titles gladly. But not Sir Kayne." Gwillym gave a great sigh. "But that was not the worst of what he suffered. The worst came but a month before he left us—a terrible thing that touched us all. I could only thank a merciful God that I was not the one who stood the responsibility for what happened. Sir Kayne was not entirely to blame, either, but he was our captain, and therefore took the blame upon himself."

"What happened?"

"I've told you that John Ipris often went out alone, engaged in some manner of spying, and what information he returned with often led us to destroy those places where our enemies were hidden. And not once—not once, mistress—was he ever in error about such things, so that we never made the mistake of killing innocents. But there came a day when John Ipris was taken ill, and another was sent in his place to see what might be discovered about a small village that Sir John Fastolf wished to take."

Even without hearing the full of the tale, Sofia began to feel a sense of dread.

"This other man returned from his spying with the news that dozens of French soldiers were encamped within the walls of a small estate near the village, being harbored there by a French lord. There was no reason to doubt the truth of this, and Sir John Fastolf gave orders accordingly to my lord, Sir Kayne, that everything within the walls of the estate was to be burnt to the ground.

"It was our way," Gwillym continued, distractedly fingering the goblet he held, "to start such blazes very early in the morn, while 'twas yet dark, and by this means catch our enemies more fully unawares. This had worked to our benefit many times before—at least when John Ipris had been our guide—and this is how Sir Kayne set about fulfilling Sir John Fastolf's orders."

"But it was a mistake?" Sofia whispered.

"Oh, aye," Gwillym said grimly. "A vile, horrible mistake. For there were no soldiers within those walls that we set flame to—making certain when we did that no one should come out alive. There were only a few women and a great many children. 'Twas a convent, you see, and, because of the war, also a refuge for orphaned children." He closed his eyes at the memory. "None of them survived the blaze. We heard them screaming behind the walls, crying for mercy and rescue, but 'twas impossible to save them. Sir Kayne tried—God above knows the truth of that. He sent Tristan time and again into the flames, striving to make his way past the gate, but each time failed. At last, only Sir Senet and Sir Aric could keep him from trying once more. If they had not done so, I believe my lord would have perished in the blaze, himself."

"Merciful God," Sofia said, setting trembling fingers against her lips. "Now I understand why he risked all to save Harold Avendale and his family from fire. And why he was visited by so many nightmares."

"Nightmares, mistress?"

"Yes, during the nights following a village fire from

which he saved an entire family, at great cost to himself. But surely you've seen the scars he bears for yourself, having been with him these past two days. I was the one who cared for him until the gravest dangers had passed. He was in terrible pain, and rest was hard-won, but even when he slept he was tormented by such dread nightmares of fire and death. I thought he dreamt of the fire in the village, but now...I can but believe 'twas that other fire he remembered.'' She strove to control her grief. "He suffered so greatly...but I think this must have been as nothing compared to what he suffered in France, following such a grave tragedy.''

"Aye, mistress. He was not the same man afterward. He nearly killed the man who'd given such false information, though the fellow pleaded that 'twas all a foolish mistake. But it could never be foolish for Sir Kayne. And some of the other captains who had ever been jealous of my lord began to hail him aloud by those names that he hated so—Kayne the Bloody, and Kayne the Destroyer.''

"Cruel, wicked men,'' Sofia uttered furiously. "'Twas no fault of his own that any perished!''

"'Twas not,'' Gwillym agreed, "but Sir Kayne would not have it so. He blamed himself and said nothing when those names were spoken, for I think he had begun to believe they were true.

"He disappeared for a full week after the fire, and no one knew where he had gone, not even Sir John Fastolf or his close companions, though they diligently searched for him. He returned just as suddenly and took up his duties again without a word, so solemn and dispirited that we none of us dared to question or disobey him.

"Then, perhaps a fortnight later, he vanished again, but this time with Sir Senet and Sir Aric and John Ipris. One of my brothers was appointed captain over Sir Kayne's men, but even he did not know where Sir Kayne or the others had gone. No one spoke openly regarding them, though there were rumors among the men that they had left the King's service and returned to England. But those of us who had been beneath Sir Kayne's command could not stop our fears and worries for him, and we determined that we must know what had become of our lord. To this end, I gathered up all my courage and approached Sir John Fastolf myself, asking the bold question. He rebuked me most angrily and sent me away, telling me not to pry into matters that were none of my concern. It convinced us—all of Sir Kayne's men—that our worst fears were true. Our captain never would have left us in such a manner, with no word, if all had been well."

"He should have bidden you farewell," Sofia agreed. "'Twas wrong of him not to do so."

Gwillym shrugged and shook his head. "He was not himself, mistress. Indeed, I think he was not whole for many months, even after returning to England, until he came here, to this small village, and found a measure of peace."

"Is he a nobleman, then? He could not have gained knighthood, otherwise."

"I have told you that I do not know the full of who or what he is, mistress, only that part which I knew of him in France, but I do not believe he is a nobleman. He has only spoken of the place where he was fostered, which is called Talwar, and of the lord who trained him for knighthood, Sir Justin Baldwin. Have you never heard of it or him?"

The names were vaguely familiar to Sofia, but she frowned and shook her head. "Perhaps, but I cannot remember."

"Sir Justin Baldwin has gained a wide reputation for fostering boys who are from poor families—or even those

that are basely born, with no family at all—and training
them for the knighthood. This is the only way in which
such boys could ever hope to attain such stature, and Sir
Kayne was among them, though I do not know which.''
Then he added, somewhat more dolefully, ''He has never
spoken of a family name, but only his Christian one—
Kayne. And even here he is called Kayne the Unknown, is
this not so?''

''Yes,'' she answered with a sigh. ''He has only ever
given his one name, and no other. And he would not say
where he had come from, much to the frustration of the
villagers. If they only knew that he is a famed knight of
the realm, how amazed they would all be. Even I am yet
amazed, though I knew he was not like other men.''

''He is not, but my lord is no longer of the knighthood,
mistress,'' Sir Gwillym reminded her gravely. ''He put
such honors aside when he came here, and has made solemn vows—before a priest, yet—that he will never again
take up arms against another man, unless it is for his own
defense or that of the most innocent and helpless, most
especially women and children. In this way he means to
make some amends for what he yet believes was his fault
in the burning of the convent.''

''Yet, though he has put away that very thing which
would have set him amongst the nobles, you still call him
'my lord,''' Sofia said softly.

Sir Gwillym met her direct gaze. ''Aye, mistress, and
will ever do so. He was, and will remain, the man to whom
I owe my very life. Even two nights past, he could have
readily killed me. Do you not think I wondered in all
amazement to find myself bested by a man who so easily
evaded my greatest efforts?''

Sofia gave a laugh. ''You are too humble, sir. It did not

look easy. Indeed, I thought you would kill him several times over, for he did naught save defend himself.''

''Then you do not know much of such contests, mistress. For all my efforts, I *should* have killed him, but he slipped from my grasp over and again, until I began to think him some kind of spirit called up from the ground in the magic of Midsummer Night. The truth of it is, I am the one who is fortunate to be alive after our encounter, and know it well. Apart from that, he saved me from public disgrace before Sir Griel and the people of Wirth, at no small cost to his own sense of honor, for, as I told you, 'twas the first falsehood that ever I heard pass his lips. A man such as that is worthy to be called 'lord,' mistress, whether he has put all titles aside or not. 'Tis a great honor to name him thus.''

Something suddenly occurred to Sofia as Sir Gwillym spoke—something astonishing and wonderful.

''Kayne is of the knighthood,'' she said, staring wide-eyed at her companion. ''Whether he is of noble birth or not has no bearing—and no one need ever know of it even if it did. My own father is not descended of any noble line, nor was my mother. And, come to that, neither is Sir Griel. Kayne is as good as any of them, and—if all you say is true—he is possessed of some money. Why, this very dwelling,'' she said, standing up and looking all about her at the fine, expensively built home, ''is proof of that.''

''Mistress Sofia,'' Gwillym murmured in a warning tone.

She ignored him and continued, wonderingly, ''There is no reason why we cannot be wed, Kayne and I.''

''Mistress…''

''Even my father must surely see that 'tis true. Indeed,'' she added, turning back to look at Gwillym, ''no one could dispute it—neither Church nor Crown nor anyone in Wirth.''

Gwillym laughed and set his wine goblet aside. "I would not dare to do so, then, either, mistress. But you might wait to perceive what Sir Kayne wishes before making such declarations. I do not think he will take up the knighthood again, having set it aside, and if he does not his fitness to wed you will fly away once more."

Sofia thought of all that had occurred between herself and Kayne, and remembered his kisses. He had never told her that he loved her, but surely he felt as she did. She had recognized how he'd struggled to restrain himself in the forest on Midsummer Night. His longings then had matched her own—Sofia was certain of it. She had not spoken openly of her love, either, and yet love him she did.

"He'll take up the knighthood again," she murmured. "I know that he will, once I've explained all to him."

"And what of the vows he has taken never to fight again, nor to bring harm to any man save in the direst circumstances?" Gwillym asked. "Such as that is not the way of the knighthood, especially to a man in service to the king, as Sir Kayne was. And what of the smithy? Sir Kayne has gone to great effort to secure the peace he's found here. You would ask him to give it up for your sake?"

"Nay, never," she said fervently. "I am content to dwell here, and to let Kayne follow his heart's desire, until my father, may God keep him, passes on. After that, we must do what is best for the people of Wirth, and Kayne would agree that this would be so."

"Move into Ahlgren Manor and become lord of the estate?" Gwillym asked. "He would make a fine lord, I grant you, but whether he would wish to be one is another matter."

"He will," Sofia said with a nod. "By then, he will have wearied of smithing, and will accept what he must do."

Sir Gwillym looked unconvinced. "You are very sure of yourself, mistress."

"Oh, aye," Sofia agreed, smiling at him, "where Kayne the Unknown is concerned, I am certain of all things. Have no fear for that, sir. I know what I am about."

Chapter Nine

The last thing—or person—Kayne expected to see when he returned to Wirth on a sunny afternoon twenty days after he'd left on his journey was Sofia, standing in the center of the village, covered head to toe in mud and caught in the midst of a rampaging herd of cattle. Every man, woman and child in the village—including Gwillym—was either screaming wildly, jumping about helplessly, or, as in Gwillym's case, striving desperately to gain some measure of control of the cattle and rescue Sofia. But it was to no avail. Sofia was well and truly beyond the reach of their hands, and no one could push through to save her. She was being knocked in every direction, close to being trampled to death. When the realization of this struck, Kayne's heart nearly stopped.

Without thinking upon what he did, he withdrew the small sword at his side and took Tristan's reins in a strong, steady grip. Tristan would not want to enter the tight, pressing confusion of the loudly protesting cows, but he was too well trained to disobey commands. Any smaller, weaker steed would never have been able to withstand the butting and shoving of the heavy cattle, but Tristan, calling upon his great strength, plowed into the midst of them and, striving mightily, forced a path. Kayne helped as best he could, shouting orders to the villagers to herd the beasts to the south and reaching down to thump the half-maddened creatures on their heads with the hilt of his sword.

Sofia saw him coming, but had little reaction. Clearly suffering both shock and fear, she but stared at him wide-eyed. Gwillym, from Kayne's left, understood at once what was best to be done, and he physically reached into the frantic, directionless herd and grabbed the head of the nearest cow, forcibly pulling it away from the rest and driving it south. Giving loud protest, the creature ran mooing down the street. Two others blindly followed behind it.

Gwillym grabbed another cow, wrestling with it until it at last turned and ran after the first three. Immediately, every man who dared joined him in the task.

Kayne continued to force Tristan forward, bringing his hilt down on the cows' great, lumpy heads to make them move as he inched a path toward where Sofia stood. Her slender, muddied form swayed against the force of the great, heavy bodies that buffeted her. Her face was white, and Kayne knew that she was very near to fainting.

"Sofia!" he called out to her. "*Wait*…wait for me. I'm coming."

He spurred Tristan on, and the brave steed responded nobly, straining even harder to push forward through what seemed like a never-ending sea of bone and flesh.

Almost at the same time as Kayne neared Sofia, reaching down one long arm to scoop her up, the cows finally began to disperse, thanks to the efforts of Gwillym and the others. The confusion and pressing turned into a stampede, all going southward, but by the time it began Kayne had Sofia safely before him on the saddle, cradled against his chest. She lay limply, saying nothing, but he could hear the gasp-

ing of her breath as she strove to draw in air, and feel the
trembling of her body.

Gathering her more closely, he shouted back to Gwillym,
"I'm taking Mistress Sofia home!" and, without waiting
for a reply, he set Tristan into a firm, steady trot out of
what remained of the herd and the village in the direction
of Ahlgren Manor.

"Are you all right, Sofia?" he asked once they were well
out of the village. "God alone knows how you came to be
in the midst of such a dire circumstance." The hand that
held her patted along her shoulder and arm, as if to discover
whether anything was broken. "Were you hurt?" He kept
patting, striving to reassure himself that she was well. "By
the Rood! What were you doing there? How came you to
be in such danger—and with Gwillym standing there like
a very fool, when I commanded that he never let you out
of his sight."

"T-take me to the r-river," she stammered, still trembling fiercely.

Kayne was certain that he'd not understood. "What? To
the river?"

"Aye, t-to the r-r-river. P-please, Kayne."

"To the manor is where you should go," he told her,
but he was not proof against her pleas. When they reached
the forest, he turned Tristan into the trees and rode toward
the river, coming to the place where they had set the small
boats bearing wishes afloat on Midsummer Night.

Sofia hardly waited until he'd brought Tristan to a halt
before she pushed out of Kayne's arms and slid down from
the saddle. Without so much as glancing at him she rushed
into the darkness of the forest, leaving Kayne in a state of
utter bewilderment.

"Sofia?" he called out as he dismounted.

"I'm all right," she shouted back from somewhere behind the trees.

Kayne wasn't quite so certain, especially when he heard a great deal of rustling. What in the name of heaven was she doing? With a sigh and a shake of his head, he led Tristan to the water and let him drink.

"This is not the manner of welcome we had thought to have, is it, old boy?" he murmured, patting the great steed upon the neck. "But, considering it was Sofia involved, 'tis no great surprise. Eh? She has a way of—"

A loud splash of water farther downriver made him jerk his head about in alarm. The next moment, he had dropped Tristan's reins and gone racing toward the sound.

"Sofia!" he shouted frantically, pushing through where she'd disappeared into the trees. "Sofia!" Her surcoat and soft boots, both yet heavy with mud, had been thrown across a low branch near the riverbank. The sound of more splashing confirmed his worst fears—that Sofia had somehow fallen into the river and was desperately striving to stay afloat.

Kayne knew how to swim, but was full aware just how rare a thing that was. Death by drowning was among the most common occurrences in the land—and it happened very quickly.

Without hesitating a moment to pull off even his boots, he flung himself forward, through the screen of trees and straight into the wide river, thanking a merciful God as he splashed through the cold water that it was slow-moving and not too deep.

He was up to his thighs in water when Sofia, who was in the midst of rinsing her hair of mud, stopped what she was doing and looked up at him with surprise.

"Why, Kayne," she said, her eyes wide with amazement, "what is amiss?"

He was momentarily shocked beyond all speech, and stood where he was, water swirling all about him, and stared.

She was clothed only in a white linen chemise, which had become nearly invisible in the water, though she was very modestly sitting deeply enough in the water so that everything below her shoulders was covered. Not that it mattered to Kayne. The sight of her thus, nearly undressed and sitting such a short distance away, made him forget almost everything else.

"I thought you were drowning," he said stupidly, blinking and striving to pull his gaze from her wet arms and shoulders. She might not have been wearing the chemise at all for the good it did in hiding her flesh.

She smiled and calmly began to wash herself again, rubbing her fingers through her long, golden-brown hair to rid herself of mud. "I'm sorry if I gave you a fright," she said, carefully leaning back to rinse her scalp the better. Kayne watched, fascinated, as the swell of her breasts rose from the water at the movement, just enough to tease and tantalize and make him feel maddened.

"I learned to swim as a child. My father insisted upon it, though many of the villagers declared it a great evil. You know how 'tis said that the devil lives within the water, only waiting to snatch away the spirits of those who dare to enter." She closed her eyes and disappeared briefly beneath the water, resurfacing faceup so that water glistened on her skin and eyelashes, and her hair was sleek and wet. "Ah, 'tis better now," she murmured with clear contentment. "Much better." Her eyelids opened and she looked at him, all blue-eyed innocence. "Will you fetch my gown and shoes for me please, Kayne? I wish to wash them, as well. My father will be furious if I do not make myself clean before entering the manor. 'Twill not be pleasant to explain how it is that I come to be wet, but he has ever had a special dislike of filth.''

Glad for a reason to hide the proof of his burgeoning desire, Kayne abruptly turned about and climbed out of the stream. A few moments later he returned, but rather than leave them on a rock where she might fetch them, he walked back into the river, mindless of his boots and clothes, and waded in until he stood nearly beside her.

Now it was Sofia's turn to stare in shock. ''Kayne! I did not mean for you to become even wetter than you were before. Pray, leave them here with me and get you out to dry.''

Ignoring this, he handed her the heavy surcoat, and then began to clean the boots himself, careful not to lose one or the other as he scrubbed the mud from each.

''The water is good for me at present,'' he told her. ''And as it is cold, much the better. Now, tell me, Sofia, how you came to be in the midst of all those cows.''

''Oh, 'tis such a foolishness that I cannot think you wish to hear the tale,'' she replied, busily rubbing at a particularly bad stain on her surcoat. ''They were Mar Halliway's cattle, I think, for I seem to recall that he meant to drive them to the Portertown market today. They came running into the village in a mad rush, with a dozen dogs or more yipping at their heels and causing an even greater confusion. Gwillym and I had been out making my daily visits, and had just left Mistress Losley's—you know how painfully she has suffered the gout these past many months—when we saw them coming toward us.''

''Did Gwillym not try to keep you from harm?'' Kayne asked, unable to believe that his former soldier had done anything less.

''Oh, aye, he did,'' she assured him, glancing up from her work, ''and most valiantly, I vow. But the cattle were maddened and causing every manner of damage, and no one could stop them, or was even brave enough to make the attempt.'' She looked up at him once more. ''Though I do believe Sir Gwillym would have done so, if I'd only had the sense to give him the chance.''

''You thought you could stop a herd of maddened cows,'' Kayne stated flatly, most unhappy at the idea of such misdirected bravery, regardless how greatly he admired the quality. She could have so easily been killed, and the very thought made his heart ache with a deep distressing pain.

''I know 'twas all foolishness,'' she admitted, frowning at the stain which stubbornly refused to go, ''but I was in the midst of the cattle before I had truly thought of what I did. And then 'twas too late. I thought—I thought I would die,'' she said, her voice growing solemn and sad, ''and this saddened me not only for my own sake, but because it meant that I would not see you again.'' She looked up at Kayne, her gaze sparkling with tears, though she smiled. ''And then, what a greater fool I acted after you saved me, for I could not bear that you should see me in such a state, so covered with filth.'' She uttered a laugh. ''And so I bade you bring me to the river, and now here we are, the both of us, because of my sinful pride and vanity.''

Reaching out, she touched his hand, which had fallen still in the task of cleaning her boots. He had simply been standing, gazing at her.

''I did not tell you yet, Kayne, but I am so glad you are home. Each day I prayed for your return. I had meant our first meeting to be far different than it was, but that cannot be helped now. There is so much I have to tell you. Did you have a pleasant journey? And to where did you go in such a hurry?''

Whatever measure of control he'd held upon himself

melted away, leaving Kayne defenseless against what he felt. Without a word, he turned and strode back up to the bank, water swirling all about him, and set Sofia's boots upon a large, safe rock. Then he walked back out into the river again. Sofia had no warning for what was to come, but, then, Kayne reasoned, it was the same for him. He was helplessly in love and helplessly aroused, and it was all her fault.

"Sofia," he said as he neared her.

She was yet smiling up at him. "Yes, Kayne?"

"Come here."

He grabbed her shoulders and pulled her up against him, half out of the water so that her wet chemise dampened what little of him was left dry. His mouth found her own and he kissed her with the fervent need that had haunted him for the past twenty days and nights. She responded with equal need, and, murmuring against his lips, slid her arms about his neck and held him tightly.

He had no idea how long it went on, though it seemed like hours. Long, lovely, blissful hours. His hands moved restlessly over the thin, wet cloth covering her body, caressing, stroking, barely constrained in seeking out those places that he most longed to touch. When he touched her lips with his tongue she opened for him—first shyly, and then more eagerly as he showed her how that sweet manner of intimacy was shared.

Her hands moved over him, too—indeed, her whole body did. It was as if she were trying to climb onto him, into him, and Kayne didn't discourage the attempt. Instead, he helped, pulling her closer, kissing her even more ardently.

In time, the kiss came to an end, not because Kayne wanted it to. Far from it. But because Sofia at last pulled away and, with a happy sigh, rested her cheek on his shoulder.

"My gown has floated off," she told him, as if the news didn't distress her in the least.

It distressed Kayne, however, and most greatly.

"By the Rood!" he swore vehemently, coming to his senses and setting Sofia away. He looked all about, ready to swim after the accursed surcoat in hopes of regaining it, but it was nowhere to be seen.

"It's gone," Sofia told him simply. "I lost hold of it several minutes ago."

"But why didn't you tell me?" he demanded.

Her smile was openly amused. "I fear that I was most distracted, Master Kayne, by far more important matters."

Kayne set a hand to his forehead and groaned, wishing he'd never given way to the temptation to touch her, no matter how strong it had been.

"Sofia, you cannot return to Ahlgren Manor so unclothed, and certainly not when you left the village in my escort. Any and all who saw you in such a manner would believe that we had...that I had..." He couldn't even think of the way to finish what he meant, so close it was to the truth. "God help me," he muttered, turning and striding out of the river. "You make me crazed, Sofia. You drive every bit of sense and forbearance from my head."

He could hear her behind him, splashing to keep up. "But there is no trouble with that, Kayne. Not now, when I have learned the truth of who you are...or once were. Gwillym has told me the full of all that he knows, and it is more than enough. You are not a commoner, and there is naught to keep us from—"

He abruptly turned. "There is everything—" he began, falling silent at the sight of her body, now fully revealed as she stood out of the river, the wet-tight chemise molded against her form. Swinging about again, he grit his teeth together and tried mightily to push the vision out of his mind. If he hadn't been wet, and cold, it would certainly have been a losing battle. "There is every reason why we cannot come together—ever."

"But, Kayne—"

"Wait here," he commanded curtly, striding toward where he'd left Tristan, praying that the steed hadn't wandered off. "I will fetch a blanket so that you may cover yourself, and then you will sit in the sun until you are dry enough to go home."

Ten minutes later, Sofia sat on a large rock in the warmth of the sun, a blanket wrapped so tightly about her that she could scarcely move. Kayne had done the wrapping, not looking at her while he did it, with such deftness and vigor that she had felt more like a child being swaddled than a woman full grown.

Kayne had removed his boots and some of his own wet clothes—his cloak and tunic, so that his chest was bare. He had unpacked and unsaddled Tristan and let the horse graze in the tall grass nearby. At present, he was kneeling on the ground, digging through one of his bags. Finally, he drew out a small, cloth-wrapped bundle and tucked it under one arm. Then he picked up a leather wineskin and rose.

"Drink some of this," he said, uncorking the skin and holding it out to her. "'Twill keep you from falling ill."

With great difficulty, Sofia extracted one of her arms from Kayne's wrapping, and took the wineskin from his hand.

"Is this the same man who scoffed at the superstitions held on Midsummer Night?" she asked, putting the wineskin to her lips and sipping a small amount. The wine was dark and rich, of a fine quality, and she drank of it again before handing the wineskin back. "A little water will not make me ill."

Kayne knelt upon the ground again and untied the bundle

he'd carried from his bag. A small loaf of bread and a hunk of soft white cheese were within, and Kayne withdrew a dagger from the belt at his waist to cut them into even smaller portions. Sofia watched as he bent over the task, his blond hair white in the sun, long and silky, falling over his heavily scarred but well-muscled shoulders. Except for the scars, which showed white, he was as darkly tanned as a field worker might be, and she thought of how many hours and days and months he'd labored upon a far different kind of field—one of battle.

He set a slice of cheese upon a bigger slice of bread and handed it to her. Sofia held his gaze for a moment as she took it, staring deeply into his blue eyes.

"Kayne," she said, carefully unearthing her other hand so that the blanket did not fall below her breasts, "I saw the hidden closet in your dwelling. The one with the armor and sword and other…things. And Sir Gwillym told me the truth of what you once were."

"I know," he said, busying himself with preparing his own modest repast. "I knew that you would ask a great many questions of Gwillym, and perhaps rightly so. I gave him my leave to tell you what he would. And now you know the truth."

Rising, he took his share of the bread and cheese and the wineskin and moved to sit behind her on the rock. She felt his warmth, so near, but wished that she could see his face.

They ate their meal in silence, with the wineskin set between them so that she could easily reach it when she wished. The sun above was pleasant and warm, and she felt her chemise begin to dry. When she had finished the bread and cheese, she parted the blankets a bit to let the greater length of the garment dry. Beneath her feet, the grass was soft and inviting. A breeze picked up the scent of the river caressing her face, and over her head, clouds, white as snow, drifted lazily across a brilliantly blue sky. To be here with Kayne on such a day, in such a way, should have brought nothing but joy. Yet Sofia could feel only fear.

She had confessed that she knew the truth, but his reaction had not been what she'd expected. Did he not realize, then, what it meant? That there could be no obstacle to part them now? Or perhaps…perhaps he did know, but did not care. Perhaps he did not *want* to wed her…perhaps he did not even love her, as she had thought he must.

The idea was worse than the knowledge of a certain and painful death. Indeed, she thought such a death might almost be preferable.

"Kayne," she whispered, her voice trembling badly, just as all of her trembled, and her heart pounding with dread foreboding in her chest. "Kayne, you must only tell me, if you…if you do not…"

"I love you, Sofia," he said so softly that she almost didn't hear it. Reaching back, she felt him searching for her hand. With a sob of relief, she offered it, and his fingers closed about her own tightly. She leaned backward against him, and felt, with an indescribable joy, him returning the loving pressure. "You need never fear or worry for that. I love you as I have never loved a woman before. In truth, I had begun to think I was not capable of caring so deeply for anyone. But I loved you almost from that moment after the fire, when I opened my eyes and found you hovering over me like a very angel. My angel. Each day since then, I have loved you even more greatly. And will continue to love you until that day upon which I last draw breath."

"As I love you," she murmured, able to breathe once more, her eyes filling with tears of relief and thankfulness.

"But it matters not," he continued in a tone both sad and weary. "We cannot wed, Sofia. I would not ask such a thing of you, to bind yourself to a man as I am. You are filled with light and goodness, while I am filled with naught but darkness. You cannot begin to know how.''

Sofia scooted around to look at him, and saw the dispirited set of his handsome features.

''I love you,'' she repeated. ''I know some of what you suffered in France.'' She pushed her fingers between his own, sealing their hands together tightly. ''If there is light within me, then let that light—and the love I bear for you—dispel this darkness you speak of.''

''I fear it would not be so. In truth, I think 'twould be the other way. That I would bring naught but darkness into your sweet life. That I could never bear to do, Sofia.'' He released her hand and stood. ''Never, may God help me.''

He walked a few steps away, running both hands through his hair, then at last turned to face her.

''You wish to believe that I am a good man, perhaps even a noble man, but I am bastard born, a commoner among commoners, even though the man who sired me was wealthy and well-born. I come from a place called Briarstone. Do you know of it?''

''Nay,'' she said, giving a shake of her head. ''But I thought you were fostered at a place called Talwar, or so Sir Gwillym told me, with your close companions, Sir Senet and Sir Aric and a man named John Ipris.''

''Aye, and that I was,'' he said with a somber smile. ''But before we went to Talwar, John, Aric and I were raised at the nearby estate of Briarstone. 'Tis a singular place, where any who are alone or poor or hungry are welcomed and given the chance to earn a plot of land and a dwelling in trade for work. None who come are turned away, unless they are of a violent nature, and none are asked to give an accounting of themselves.

''Women, most especially, are welcomed, and even moreso those who have no other place to go. Whores, thieves—criminals of every kind, I vow—and any who have been cast aside, as my mother was. All are given a place at Briarstone. These, Sofia,'' he said, gazing at her very directly, ''are the ones who raised me from a babe. They are my people, my family, who I shall ever name my own. Can you tell me now, looking into my eyes, that you would welcome such a family? That you would wish to visit at Briarstone and be embraced as a daughter by such people? Can you think that your father—or the people of Wirth, so upstanding and right—would accept that you had taken criminals and harlots to your bosom as relatives?''

Her heart told Sofia to say the word at once—yes—but her mind, so treacherous and logical, made her hesitate. She had been prepared to hear that Kayne was basely born, but to know that he had been raised by such people—the very lowest in society, scorned by one and all, most especially the Church—this she had not expected.

Kayne's face showed that he understood her feelings well. He gave a curt nod and looked away.

''I went to Talwar from Briarstone, as did Aric and John and many other boys. The two estates are very close, and the lords of them like brothers. They have a common goal—to make a better way for all those who are less fortunate. Sir Christian, who is the lord of Briarstone, oversees the raising of promising boys, and Sir Justin Baldwin, the lord of Talwar, takes them on to train them for the knighthood. Whether these lads attain the knighthood or not is their own decision, but the chance for it is there, and a guidance and encouragement that could scarce be had from any natural father.''

''Sir Gwillym told me something of Sir Justin Baldwin,'' Sofia murmured. ''He is a very great man, I think, to do what he has done.''

Kayne looked up at her again with a fierce expression such as she had never seen on him before. "He is the finest man on God's earth," he declared, "and I have named him my lord and will ever do so. Even when I served the king in France, 'twas truly Sir Justin I served. He gave me all that I have, even Tristan, who was his parting gift to me when I left for France. What I know of blacksmithing, Sir Justin taught me—aye, and all those who are fostered in his care, for he knows full well that few attain the knighthood, but many may be blacksmiths. If it had not been for Sir Justin and Sir Christian, I would have been as naught, for that is my birthright. I might have become the basest manner of criminal, a man you would scarce deign to look upon, Sofia, unless you could avoid looking at all."

It was true, she thought with growing distress. All that he said was true.

"But you are not a criminal, Kayne. You became a great knight—a captain in the king's army, commanding hundreds of men. And your father…you said that he is a rich man, and also well-born. Surely his lineage is acceptable, even if he is but a merchant."

He uttered a humorless laugh. "Oh, aye, his lineage is fully acceptable. He is a great lord of a fine estate. Sir Ronan Sager, who is also called Baron Renfrow, the master of Vellaux."

Sofia's eyes widened. "Lord Renfrow is your *father?*" she repeated, hope welling up once more.

"My sire, as I have ever called him," Kayne replied curtly. "My mother was a servant in the castle at Vellaux, and very young when she took her place there. Lord Renfrow had made her his mistress before she had attained sixteen years of age, and soon thereafter got her with child. But this is a common tale. I doubt it surprises you."

"Nay," she admitted. "'Tis not unknown to me that this is the fate of many young women."

He gave her a long, searching look. "Of poor young women," he said. "Of common village girls, as my mother was. No man possessed of any sense of honor would defile a born lady in such a manner, but he will not hesitate to take his pleasure of someone like my mother. She thought Lord Renfrow loved her, as she loved him, and she believed, when she agreed to lie with him, that he would never abandon her. But while he was bedding so innocent and ignorant a maid he was also courting a young and proper lady to be his bride. 'Twas his great misfortune that my mother happened to get with child just when the proper lady had at last agreed to be his wife, for he could not have brought her to share the same dwelling with his whore and bastard child."

"But surely," Sofia murmured, "surely he could never have sent your mother away to Briarstone? To a place filled with thieves and harlots? Could he have been so heartless?"

Kayne's blue eyes, which had grown so very cold, softened a small measure. "Until only a few days past, I believed that he had been so cruel, though I love Briarstone dearly, and would not name it so harsh a place as it sounds. My mother never told me the truth of what had occurred, that she learned Lord Renfrow meant to make her leave the castle, and in her grief ran away from her family and her great shame—and most especially from him.

"Thanks be to a merciful God that she found her way to Briarstone, where she was safe from the dangers that so often befall such young women. For his part, Lord Renfrow was greatly distressed to find his mistress flown, and in desperation searched for her, meaning to bring her back to Vellaux and settle her in a dwelling of her own near the castle, with servants to care for both her and the child she carried, and to provide them with every manner of luxury. It was his intention—or so he swore to me in holy oath only a few days past, for it was he I journeyed to see—to maintain her as his mistress, even after the child was born and despite his marriage, and to raise the child with full acknowledgment, though certainly as his bastard. It was, I grant, an understandable determination for a man who had every expectation of gaining legitimate children out of his young wife. I would fault him for it if I could, but I cannot."

"Nay, for that is the way of men, to desire legitimate heirs," Sofia said sadly. "He must have loved her a little—your mother—to be willing to do so much for her, and to acknowledge you as his son, though bastard-born. Not every man will do as much."

"This is so," Kayne admitted. "For many years I thought he had abandoned us both, but now I believe that he meant only the best for my mother and me, and to do as much for us as he could. If she had not run away to Briarstone, and if she had agreed to return to Vellaux when Lord Renfrow at last found her, her life would have been very different than what it was."

"And yours, as well," Sofia said. "She would not return with him?"

He shook his head. "She could not bear to see him living with his beautiful new wife. She loved him too greatly to do so. And 'twas as well, I vow, for we were content at Briarstone, being among our own kind."

"Oh, Kayne," she said miserably, "they are not your people, though you lived among them. Your father is a great and most noble lord."

"And my mother the daughter of a lowly vassal. You cannot make me what I am not, Sofia. I am bastard-born, and naught can change that, despite my father's desire that I attain the lordship of Vellaux one day—"

"Attain the lordship?" Sofia repeated, sitting upright. "Your father has acknowledged you? He desires to make you his heir?"

Again, he nodded. "I am the only living child born from his flesh. His wife gave him no children, and the two other bastards born to his mistresses died in their youth. This being so, it is Lord Renfrow's desire to petition the crown that I be made his legitimate heir. But, Sofia," he went on firmly as she rose, filled with complete joy at the knowledge, "it yet makes no difference to us. Lord Renfrow will not make me legitimate unless I once again embrace the knighthood, and that I cannot do." His expression was somber. "When I put that holy ordination aside, 'twas forever. And thus I vowed before God, for the sake of the darkness within me."

"But 'twill not be thus forever," she murmured. "One day, this darkness you speak of will leave you—if you desire that it be so."

"I desire it above all things, but I cannot see how 'twill ever be changed. It is a part of me, perhaps even born of me. You cannot begin to know what manner of man I am."

Sofia pulled the blanket modestly about her, and walked straight up to him, staring him in the face.

"I know far better than you what manner of man you are, Kayne the Unknown, and despite all that you have told me, my love for you has not altered in the least."

"That is because you do not know the full of it," he murmured, lightly touching her cheek. "I am a foul murderer. My hands—these very hands," he said, lifting them up, "are covered with the blood of innocents. Women and children and more fighting men than I could begin to number. Hundreds upon hundreds I have sent to God—plucking them away from their families and those who loved and needed them. And all,'' he said in a husky tone, the words hard to speak, ''for naught but the vanity of fancy noble-men who dream of conquering thrones, not knowing or caring what the cost may be. Those dreams came to naught, for France is lost, and every man and woman and child who died upon her soil lost their lives for nothing but fool-ishness.''

''Kayne, you have no part in that. You were a soldier,'' she murmured tenderly, setting a gentle hand against his bare chest, in the place where his heart beat most fully. ''You did as a good soldier must do, and served your king with perfect obedience. No one can find fault with that, or blame you for doing as you were commanded. I will never blame you.''

He set his hand over her own, pressing it hard against his chest.

''You don't know, Sofia.''

''But I do,'' she insisted. ''Gwillym told me about the convent, about the mistake made by the man who'd taken John Ipris's place. None of that was your fault.''

He lowered his head. ''I was the captain of those men. I led them. And I am the one who must take the blame for what occurred. I should never have trusted any man's word apart from John's. I should have made certain of the truth.'' He closed his eyes, squeezing them tightly shut. ''I hear them still, when I dream at night. The screams. So many children—screaming for someone to save them—and babies crying, and the nuns praying and weeping…''

Sofia lurched forward, throwing her arms about his neck and hugging him tightly, not caring that the blanket fell to the ground, pooling about her bare feet.

"Don't think of it now. Don't speak of it. I won't let you."

"You can't stop it," he said harshly. "There's too much darkness within me to stop it. Nay, Sofia." Taking her shoulders in his hands, he gently pushed her away. "You cannot begin to know the half of it. Ten years I was in France. Ten years killing." His hands slid from her shoulders to her wrists, and he gazed at her solemnly. "The memory of it will never go away, no matter how you or I or even my father may wish it. And without the knighthood, I am but a commoner, whom you can have no part of."

"I don't believe that," she told him. "I *will* not believe that."

"There can only ever be friendship between us. And if you cannot accept that, then I must leave Wirth."

Slowly, she shook her head, filled with both anger and pain. "I'll not let you leave. You promised to be my champion against Sir Griel, and I will hold you to that promise until your dying day, may it be many long years in coming."

Kayne gave a solemn nod. "So be it. I will remain and be your champion, but you must no longer come to the smithy to speak to me, Sofia. I cannot seem to master myself when you are near, and therefore the temptation must not be placed before me. If I see you coming to me, even with custom, I will lock my gate against you."

"You would not!" she cried with disbelief.

"I will, indeed. Now, set the blanket about you once more and I will fetch your shoes. 'Tis time for you to return to the manor."

Chapter Ten

The trouble with Sofia, Kayne discovered within the following weeks, was that it was almost impossible to see her coming before she was already there. She was silent and sly and obviously had no care either for his insistence that she stay away or for the gossip that already spread like an unchecked fire throughout Wirth and the surrounding villages.

He had thought, after the day he returned to Wirth, that his life would become what it had once been. Quiet, calm, peaceful—and lonely. But that was part of the penance he knew he must serve. What right did he have, after all, to the kind of happiness that other men might know—most especially with a woman?

The day following his return from Vellaux, Kayne sent Gwillym to Lomas to make his vow of fealty to Senet, who would be a master worthy of such service, and the day after that he opened his gate to receive custom. A great deal of work was brought to his door and Kayne was glad to have it, for it kept him busy and left him little time to think of Sofia—though God knew he still did.

She made no attempt to try to see him during the first week, and Kayne, telling himself that he wasn't miserable

for the lack of her or sorry that he'd forbidden her the
smithy, let his life fall back into its regular pattern. He rose
early each morn and, kneeling in his prayer closet, made
his recitations to God. Then he washed and shaved his face
and dressed in his working clothes before breaking his fast
with a simple meal of bread, cheese and ale. Occasionally,
if he had butter and a little sugar, he would boil a pot of
oats to enjoy, instead. Afterward, he went out to the stable
to begin his day of work.

He first cared for the horses and other livestock, milking
his one cow and setting the covered buckets in the shade
outside his smithy gate. His nearest neighbor, Mistress
Kading, would fetch them within the hour and turn the top
cream into sweet, fresh butter, which she kindly shared with
Kayne. Having fed his cattle, Kayne next drew plenty of
fresh water from the small well in his yard to keep all of
them, and himself, through the day, and then he opened his
gate for custom. He spent several minutes standing in the
doorway, looking first in the direction of Ahlgren Manor,
then back toward the village, before turning into the darkness of the stable and heading directly to his forge to stoke
the coals until they were red-hot.

Horses that had been brought for shoeing were cared for
first. Afterward he saw to repairs that affected the liveli-
hood of any who had come to him, such as plows or
scythes. Last of all came those items that were of lesser
importance, pots, kettles, ladles, nails, latches, knives and
the like. If he had a moment of leisure, Kayne gave way
to his personal pleasure and used his own stock of fine,
expensive metals to fashion plates, cups, pitchers and tall
vases. This was very much like the elegant and exacting
work that his master, Sir Justin, had trained him and the
other fostered boys in, during those days when they had

learned in the smithy, rather than in the fields, practicing for battle.

Sir Justin's own favorite pastime had been the making of choice swords and daggers, and his skill in this was rare, indeed. The jeweled dagger that Kayne sometimes carried at his waist had been a precious gift from Sir Justin, as had the exquisite sword that he'd carried through France. Kayne cherished them both and knew their value, and, yet, he could not bring himself to fashion like weapons, though he believed he had the skill. He had made the attempt a time or two since he had taken up smithing, only to find that his nightmares haunted him even more fiercely. He had finally given way, knowing that he could not be a man who fashioned instruments that might lead to death. He had already caused far too much of it in his life.

He returned often to his gate during the course of the day, usually to accept custom or deliver finished work to one of the villagers who had rung the large bell hanging there. Occasionally his purpose was merely to gaze up and down the village road. But there was never a sign of Sofia, nor of her father or any of the servants from Ahlgren Manor. A time or two during that first week Kayne thought that he should send a missive to the manor, only to make certain that Sir Griel and his men had been leaving Sofia in peace. He hadn't well considered that he could not keep a very close watch over her if she was barred from his presence. But, then, he'd not thought well or clearly that day by the river at all. It had been one of the worst hours of his life, telling Sofia the truth of what he was, and of why they could not come together. He could not think of it without feeling again the loss and pain.

In the afternoons, when it was time to take his midday meal, Kayne would go into the village for fresh eggs and bread and, if his shelves were bare, more wine and ale and cheese. When his simple repast was complete, he would take a few moments before returning to his labors in the smithy to consider what he might have for his evening meal. In his larder he kept a good supply of salted meats and fish, and if he found vegetables for sale in the village during his afternoon visit he would set a pot of stew to simmering over the coals in his hearth so that it would be ready for him later.

The afternoon hours were long and wearying, and Kayne's hands and arms and shoulders ached from the never-ending hammering he did. During those few—and far too brief—moments when he stopped to refresh himself with a draught of cool water and to wipe the sweat from his body, he would wish, sinfully, that Sofia might suddenly appear to take some of his misery away. He had used to live in anticipation of such visits, though he was careful never to let her know how much. Now, thanks to his own foolish stubbornness, he would never have the pleasure of them again.

When darkness began to fall, Kayne set his work aside. He banked the fire in his forge and added fresh coal to feed it through the night so that enough heat and embers would be present in the morn to start the fire anew. He cleaned his tools and washed the smithy down with several buckets of water, and then gave his attention once more to his animals. Once they had been fed and watered and cared for, he at last tended to himself, going to a large tub in the yard behind his dwelling to scrub the filth of his daily labors away. His hair, face, arms and chest were given equal care, for he had never been able to abide sleeping while covered with soot from a coal fire.

Cleaned and dried, Kayne took an extra moment to wash the shirt he'd worn—or not worn, as was his more usual state while working—and took it back into the stable to toss over the gate of Tristan's stall, where, God willing, he would find it dry enough to wear again come morn. Once each week he took all of his dirty garments to the village laundress, and gladly paid to have them properly cleaned. His own efforts were ever woefully lacking.

Having done this, and satisfied that all was well with both animals and smithy, he made his way into his home and went directly abovestairs to fetch a fresh, clean shirt before sitting down to his evening meal.

When the last remnants of his repast had been cleared away and the dwelling was in order, Kayne would take out one of his precious books and sit by his fire to read for an hour before retiring, or perhaps he would bring out ink and costly parchment to write missives to those he held dear, Sir Justin and his wife or Senet, John and Aric. Some nights, when he felt most restless, he would put on his heavy cloak, saddle Tristan, and ride out into the dark night, striving to weary himself beyond all thoughts of Sofia or France or his dying father.

His father, Lord Renfrow, whose face and voice and touch he now knew, and who he could not force from his mind despite every effort.

Their first meeting had not been in the least what Kayne had expected, and had unsettled him far more than he'd believed it would. Ten years of killing in France had hardened Kayne to a diamond strength, but he'd felt almost as a child again upon meeting the man who was his sire—a man he'd hated his whole life as he'd never hated anyone else. The experience was etched fully in his mind, as were the two days he'd spent in his father's company, and could not be chased from his thoughts regardless how hard he might push Tristan in the cold darkness of night. Just as thoughts of Sofia could not be chased away.

It was almost two full weeks before Kayne felt that peuliar tingling along the length of his spine that spoke of ofia's presence in his smithy. He'd felt it too many times efore to mistake the sensation. He was in the midst of haping a horseshoe, but the hammer in his hand fell silent lmost of its own accord. His entire body fell still. He losed his eyes and drew in a deep breath, and then straight- ned, opened his eyes, and turned to see her standing only few feet away.

She was beautiful—a sight to bring pleasure to both the yes and the soul. He was torn between sorrow at how trong the bond between them was, that it should pull her ack to him despite the certain destruction it offered, and ure joy to simply be with her again.

Somehow he forced himself to move, to make himself resentable for her, as he ever did when she arrived at the mithy without warning. He set his work aside and washed is face and sweat-covered chest, then dried himself with . cloth and put his shirt on. Then, ordering his overlong air with his fingers, he turned to face her once more.

"Mistress Sofia," he said, distressed to hear how thin nd wobbly his voice was. It was only by the greatest re- istance that he held back from leaping forward to gather er up in his arms and hold her body against his own.

"Master Kayne," she greeted with what sounded to him ike perfectly cool reserve. In her hands, she held a long- andled basket, which she swung back and forth with a mall, quick motion of her fingers. She lifted her chin. 'I've brought your midday meal."

Kayne knew that he shouldn't accept it. If he did, he vould also have to ask her to share it with him, as propriety lemanded.

"You are very kind," he said, striving to breathe more iormally. "Thank you. Will you…join me in partaking of t?"

"Nay, I thank you," she replied so primly and readily that Kayne felt his whole being contract with disappointment. She set the basket upon the ground near her feet. " am wanted in the village. Pray, sir, enjoy the meal."

With that, she turned and departed, not looking back leaving Kayne gazing longingly after her. If she had wanted to punish him, she could have thought of no better plan He took the basket up, gazed at the contents within—a roasted breast of pheasant, delicate cheese tarts, a wonderfully light cake smelling of almonds, and a skin of what he knew must be excellent wine from her father's cellar—and found no pleasure in them.

It was the same for the next thirteen days, sparing the Sabbath. Sofia arrived unannounced, always very proper and always bearing a basket filled with fine foods and delightful wines. Each day she was more beautiful than the day before, if such a thing was possible, and each day he felt as if he had been gifted with but a taste of her delicious presence—enough to be fully hungered, but never sated.

On the fourteenth day, he was waiting for her, already cleaned and dressed and combed, determined that there would be an end to such foolishness once and for all.

But she did not come herself. Instead, one of the men servants from Ahlgren Manor arrived with a short missive Kayne waited until the young man had taken his leave before breaking the wax seal and reading the contents.

"Meet me in the forest, beside the river. I await you there—Sofia"

Kayne frowned and gazed at the missive with a measure of disbelief. How could she tempt fate in such a manner? Simply coming to the smithy each day had been enough to fuel every manner of gossip in the village, but this...God's mercy, if he went, and if any heard of it...her very reputation might be ruined. Aye, even beyond what it had already suffered since all that had occurred on and after Midsummer Day.

He would send another missive, he decided at once, folding the delicate parchment note. Mistress Kading's youngest boy would run to the forest and deliver it for him. 'Twas without doubt that Sofia would be full angered, but mayhap that was for the best. Mayhap then she would cease coming to the smithy every day and tormenting him. If she did not, he could not answer for what love and desire might press him to do.

Determined upon this course, he made his way into his dwelling in search of ink and parchment.

It was a beautiful afternoon, and not too warm for August. A soft but steady breeze coursed through the forest trees, bringing the scent of the nearby river and cooling the day.

Sofia stood and gazed down at the food she had arranged on a large square cloth laid upon the forest floor. There was fresh herb bread, still warm, and moist salmon smoked in apple wood to a delightful sweetness, and fresh goat's cheese, soft and tangy. Cook had included several of her famed meat pasties, and enough tiny fruit tarts to feed a small army. And there were two wineskins filled with her father's best wine, and goblets set nearby. A wonderful feast, she thought with satisfaction. Now all it needed was Kayne's presence to make it complete.

Sofia wasn't entirely certain that he would come. Indeed, she'd been sure of nothing since the last day they'd spent together in almost this very same spot. But one thing she did know—she could not allow matters to go on as they were. She was miserable, and Kayne clearly was, too, if his looks over the past many days during her visits to the smithy were anything to go by. More than once she'd thought he might even lunge at her, so hungry and desolate he had appeared. And if he had, Sofia would have gladly given way to him. She was hungry and desolate, too.

She had never known such wretchedness. Each day, when she'd gone to the smithy with an offering—fully humiliated at the awful need that drove her to do so—she had suffered at the mere sight of him.

But she knew herself well. She was far too stubborn to put him out of her life, or to let him refuse her. Love was too rare and precious a thing to be treated so lightly, and today she meant to make him understand that. She was ready to compromise, if he was. Surely they could find the way together, if they both desired it enough, as she believed they did. And apart from that, her arguments and proposals for the matter would leave him little room for sway. He had told her that he loved her, and that, coupled with her determination, would be enough.

The sound of horse's hooves made her look up expectantly toward the open field, from which Kayne would approach. Listening, she frowned. There was more than one horse coming. Indeed, it sounded as if there must be three or more. But surely Kayne would bring no one else with him—at least, she prayed that he would not, after she had gone to so much trouble to be fully alone with him, having sent even her maid back to Ahlgren Manor to await her return.

Was that the sound of a hawk overhead? she wondered, casting her gaze upward, searching through the few slivers of blue sky to see such a bird. She was certain that she had recognized the cry of the bird, even if she could not see it.

She understood at once, with sinking clarity, what it meant. A hunting party was about to enter the forest in search of prey, following the bird's course, and would very likely trample right over the meal she had so painstakingly set out.

Only moments later the hunters came, black figures on horseback charging into the trees at the forest's edge a short distance away. Sofia's hopes rose as the riders checked their progress in deference to the thickening foliage, looking for the best way through the trees, and accordingly changed course to head toward the river and the bird's resounding cry. They did not even appear to see her…until the very last moment, when they had nearly ridden out to the riverbank.

Suddenly, the man in the lead pulled his horse to another halt and stared hard in Sofia's direction. She stared, too, wondering who it might be and whether she should be afraid. When the man turned his horse about and began to move toward her, the hairs on the back of Sofia's neck prickled forebodingly. She drew in a sharp breath as the man neared and she told herself to run—to run *now,* out of the forest and to safety—but fear paralyzed her limbs.

Sir Griel's ugly face sneered in the semblance of a smile.

"Mistress Sofia," he said in a low, laughing tone, "how fortunate that I find you here…and all alone." He glanced at the meal she had spread out upon the ground. "But you await someone? Could it likely be Master Kayne, the blacksmith? Do you meet in the forest to cuckold me, Sofia? Has he enjoyed you often? But it must be so, else you'd be surrounded by the safety of both maid and manservant. Tell me, Sofia, do you prefer being taken by rough, common men? If I had known, I would have been glad to pleasure you in such a manner."

Sofia stepped back unsteadily, both her mind and heart racing. His two soldiers had joined him, and sat upon their steeds, leering down at her in the same manner as their master.

"He has not yet joined you for your secret tryst?" Sir Griel asked. "But it will be soon, will it not?" His small, black eyes narrowed within the frame of his heavy beard and eyebrows, and he began to dismount. "We must make certain to surprise him with some form of entertainment, do you not agree? I think he will like to see how a true man can make a woman such as you howl with pleasure, Sofia." The men behind him laughed.

Just as his booted foot touched the earth, Sofia fled. She did not think where she went, nor consider what her safest course would be. Fear drove her; that same fear blinded her. Sir Griel would rape her without mercy, and the truth of that spurred her onward in a frenzied panic. Trees rushed past as she set one foot in front of the other, striving not to stumble or strike a tree or rock, praying that she'd get away. Behind her were the sounds of shouts and horses' hooves, coming nearer every moment.

The two soldiers came up on either side of her, then moved together to cut off the path she had taken. Without stopping, she changed course to another direction, and then, finding the way stopped by Sir Griel, to yet another, and another, moving in a desperate circle, panting from both fear and exertion. When the horses came so close that she could not move beyond them, she drew in as much breath as her aching lungs could manage and cried out aloud, "Kayne! Kayne!" and kept shouting the single word even as Sir Griel dismounted and approached, fury in his set features.

"Slut!" he said angrily, raising a hand to strike her. Sofia raised her own hands to ward him off, fighting like a wild animal and still screaming Kayne's name. Sir Griel swatted her blows aside as if they were naught, and brought his gloved hand down hard across the side of her face.

"Bitch!" he spat out as she fell to the ground. "Whore!"

Dizzy from the blow, Sofia tried to sit up. Sir Griel struck her again, harder this time, and as she fell upon the ground her mind whirled with pain and darkness. She tasted blood in her mouth, and heard someone groaning, but was too confused to know who it was. Again, setting one hand flat against the cool, damp ground, she tried to push herself up, blinking to clear her blurred vision. A booted foot caught her in the stomach, kicking her over onto her back, where she lay, gasping. Two more kicks followed, hard and savage. Somewhere overhead, Sofia heard the sound of laughter. He was enjoying what he was doing. He would laugh even as he killed her.

Powerful hands grabbed her, steely fingers dug into her skin, and dragged her along the rough ground.

"I warned you, Sofia, what would happen to you if you should displease me. And I am most displeased, indeed. Now I must teach you a lesson you will never forget."

Blindly, she tried to push him away, managing to thump her fist across his broad forehead. It availed her naught. He gave a harsh laugh, lifted her up, and slammed her full length against the trunk of a tree, so brutally that she lost all consciousness for the space of several long moments.

A cold draught of water poured over her head—coupled with severe shaking by Sir Griel—brought Sofia unwillingly back to her senses. She coughed and blinked and, with what little remained of clear thought, prayed for Kayne to find her soon, and if that was not possible, then please God bless her with a quick and merciful death. Her back, shoulders and neck contracted with pain from where they had struck the tree. The slightest movement was agonizing.

"Ah, good, she has come awake again," Sir Griel said,

very near her face, so that she could both feel and smell his sour breath. "I want you full aware of what I'm going to do to you. Every moment of it, so that you'll remember, and never again cross my will." He lunged forward and set his mouth against her own, pressing so hard that her lips were ground against her teeth, filling her mouth with blood anew. His heavy beard consumed her face almost entirely, even tickling up into her nostrils so that she could scarcely breathe. Then he forced her mouth to open wide beneath his own and thrust his thick, seeking tongue inside, swabbing her mouth with such violence that she gagged and was nearly ill. He felt her convulsing, and wisely pulled away. Sofia had never known such relief, and gasped for air.

But relief was short-lived. With a rough, sickening movement, Sir Griel picked Sofia up and threw her face-down upon the ground. The force of impact knocked the breath from her body, and Sofia opened her mouth wide in a plea for air. Dirt mingled with blood in her mouth, but she was beyond caring for that. Sir Kayne's hands were on her skirts, pulling them up above her waist, baring her cotton leggings.

"No," she murmured, pleading. "Do not...please God..."

"I like to hear you begging," Sir Griel said, panting now with clear excitement. "It arouses me as nothing else could, Sofia." He suddenly lay fully atop her, his heavy weight squeezing the breath from her lungs, grinding the hard ridge of his manhood against her bottom in an obscene manner. Somewhere nearby, she heard his men laughing with approval.

"I will ride you like the bitch you are, Sofia," Sir Griel murmured against her ear, thrusting up against her in a lewd rhythm. "And in the backward manner of a dog with his bitch in heat, just as you deserve. Oh, aye, this first time, you'll have your due. I'll give you all you want, and when I'm sated, I'll let my men take their pleasure of Mistress Sofia Ahlgren. Kayne the Unknown won't touch you after we've done with you, not even for a fortune. You'll be my whore, Sofia. Mine, and no one else's. Do you feel that, bitch?'' He shoved his manhood hard against her, and his cruel fingers dug into the waist of her leggings, ripping the cloth to pull it down. "That's going to ram you so hard that you'll not walk for a week without remembering it. I promise you—''

Suddenly, Sir Griel gave a loud grunt and fell heavily on top of Sofia—but only for a brief moment. Almost at once, he was lifted away and tossed to the ground beside her, landing with a resounding thump.

"Sofia.'' She heard a dear voice, filled with harsh emotion, murmuring her name, and knew that she was safe. The relief made her begin to weep, as she'd not yet been able to do, even with all Sir Griel's terrors.

"Oh, my love.'' A hand gently smoothed her skirts down, and then she was tenderly turned over and lifted into strong, soothing arms. From the corner of one swelling eye she saw, blearily, one of Sir Griel's men lying not too far from his master, clearly insensible. Sir Griel and his minions must have been too occupied with his evil to hear Kayne's approach, and thereby to stop him.

"I have you,'' Kayne murmured, cradling her against himself. "He cannot harm you now.'' Careful fingers pushed the hair from her face, and then he was still for a moment, very still. She heard him draw in a tight breath. "I will kill him for this, Sofia,'' he said, his voice trembling. "I make this vow to you, and before God. I will have him dead. But not now. Not when he is insensible, and cannot suffer as I shall make him suffer. Now, I hold you in my arms and will not let you go for the sake of any man, or for any reason, until I have you safe.''

Sofia felt herself being lifted, and with a sigh she turned her face into the immense comfort of Kayne's muscle-hard chest, letting herself drift back into the beckoning darkness.

She did not know how long it was until she woke again, her body wracked with pain, to find herself riding on Tristan, still held securely in Kayne's arms.

''Kayne,'' she said, distressed to hear how gravely and horrid her voice sounded.

She felt him look down at her, and he shifted her slightly upon the saddle. The movement made her groan aloud.

''Forgive me,'' he said, adding quickly, ''Nay, do not try to move or open your eyes. You are grievously bruised, love, and 'twill give you great pain to move at all.''

He was right. Her eyes were swollen nearly shut, and she hurt everywhere. But her mouth was terribly dry, and she begged for a drink of anything. Kayne's hands moved, but always carefully supported her, and soon, not slowing Tristan's steady stride, he set a wineskin to her lips. She sipped eagerly, only to discover that even that small effort hurt. Her mouth was swollen and the taste of blood and dirt yet strong on her tongue. Kayne took the wineskin away and gently dabbed her lips with the tip of his cloak, in which Sofia discovered that she was wrapped.

''Try to rest,'' he advised softly, cradling her nearer. ''We will be there soon, and all will be well.''

''Where?'' Sofia managed to whisper, cracking her eyes open enough to gaze up into his taut expression.

''To a dear and trusted friend,'' he replied, holding his gaze steadily upon the road before them. It occurred to Sofia for the first time that they were surely being pursued by Sir Griel and his men, who would have followed after them as soon as they had wakened from the slumber Kayne had gifted them with. "No man—nor any army—will be able to touch us once we are safe within Aric of Havencourt's gates."

Chapter Eleven

When Sofia next awoke it was to find herself being lowered with great care into the arms of a huge, dark man who
was shouting instructions at the top of his voice, "Shut the
gates at once, Harry! Richard, take Sir Kayne's mount and
have him properly stabled. Domnal, have the walls fully
manned—weapons at the ready and every torch and fire lit!
Philip, count the arrows we have in the storeroom and give
every man a shared measure. We'll give the scoundrels a
welcome they'll not soon forget!"

It sounded as if he were preparing for a terrible battle,
and was most gleeful at the prospect.

Sofia groaned and tried to open her eyes, and the dark
giant's voice lowered at once.

"She's stirring," he said, to which Kayne replied, "The
dead would stir at all your shouting, Aric. Here, give her
to me gently...gently, man."

She was transferred to Kayne's arms, and the other man
said, "God's mercy, but she's been sorely abused. I'll fetch
Magan at once. She'll know what to do. And Lady Katharine can be called for if need be. I'll send one of my lads
to Senet once we have your good lady settled. And to John,
as well, by the Rood." His voice began to rise again.

"We'll teach the bastard who did this vile thing a fearful lesson, I vow."

"Only lead me to Magan before you start your war, Aric," Kayne said impatiently. "I want Sofia made comfortable at once."

She drifted in and out of awareness for the next hour or more. She recalled the soothing sound of women's murmuring voices, and very gentle hands caring for her. She protested as she was unclothed and bathed, for the pain of being moved about and cleansed and having her wounds tended to was nearly unbearable, but to no avail. Soon enough, however, Sofia was laid upon a soft, cool bed and covered with a very light sheet. She nearly drifted to sleep again, but was roused by the sound of Kayne's voice, saying gently, "You must drink this, Sofia. I know 'tis difficult, love, but you must do the best you can."

She made a murmuring protest as he slid an arm beneath her aching shoulders and drew her up to sit. A cup was pressed to her swollen lips and tilted until the bitter contents filled her mouth. It tasted awful, but she recognized the potion as being very like one of her own medicinal remedies, and was grateful for the benefits that would soon follow.

When she had drunk it all, Kayne lowered Sofia to her pillow once more, and she gave a sigh of relief and contentment. On the morrow, she would likely suffer even greater swelling and soreness, but it did not seem that Sir Griel had done any greater damage than to badly bruise her. Nothing felt as if it was broken, leastwise, though a couple of her teeth felt loose. Still, the outcome might have been far worse, and certainly would have been if not for Kayne.

Kayne took her hand and squeezed it lightly, and Sofia managed to open her eyes a bit. The chamber she lay in was dark, save for the light of a hearth, but she could see the worry and unhappiness etched on Kayne's handsome face as he gazed down at her. She must look a dreadful sight, to elicit such concern. Ignoring the pain that the movement gave her, Sofia smiled and murmured, "I'm glad you came today…but sorry it turned out so…poorly. I meant to feed you a grand meal…not give any trouble."

He squeezed her hand more tightly and bowed his head low. "I very nearly did not come to you today, Sofia," he said in a voice both tormented and sorrowful. "I nearly sent a boy with a message, to tell you that I would not meet you. 'Twas only by the mercy of God that I changed my mind at the last moment. When I think of what you suffered at the hands of that brute…when I think that I might have kept it from happening if I'd only gone to you at once, if I'd never been so damnably foolish in turning you away as I did…"

"It wasn't your fault," she whispered, rubbing her thumb lightly over his hand. "Kayne, you saved me from him…not for the first time." She drew in a shaking breath, afraid that he was weeping. "Please, Kayne…do not…"

He shook his lowered head. "I vowed to be your champion, to keep you from harm. I vowed that he would never touch you again. He was going to rape you, Sofia. He might very well have killed you in the doing of it." He raised his face at last, taut and filled with a violence she had never before seen. "But he will never have the chance to do so again. I am taking you to Vellaux as soon as you are well enough to travel."

"Vellaux?" she repeated, utterly confused. "My father will be afeared…to know what has become of me."

"Aric has already sent two of his swiftest riders on their way to Ahlgren Manor to allay your father's fears and inform him of my plans. It was necessary that they take the longer road, for Sir Griel and his men are very near to Havencourt now, but they are good men, riding Aric's strongest mounts, and will reach Wirth before dawn. Once there, they will remain at my dwelling and care for my animals until I've returned. You must fear for nothing, Sofia, not even for your father's worries. Only rest, and know that you are safe here.''

"I do not fear for myself, Kayne. But…I will not be easy until you take back your vow…that you will kill Sir Griel.''

His skin darkened. "That is a vow I will keep, before God and man. I will kill him. Indeed, I pray that I may do so this very night—even within the hour.''

She was full distressed at the words, and with her feeble strength gripped his fingers.

"Nay, you must not, Kayne. I will make charges against him…and he will be justly condemned for what he did this day. But you must *not* go against the vow you have made when you gave up the knighthood.''

"Then I will take up the knighthood again,'' he said, his blue eyes hard and cold. "If only to kill him, I will do it.''

Sofia could scarce believe such words. To kill again, especially from a rage born of hatred, would shadow him forever, and in time he would be burdened with awful regret.

"No, Kayne. Not for that reason. Never for such a reason. 'Tis not what the knighthood is for—merely to kill.''

"Is it not?'' he asked bitterly. "I was a knight for many years, Sofia, and spent all of them doing little else. For the first time, I shall enjoy taking a man's life. For what he did to you, Sir Griel surely and rightly deserves to die.''

"But not by your hand, Kayne.'' Tears stung her swollen eyes. "The law will judge and punish him.''

"We shall see," he replied curtly, then began to rise. "You must rest now."

Using her last bit of strength, Sofia held on to his hand, not letting him go.

"Stay with me," she pleaded.

His gaze softened and his voice was more gentle. "I will return soon, I vow, and sit here beside you through the night to tend you."

"Nay, do not go at all. How can I rest easily knowing that you go to fight and kill Sir Griel? It is a very torment to me, only to think of it. Please, Kayne. Please."

He stood for a long, silent moment, frowning at her, while Sofia struggled to remain awake against her great weariness and the powers of the potion she'd taken earlier.

With a sigh, Kayne gave way, pulling his chair closer to the bed and sitting in it, yet holding her hand.

"Very well, Sofia. To give you peace, I will stay."

"And will not leave, even when I have fallen into slumber?"

He gave her a slight smile, then leaned forward to very gently kiss her forehead.

"I will not leave you."

She released a deep breath and relaxed. "I am glad," she murmured, closing her eyes with relief. "So glad, Kayne."

The room was silent, then, save for the comforting sounds of the fire. Sleep pressed heavily upon her and Sofia, her hand held securely in Kayne's, gladly embraced it.

"For my own part, I would be the first to approve your regaining the knighthood. But, for your part, Kayne, I cannot admit to being so glad." Senet Gaillard set his hands behind his back and held Kayne's gaze. "You have been happier since putting aside your ordination, my friend. You have even gained that measure of peace which you so dearly sought—at least for a time it seemed thus. Since coming here yesterday, I have seen only a return to that man who you were when we left France, and it fills me with sorrow."

From across the room, Kayne fairly well scowled at him. "I do not begin to know what you mean. I am but myself."

John and Aric, sitting at a large round table in the midst of the private chamber, both looked at him with a measure of surprise.

"You have seemed tense, Kayne," John said, taking up his tankard of ale to sip at it. "And unhappy, as you were when we left France, though I admit 'twas far worse then."

Aric uttered a laugh and leaned back wearily in his chair, taking up his own tankard. "You've been as pleasant as a mad, starving bear with a thorn in its paw," he said. "No need to put so fine a point on it. That's the truth, well enough. 'Tis a mercy Mistress Sofia kept you by her bedside while Sir Griel and his men made their attempt upon Havencourt, else I would've been obliged to knock you on the head and have you dragged off, just to keep you from doing something foolish."

"I had every just reason to confront Sir Griel," Kayne said coldly. "I was not out of my senses."

"Aye, but you were," Aric insisted. He looked at Senet and John, who had arrived with their armies after the fighting had begun. "He was, and if Mistress Sofia hadn't made him promise to stay by her side through that first night, he would have been naught but the greatest trouble to us all. And him being one of the finest men in the field we've e're known before now, aye?"

"'S'truth," Senet said, nodding.

"Aye, indeed," said John.

"I was but full angered, and with every good reason!"

Kayne insisted furiously, striding to the other side of the chamber. "I was not outside of temper or judgment—I was but briefly maddened by the day's events."

Senet moved to stand beside him, and set a hand on Kayne's shoulder.

"And what of now, Kayne? Sir Griel and his knaves ran away yesterday morn, but you have not yet given way. Even though Mistress Sofia improves greatly, you snap and growl and are ready to quarrel at every turn. This is not like you."

Kayne wanted to deny his friend's words, but could not. From the moment that he had ridden into the forest at Wirth to find Sofia being brutally accosted by Sir Griel and his men, he'd been lost in a darkness so fierce and overwhelming that he did not know if he would ever find the way out of it.

He had never wanted to kill before, though he had done so hundreds upon hundreds of times. But he wanted to kill now. It was all he had thought of for the past many hours, apart from Sofia.

She was better now. Much better, thanks to the care of both Magan and Senet's lovely wife, Lady Katharine. The day following her attack had been the hardest for her to endure, as they all had known it must be, for she had been stiff and sore and so painfully bruised that it had been difficult simply to look at her, let alone touch and give additional pain. Sir Griel had struck her across both sides of her face with such force that her lips and eyes had swelled badly. It was only by the mercy of God that he'd not broken any of the delicate bones there which formed her particularly fine beauty, or permanently scarred her with his rough gloves.

The bruises along the length of her back were even worse, or so Lady Katharine had told Kayne after she had carefully examined Sofia. They would heal, in time, but the damage within would take a great deal longer, and would give her much pain, even in so simple an activity as walking. But at least she *could* walk, even if very slowly, and that in itself was a blessing. Kayne had known strong men who'd had the grave misfortune during battle to fall in a like, fierce manner against trees and walls and other such solid objects, and had thereafter lost the ability to walk or move altogether, if they survived at all.

He had kept his word to Sofia and stayed by her side, even when Sir Griel and his small army of men had made their attack on Havencourt. It had been foolishly attempted, for they'd been met by Aric's fostered lads, whom he had trained for battle just as Sir Justin trained him, and with the advantage of Havencourt's sound walls and excellent weapons such enthusiastic warriors could scarce be matched even by seasoned fighting men.

But Sir Griel and his men had striven through the dark hours, driven, surely, by Sir Griel's unchecked wrath and determination not to be bested. Just before dawn, answering Aric's summons with astounding speed, both Senet and John arrived with their own respectable armies, and Sir Griel had finally had no other recourse save to call his men together and run away, back to Maltane.

Kayne had little doubt that he would rest peaceably, however. Any man who would treat a woman as Sir Griel had treated Sofia was mad and intemperate, and they'd not be finished with him until he was either forced to accept peace or dead.

Sofia desired the former, Kayne the latter. She yet believed that Sir Griel would be tried and appropriately judged for what he had done to her, but Kayne knew better. A wealthy knight of the realm, a man possessed of a vast and valuable estate, who had powerful friends in the king's court, and who spent a great deal of money each year to make certain that those friends remained true—such a man would never be justly punished for any crime he might wish to commit. Certainly not for accosting a woman, even though she was a gentle lady and the daughter of a landed knight.

Sir Griel would claim that she had driven him to madness after he, with every honorable intention, had offered her marriage, only to have her tease and torment him. He would bring forth witnesses to tell that Sofia had been observed in unseemly conduct with the village blacksmith, that she had even gone—alone—into his smithy and remained there unattended by maid or manservant. Sir Griel himself could testify—with his soldiers to agree—that he had found Sofia in the forest, alone and with clear evidence that she was awaiting her lover for a secret tryst. Any man, he would argue, who had dealt so honorably with the woman he desired for his wife, would understandably be driven to violence.

In this light, Sir Griel would be viewed as a man much to be pitied, while Sofia would be publicly humiliated and forever branded a creature of shame. And as Kayne would never allow this, Sir Griel would have to be dealt with—by him.

But first, he would take Sofia to Vellaux just as soon as she could travel. He would accede to his father's wishes and take back the knighthood; his father would know how it could be quickly done. And he would agree to be made his father's legal heir. Afterward, he and Sofia would return to Wirth to gain her own father's permission for their immediate marriage. The moment Sofia was his wife, but one unchivalrous word falling from Sir Griel's lips and Kayne would be free to kill him, and be approved in such action by both Church and state. For then he would be a powerful man, as well, being heir to Vellaux. No man would gainsay him. He had but to bait Sir Griel, and wait.

Until that time, Sofia would not be safe, and Kayne, though he would give his very life for her, held no false pride that he alone could keep her perfectly protected. He needed his friends now as he had never needed them before, and had brought them all to this room to set his case before them and ask for their aid.

They had at once agreed that they would accompany him, with all their best fighting men, and make certain of Sofia's perfect safety until all had been accomplished. Their combined forces would create an estimable army that Kayne hoped would temper the madness of even an intemperate man such as Sir Griel. But despite their willingness to help him, Senet, John and Aric had surprised—and aggravated—Kayne with their concerns for his state of mind. He was in perfect possession of his senses. Fully and completely, and they had no cause for any such worry—even if he could not argue the matter.

"Mayhap 'tis not like me," he said, "but 'tis how I am at present, and if you do not desire to accompany me in this state, only tell me now, and we will part ways from Havencourt."

"Kayne," Senet murmured, a mixture of hurt and chiding in his tone. "We do not deserve that of you. Have we not said that we will stand by you?"

"Aye, as we have ever done and ever will do," John added. "We are brothers in all this."

"No matter how foolish one of us may be," Aric put in more bluntly, "and despite such insults as a man might take rightful offense at, if he was of any mind to do so."

Kayne knew a deep measure of ~~shame~~ he had grievously insulted his dearest friends—men who had, just as

John said, stood beside him as brothers through both hard times and good, even in the midst of direst battle.

"Forgive me," he said, not able to look at any of them. "I should not have spoken thus. 'Twas unjust…and wrong. I pray you all…forgive me for it."

"It is only for your sake that we are anxious, Kayne," Senet said. "To see you like this is hard. Very hard. You have ever been the best among us, except, perhaps," he added teasingly, "for John, who, now that he has become a great lord, is fast winging his way toward sainthood with all his good works."

At this, John laughed out loud and Kayne felt some of his shame lessen. He was able to smile and turn to look at his friends.

"You are truly my brothers," he told them, "and I am thankful for each of you beyond any manner of speech to tell how so. If I am not myself for some few days, I pray you, forbear. Once I have Sofia for my wife, and know that she is wholly safe, I will return to myself. Of this I am certain." But the words were spoken with all this discomfort he felt, for in truth, he was sure of nothing in that moment, save that he could not let these men down at any and all costs.

"We would not desert you, Kayne, for any reason," Aric said. "Until Mistress Sofia is safe and beneath your care, we are your men. Nothing on God's earth could be more certain."

"For this," Kayne murmured, "I am fully glad and grateful. Thank you all."

Senet's hand was yet warm on his shoulder, and he gave him a friendly, reassuring shake.

"We decided long ago never to speak of thanks to one another, nor of any manner of gratitude. We will see this thing through together, as we have always done. Now cease all this foolishness, and sit and have a tankard of ale. We have many plans to make for the coming journey to Vellaux.''

Kayne nodded and gladly let Senet lead him to the nearest chair. John poured him a tankard of ale and pressed it into his hands, Aric unfolded a large map and laid it upon the table before them all, and they began to speak as they had once done in France, planning routes and stops and the way to move many men as an army. Despite the goodness of being with his comrades once more, Kayne felt the darkness within him feed and grow, becoming more cold and bitter with each word. He was going back into war again, back to killing, but this time his heart was beyond being touched by what was to come.

Chapter Twelve

Sofia was in awe of Lady Katharine Gaillard, wife of Sir Senet Gaillard, the lord of Lomas. But she supposed that everyone, even Lady Katharine's own husband, must be as well. She was very beautiful, with red-gold hair the color of a glorious sunset, and was taller than almost any woman that Sofia had ever seen. She had a regal manner and bearing that made her as commanding as a queen might be, and all those in her presence reacted accordingly. When Lady Katharine spoke, every eye turned immediately toward her, and when she gave commands, servants raced to fulfill her bidding.

"You will not walk at any faster pace than this, Sofia. I will speak to Kayne and make certain of it. Your back will not be strong for many weeks, and any more rapid step will cause you to suffer such spasms as you had yesterday morn, and a like incident must be fully avoided. Apart from the pain and distress it gives, 'twill also diminish any improvements you have made. You must take every care to allow that no further damage be done by walking at a greater pace."

Sofia, who was slowly moving in a very unsteady line, being held up on one side by Lady Katharine and on the

other by a young serving maid, replied, "Yes, my lady."
Such docility and obedience were strange to her, but thus
it was when Lady Katharine spoke. It would have been
impossible to do anything but agree.

In the far corner of the chamber, Mistress Magan, the
wife of Sir Aric, looked up from nursing her infant son. "I
pray you, my lady, do not overtire Mistress Sofia, else she
may fall ill again."

"And if she lies abed all day," said Lady Katharine,
"she will entirely lose the use of her limbs. Nay, though
she is wretched and bruised, she must walk every third
hour, for a quarter of an hour. Mark me well, 'tis the quickest way for her to regain the balance of all her humours.
Do you not feel better for the exercise, Sofia, despite the
discomfort?"

Sofia was simply glad to be walking at all. Yesterday
morn, when she'd come awake from her stuporous slumber
to find Kayne asleep in his chair beside her, she'd felt so
stiff and sore that she'd had not the least desire to move—
ever again. But from her own experience in healing the
wounds of others, she had known that she must face the
unpleasantness of sitting up, getting out of bed, standing
and walking. The greatest difficulty, apart from her physical
pain, would be in opening her eyelids enough to see where
she would be walking to. They were swollen nearly shut,
and it would be several days more before that swelling
lessened in any great measure. But that could not be helped.

Sofia had lain silently for a long time, not letting herself
remember what had happened the day before, gazing only
at Kayne through the thin slits that her eyes were allowed.
She had watched him sleeping just so when he had been
ill following the fire, save that he'd not been sitting in a
chair and looking so uncomfortable. His blond hair was in
disarray, and a long swath of it fell soft against one cheek.

She wished he were close enough that she might touch him, but knew that even if she could, she would not for fear of waking him. And so, instead, she spent the next half hour occupying her mind with pretending that she was not a patient, but the healer of such a case as she provided, and determining what various remedies she would use for the best and fastest healing.

She had only just decided upon what the best medicinal rub might be to soothe aching limbs when Kayne gave a sigh, turned his head back and forth once upon the back of the chair, and opened his eyes. He blinked up at the bed curtains for a long moment before collecting himself and sitting forward. He was clearly surprised to find that she was already awake and reached for her hand with both of his.

"Sofia, are you well?"

She did her best to smile at him. "Far better than I look, I think."

"You look very beautiful," he said, "as you always do." He lifted her hand to his mouth and kissed it gently.

"You are a dread liar, Kayne the Unknown," she told him, yet smiling, "but I am far more wicked, for I do like to hear such lies."

She expected him to smile, in turn, but he did not. Indeed, his countenance, as he gazed down at her, was as severe and darkened as it had been the night before, so that he appeared, moment to moment, almost like a stranger rather than the man she had known in Wirth.

"Kayne—" she began, but he released her hand and stood, saying, "You will be thirsty, perhaps hungry. I will fetch Mistress Magan at once. If you need me, Sofia," he said as he neared the door, "only call for me, and I will come at once."

Once the household was made aware that she was awake,

Sofia was descended upon not only by Mistress Magan, but also by a small army of female servants, all of them clucking and shaking their heads and treating her as gently as a frail, tiny child. With slow care she was propped up on several pillows and fed a bowl of weak broth. She had only just finished this and begun to think that she wouldn't mind going back to sleep once more when Lady Katharine and a contingency of her own maidservants arrived.

Within minutes, Lady Katharine had taken charge of Sofia's care, declaring that she must be gotten out of bed and bathed and have each wound fully examined and tended to according to Lady Katharine's own much practiced knowledge of medicine.

Sofia understood the wisdom of Lady Katharine's commands, but was loathe to fulfill the first of them. Every movement was excruciating, and when, with the help of four of the maidservants, she attempted to rise from bed, the muscles along the length of her back contracted with such painful spasms that she could not hold back either the cry that fell from her lips or the tears that sprang to her eyes. But Lady Katharine was deaf and blind to this—or seemingly so. She would not let Sofia lie down again until she had walked the length of the room, for, as she said after making her examination, "You are not so grievously wounded that you must be coddled."

Of course, she was perfectly right. Sofia recognized Lady Katharine's superior knowledge of such matters, but that made it no easier. She had never known such relief, or better sleep, than when Lady Katharine at last allowed Sofia to return to her bed, aided beforehand by one of Lady Katharine's own medicinal draughts, which provided immeasurable relief of her pain. She drifted to sleep thinking that she must ask Lady Katharine to share the receipt for the concoction. 'Twould be a valuable addition to her own collection of remedies.

Through all of yesterday and this morning, Lady Katharine had tirelessly tended Sofia, quitting her duties only long enough to nurse or tend to her infant daughter, who had taken up residence in a small cradle within the chamber, and leaving the room only on those occasions when her husband, Lord Lomas, requested her presence. Otherwise, she slept on a cot beside Sofia's bed through the night—giving Kayne a very shocked look when he'd said that he would remain, instead, and informing him in stately tones that he most assuredly would *not*—and had taken all her meals in Sofia's chamber, as well.

"Now," said Lady Katharine, slowly turning Sofia about to head back toward the bed, "'tis time for a good rubbing of salve to heat you through and ease your pains, and then you must lie down for another rest. We will have you recovered and on your way to Vellaux in but another week or so."

Sofia readily submitted to being unclothed and rubbed along the length of her back and limbs with Lady Katharine's medicinal salve. It smelled wonderful and put off a gentle heat which was most soothing.

"Kayne is anxious to be at Vellaux, is he not?" Sofia asked, yawning. She lifted her arms without help as Lady Katharine and her maid pulled a clean chemise over her head.

"Aye, he is," Lady Katharine admitted, "though 'tis very strange in him. Kayne has ever been the most patient of men. But he has been overset by what has occurred of late, mostlike, and can be pardoned." Supporting Sofia, she guided her toward the bed. "You will travel in my finest carriage when you make your journey to Vellaux. The seats will be covered in pillows, and made the more comfortable for you.''

"Thank you, my lady," Sofia said, as much with the relief of being able to lie down once more as in gratitude for her kindness. "Is it a long journey? Have you ever been to Vellaux? I fear it must be very grand."

"Aye, that it is," Lady Katharine told her, removing one pillow so that Sofia might lie more comfortably. "But this I know only from what I have heard. I have not had the honor of visiting at Vellaux myself. But it is said to be a great and noble estate. And it is but fifty miles from Lomas, so that we will not be too far separated once Kayne has ascended to the title. But you must not think on such matters now, for 'tis always vexing to a woman to be considering the many troubles regarding a change of dwelling, even to so grand a place as Vellaux. You must have no fears, however, Sofia, for Kayne is fully able to keep you safe from both Sir Griel and his noble father—though from what I have heard of Lord Renfrow, he is a very different man from Sir Griel. And you will have Senet and Aric and John and all their men escorting you as well. Now," Lady Katharine said gently, making the bedcovers secure, "you must rest, and think only of regaining all your strength. As for Vellaux, you will be there sooner than you expect, I vow."

The words, Sofia thought two weeks later as she leaned out of Lord and Lady Lomas's fine carriage to gaze at the grand, looming Castle Vellaux, were prophetic. She almost couldn't believe she was truly there, and with her father's full blessing. Before leaving Havencourt she'd had a missive from him, assuring her that all was well at Wirth and Ahlgren Manor and that she wasn't missed or needed in the least. He'd gone to such great lengths to tell her to stay away from Wirth that she could only wonder at how greatly

Sir Griel must have frightened him. She knew too well that her father couldn't manage Ahlgren Manor without her help; he must fear for her very life to tell her in as many words to stay far, far away. It was the first time that Sofia could ever remember him putting her care and comfort ahead of his own, and she was deeply moved by this first expression of fatherly devotion. And a little afraid, as well, not only for her own safety, but for her father's. She knew how easily Sir Griel could torment and terrify him.

"Do you not find it pleasing, Mistress Sofia?" Sir Gwillym, who had been riding beside the carriage and conversing with her the last mile, asked. His own gaze, which he turned to the massive walled castle before them, was filled with admiration. "I confess I had not expected Vellaux to be so large an estate. Such a castle! I would have been in dread to attack any like fortress in France."

It was truly an imposing place, and the estate was clearly a wealthy one. She had heard a little of Lord Renfrow in passing, and knew that he was a great and very respected lord. She was rather daunted by the idea of so much power and wealth—most especially of being married to it. Kayne had once told her that he was a commoner, and therefore could never hope to make an alliance with her, the daughter of a landed knight, and she had not appreciated how he had felt. But now 'twas all turned about. She was in no way a suitable bride for the man Kayne was about to become—a nobleman, rich and powerful, who could have any highborn bride he desired.

But she was determined to give Kayne no reason for dismay upon meeting his father, nor to grieve the father upon knowing his heir's future bride. Now that she had regained so much of her strength and most of the bruises had faded from her features, Sofia felt a great deal of her former confidence returning. Save in one matter—her coming marriage to Kayne.

Somehow, they had become betrothed without her knowing it. Kayne hadn't even gone to the trouble of speaking to her about any manner of alliance. He had simply begun to refer to the coming event as if it had been long settled. They were to be wed and afterward she would be forever safe. Over and over, he said it, but never spoke of love or desire or any other feeling.

He had rarely smiled since the day they had left Wirth, following Sir Griel's attack. He had not wanted to speak to her in any lengthy matter, or to discuss anything that did not pertain to either her regained health or his plans for dealing with Sir Griel. Indeed, he did not seem to want to be in anyone's company for any longer than he need be. He was not himself at all.

She knew that he did not sleep well, for she'd overheard Lady Katharine speaking to him just outside her chamber one day, informing him that she would mix a sleeping draught for him to drink that night. He had politely declined, and then had gone away, daring in his ill humor to depart Lady Katharine's presence without taking formal leave of her. This was certainly not the Kayne she had known in Wirth, who had ever been unfailingly polite and well-spoken to everyone he met.

She could not help but worry and wonder whether she was not the one to blame for this unhappy change in his manner. He was so taut and frowning each moment of the day, as if whatever misery that had befallen him was so great that he found no relief from it either waking or sleeping, and she could not begin to know how to help him. She prayed that coming to Vellaux would work some magic. Perhaps he was merely unnerved at the thought of seeing his ailing father again, and of taking up the knighthood once more. She prayed that it was so. Every other answer she came up with was most unpleasant.

"Aye, 'tis very grand, indeed, Sir Gwillym," Sofia said. "How many towers do you count?"

"Six, and those are but what I can see from this view. There may be six more, or several dozen, for so great a dwelling. But, look, here are the gates being opened to us."

Vellaux was unlike Wirth, where the village butted almost up against the manor house, with but little spare land between them. The castle at Vellaux was set upon a hill, overlooking the walled village that circled it below. Several acres of terraced, planted fields lay between the village and the castle, and set in the midst of them, almost equally distant between village and castle, was a low-walled collection of buildings that comprised what Sofia thought must be a monastery.

It was all beautifully laid out, and Sofia did not believe that she had ever seen any estate more well-favored in its situation.

"Gwillym!"

It was Kayne, speaking in the harsh, impatient tone that had defined him for the past many days. Both Gwillym and Sofia cringed and turned to look at him sitting atop Tristan nearby. He looked as grimly irate as he sounded.

"Aye, my lord?"

"Do you mean to spend the day dallying, or are you going to lead that column through the castle gates? If you do not feel able, I will name another to do so."

Gwillym glanced at Sofia to share a knowing look, then sighed and replied to Kayne, most obediently, "Forgive me, my lord. I am on my way now." He spurred his steed forward to move to the front of the column.

Sofia gave Kayne a reproving look, but he merely looked at her evenly and asked, "Are you well?"

"Yes."

He gave a curt nod. "We will soon have you comfortable within Castle Vellaux." Then he, too, rode away.

Lord Renfrow met them in the inner bailey, and Sofia was astonished at the sight of him. He was Kayne's double, though older and far more frail. His hair was just as blond, his face just as handsome and proud. He was tall, like Kayne, and yet broad in his shoulders, despite his obvious illness. Dressed in a stately manner worthy of greeting a king, he stood at the bottom of the castle steps, supported on either side by two servants. He looked most unsteady to Sofia, but when Kayne dismounted, Lord Renfrow pushed free of their aid and walked to meet his son face-to-face, his arm outstretched to clasp Kayne's.

Kayne was stiff as his father set his arms about his shoulders, but after a moment he returned the embrace, clumsily, but very gently, patting his father's back. Sofia, watching them from the carriage's open window, smiled against the tears that came to her eyes. For a few short moments, until he stepped out of the embrace, Kayne was himself again.

The door to the carriage was opened by Lord John Baldwin, who had formerly been called John Ipris. He had recently been adopted into the powerful Baldwin clan, and thereafter made lord of his own estate, Capwell. He was quiet, handsome, and surely one of the most chivalrous men Sofia had ever met. Giving her a reassuring smile, he held out both hands to aid her in stepping down, supporting her almost completely while letting her take her time, for she could yet move but slowly. She was full glad to be quit of the carriage, comfortable as Lady Katharine had made it, and relieved to be out in the crisp autumn afternoon. She paused to draw in a deep, refreshing breath of sweet, fresh air. It was a beautiful day, cool and breezy, and filled with the delightful smells of both the season's change and the busy harvest. In the many ripe fields that they had passed on their journey, they had seen hundreds of laborers hard at work, reaping each bountiful crop in their yearly race with the coming winter.

"John!"

Kayne shouted the single word so fiercely that Sofia nearly stumbled as she took another step. She and Lord John looked to where Kayne was striding furiously toward them.

"By the Rood, man! What are you about, dragging her in such a manner from the carriage?"

"Lord John was not—" Sofia began, but John had already stepped aside and given her over into Kayne's care. "Pray forgive me, Mistress Sofia," he said, "and you also, Kayne." He bowed politely and walked away to tend his troops.

"He did naught wrong," she insisted as Kayne lifted her off the carriage steps and into his arms.

"Come and meet Lord Renfrow," he said, ignoring her comment and carrying her toward the castle. "He had my missive and has had the most comfortable chamber made ready for you."

With the greatest care, he set her upon her feet in front of his father, then with both hands steadied her as Sofia smiled at Lord Renfrow and made a careful bow. When she lifted her head, it was to find Lord Renfrow smiling back at her with shining eyes. How very much he looked like Kayne at this closer distance! Even his blue eyes were exactly like his son's. Despite his illness, he was a most handsome man, and his expression was one of such kindness and gentleness that she immediately felt an affection for him.

"My lord, I would make known to you Mistress Sofia

Ahlgren, daughter of Sir Malcolm Ahlgren of Wirth. Sofia, this is Sir Ronan Sager, Lord Renfrow...my father.''

"My lord," Sofia greeted very formally.

Lord Renfrow took her hand and smiled down at her. "Mistress Sofia, you are even more beautiful than my son's missive described, though he did well in claiming that you are most rare and fine, for indeed you are. I cannot tell you how it gladdens my heart to know that you will soon become his good lady wife, and therefore also my daughter. You are welcome at Vellaux. But, come. I can see that you are full weary, and I know that you have but a few weeks past been grievously wounded." He took Sofia's hand and tucked it beneath his arm to guide her into the castle. "Kayne," he said, "see to the settling of the men. I have had the outer bailey made in readiness for them and all your horses. When you have done, come to the great hall with your particular comrades and all your captains, and you will find food and wine waiting for you to refresh yourselves. I will see that Mistress Sofia is made comfortable."

Sofia wasn't sure which one of them was helping the other as they made their way so slowly up the great castle stairs. Servants hovered on either side of them, but Lord Renfrow was clearly a man of great pride—also like his son—and gruffly refused their aid. She could feel, beneath the hand that she held on his arm, the effort it cost him to maintain his pose of strength and ability, but she continued to let him expend that effort and guide her until they had reached the castle doors. To do anything else, especially in front of so great an army of fighting men, would have humiliated him utterly.

She looked back, once, before they walked into the castle, awed by the number of men who had ridden into the inner courtyard. Many more had stayed without, in the much larger outer bailey, but she could not yet help being

impressed by how large an army Kayne and his friends had
managed to bring together. She caught Kayne's eye, saw
how grim and concerned he was as he gazed at both herself
and his father, and she smiled at him reassuringly. His
frown lessened slightly, and their eyes met and held, his
with silent entreaty, hers with understanding. She would not
let his father exhaust himself for her sake; she would make
certain that he was comfortable, even as she allowed him
to do the same for her.

The moment they had crossed the castle threshold and
servants had closed the castle doors, both Sofia and Lord
Renfrow grasped the strong arms of the servants beside
them. They looked at each other, took in the other's pale
face and smiled.

"We are a well-matched pair, are we not, my lord?"
Sofia said. She clutched his hand more tightly, as if she felt
far more unsteady than she was. Lord Renfrow's brow furrowed with concern. "I am sorry to be so much trouble,"
she went on, letting herself sound a bit weak, "but I think
I must rest for a few minutes before attempting any greater
number of stairs. Is there somewhere we might sit in the
great hall? I confess, as well, that I am very eager to see
it, for Kayne has told me how very beautiful it is."

"Of a certainty, daughter," he replied at once, "but
would you not rather be carried to your chamber? I wish
might have the honor of doing so, but as I cannot, one of
the servants can readily perform the task."

"Oh, nay, I thank you, my lord." She gave him a grateful, very feminine smile. "I will be better in a very short
while, if I could only sit...."

"Then come at once into the hall," he commanded
gently, nodding at the servant on Sofia's side to help her
Lord Renfrow himself guided the group, ever holding and
patting Sofia's hand. "We will sit here, by the fire, in these

very comfortable chairs, and wait for Kayne and his fellows to join us. Fetch wine,'' he called to a young page standing near the fire. ''At once.'' The boy bowed low and then ran off full speed to fulfill his master's bidding.

The chair she was settled into, with the solicitous aid of the servants, was indeed very comfortable, and she saw that Lord Renfrow looked most pleased to sink into the one across from her. He was far more tired than she had thought. He must have been awaiting Kayne's arrival for many hours.

''The great room of Vellaux is very beautiful, my lord,'' Sofia said, looking about her with interest. It was truly a magnificent chamber, worthy of so magnificent a castle. And it was surely the largest and grandest room she'd ever seen, with six hearths set at intervals along the length of each long wall, and an eating area set with tables and chairs enough for hundreds of people. At the very end of the hall, a regal marble dais rose from among the more common stones that comprised the hall floor. Upon the dais sat a large, thronelike chair—clearly Lord Renfrow's chair of judgment, from which he received the people of Vellaux, heard their complaints, and made his determinations. She gazed at it for a long moment, but could not envision Kayne sitting there. At least, not as he was now, so tense and unhappy. ''All of Castle Vellaux is beautiful. I vow that I have never seen anything to compare to it.''

Lord Renfrow's smile was filled with happiness.

''I'm glad that you find it pleasing, Sofia. You will be mistress here one day, and it would mean a great deal to know that the new lady of Vellaux loves it as fondly as I have ever done. It will be harder for Kayne to care for it with any measure of affection, I think,'' he said a little more sadly, ''for I had no chance to teach him all that he must know. I was greatly relieved to know that he had chosen a proper born and gentle lady for his bride.''

"But, my lord," Sofia said with quick distress, "I am by no means a noblewoman. Indeed, I am but a commoner compared to Kayne's far more noble lineage."

"It is strange in our society," he said gently, "to think that Kayne, in but a few days, will be changed from a bastard commoner to my legal heir, the future lord of Vellaux, and a great and powerful man. And he will be a knight of the realm again. But naught can change the manner in which he was raised. Oh, he is a fine warrior, I vow, but he has no knowledge of servants and vassals and crops and tradesmen—certainly he knows nothing of the many responsibilities that face him. But you were born to these things, and from what I have heard of your life at Ahlgren Manor, you know all that the lady of any estate, large or small, must know. For my part, Sofia, I think you must be the very answer to my prayers. You will know the way to keep my son from harm."

"I am not so certain of that, my lord," Sofia told him honestly.

He looked at her with warmth and wisdom.

"I am, daughter. Quite certain."

Chapter Thirteen

The night was black with storm clouds, and bitingly cold. Rain would come soon. Kayne could already smell it, ominous in the damp night air. Uncaring, he spurred Tristan on, pushing the destrier full out along the length of the field they rode upon. When they had left the field he steered Tristan to the road and galloped headlong, heedlessly, recklessly, until they were both so spent that there was no choice save to come to a stop.

He led the winded horse off the road and into a copse of twisting oaks, then, dismounting, let him free to wander and rest. Striving to catch his own breath, Kayne leaned against the nearest tree for several long minutes until his whirling senses had begun to calm. When he at last sat down in the cool, damp dirt at the base of the tree, the first bolt of lightning from the coming storm lanced across the sky, followed seconds later by a not too distant rumbling. He heard, rather than felt, the drops of rain as they began to fall on the tree leaves overhead, soft and delicate at first, but growing steadily heavier as the minutes passed. Tristan, unsettled by the lightning and the sound of thunder, moved restlessly back toward Kayne. Being a seasoned warhorse, he would not bolt or whinny with distress, even when the storm became wild, but he would yet be uneasy, partly because of the storm, and partly because of his master's odd behavior. Kayne could hardly blame the creature. He was full uneasy with himself.

He was a knight again. The ceremony this second time had been far, far grander than the first he'd undergone. That first one, more than ten years ago in France, had taken place after his very first battle, when he was covered with blood and dirt, filthy from the killings he'd freshly committed for the sake of England. Sir John Fastolf himself had dubbed Kayne in both the name and authority of the king, right after he had finished dubbing Senet. Aric was dubbed immediately following Kayne. They had knelt together, side by side, on the outskirts of the muddy battlefield, and become knights together. John would have been knighted, as well, for Sir John Fastolf had deemed him the worthiest among the four, but he had refused the honor, and had kept refusing it year after year after year. That, Kayne thought now, must be the secret to all John's serenity and calm. He had never given himself over to be a slave for the king, or for any man. John had been far too wise for that.

Oh, God. Far too wise.

Kayne lifted his face toward the sky and let all his pain and rage come shouting out of him. Louder than the thunder, far louder. He shouted at the top of his lungs, uncaring of whether anyone heard him or even if he was full crazed for it—with all his might he brought it forth, from his very depths, until his muscles ached and burned, a long, harsh, guttural sound of fury.

He did not know how long it continued. Time was as black to him now as all else. He found himself sitting beneath the tree, weeping, with the rain falling hard through the leaves now, utterly soaking him. Tristan had moved away again, right into the rain, far more afraid of his master than of the storm.

He felt as if he were going mad. He felt as if he would gladly accept death rather than what was before him—a lifetime of blackness, with all his hard-won peace thrown forever aside—save for one thing. Death would take him from Sofia, and he could not abandon her for any reason. It was not her fault that he'd been forced upon this hated path once more. It was his own, for not taking better care of her. But that would never happen again. She would be his wife, and he would devote his life to protecting her— even from his own singular evils.

He would kill again, for her sake, and because he was now a knight of the realm and had taken vows to do the king's bidding, whatever that might be. He would take life, as he had prayed never to do again, as he had *vowed* never to do. And how could God forgive him for breaking such a vow? Surely there was no way to find sanctuary for such as that. He would deservedly end his life in hell and then be parted from Sofia forever. But it could surely be no worse, he thought morosely, than the hell he was living in now.

Lightning briefly made the sky as bright as day, and a booming crack of thunder shook the earth at almost the same moment. The skies opened with a fury now, drenching the land and everything upon it. Tristan, admirable horse that he was, stood patiently beneath the raging on-slaught, only daring to shake his mane once every few minutes. Kayne could hardly see the great beast through the darkness, but his stance was familiar and calming.

Slowly, he stood, and then began to pull the clothes from his body. A gust of wind buffeted Kayne as he tossed his tunic to the mud and, naked from the waist up, walked out from beneath the tree to stand in the open. He spread his arms wide to receive all that nature desired to send upon him, hard, stinging rain and bitterly cold gusts of wind. Another bolt of lightning cracked across the sky, and another crushing fist of thunder pounded the earth. Kayne lifted his face once more and held his arms out wide, welcoming all of it.

He wanted peace. God's mercy, how he wanted it. Only a few sweet moments would be worth all he possessed, even his very soul.

Her name was the only thought that came to him.

Sofia.

She was all his peace, all his refuge now. Only when he was with her did he feel any measure of lightness, enough that he might bear the path he had chosen to travel once more. To see her, to hear her voice and gaze upon her lovely, smiling face. That would be enough. If he must live in hell, she would be what little he knew of heaven. His love. His own sweet bride. His only reason for embracing life at all.

How beautiful she had been this day, standing so near as he took his knightly oaths and undertook the holy ceremony. Hundreds of onlookers—almost all of them soldiers—had watched the solemn rite, but Kayne had known that Sofia, with her exceedingly great beauty, had drawn far more attention than he had done.

Lady Katharine had sent Sofia a beautiful surcoat to wear for the event, made of a blue cloth that nearly matched the color of her eyes, ornamented with gold thread that highlighted the wealth of gold in her hair. She had stood beside his father during the ceremony, and Kayne had maintained his sanity only by holding his gaze upon her.

He dropped his arms and stood utterly still beneath the rain, finding pleasure in the cleansing torrent that poured over him. He had found a measure of calm here, and would treasure it. Tomorrow he would face the day, and all that it brought, anew. For now, he would seek only peace.

Sofia would give him peace. And rest—the sweetest thing of all to those who were cursed. She would keep the nightmares that haunted him at bay.

All about him, the rain poured down like a waterfall from the sky. He smiled to think of himself standing there in the midst of it, with his poor horse wretched and wet and likely thinking his master a fool.

Turning, he found his discarded clothing, and went to fetch Tristan, who didn't mind having the wet garments tossed over his already wet neck. Bare chested and soaked from head to toe, Kayne heaved himself onto Tristan's saddle and took up the reins. Setting the steed into motion, he headed through the darkness and driving rain back in the direction of Vellaux.

It was impossible to sleep. Sofia lay in the comfortable bed in her firelit chamber and stared at the bedcurtains that she had not allowed the maidservant to close. On a night such as this, when lightning filled the room from time to time with eerie light, a person would usually prefer to cloak herself securely in the darkness of the heavy curtains, closed very tightly to keep warmth in and the effects of the storm out. But Sofia had little use for such as that. She couldn't sleep, and the play of light and sound of thunder and rain were far more interesting than a blank, curtained darkness.

With a sigh, she at last gave up even the pretense of rest and slowly, carefully, pushed the heavy covers aside and got out of bed. Her back ached badly after a long day of so much standing, sitting and kneeling. Kayne's knighting ceremony had been lengthy and grand, and had been attended by one of the king's own regents. Before it had come to an end, Sofia's legs had burned like fire, and she had longed to sit down. But as uncomfortable as it had been for her, it had been a thousand times worse for Kayne. She had never seen any man more unhappy than he was as he took on again the vows and duties of the knighthood. A dozen times at least she'd wanted to cry out loud that it must all stop, that he mustn't continue with the ceremony, but the hand that Lord Renfrow had kept upon her arm seemed to hold her both paralytic and mute.

With careful steps, she moved to a tall, thickly paned window, and gazed out at the raging storm. A damp chill emanated from the heavy glass, and Sofia lifted fingertips to touch the cold, smooth surface. Few noblemen were wealthy enough to have windows in their castles, but Lord Renfrow was one of them. Wealth, power—Lord Renfrow possessed them both in great measure. And Kayne would inherit them, along with all the responsibilities of the title.

She couldn't forget the look on his face as he'd taken his vows. How cold and dark his blue eyes had appeared, so dull and lifeless, just as his voice, reciting the words, had been.

It was her fault that he had become so wretched. He had been content in his smithy at Wirth, and in his clean, quiet, spare dwelling. But now, for her sake, he had taken on the knighthood, and had let himself be made Lord Renfrow's legitimate heir. Thinking of it, Sofia closed her eyes and leaned her forehead against the cold glass. How could she have let it all happen? How could she have allowed the man she loved so deeply to take such a heavy, cumbersome burden—a burden he had only just thrown off?

But she knew why she had been too weak to stop it. She could blame no one but herself, for the truth of it was, she was afraid, and Kayne made her feel safe. For her own selfish sake, she had let Kayne make so great a sacrifice.

He had done it out of love, while she, who claimed to love him so well, had been too foolish and cowardly to make any like sacrifice for him.

Suddenly, the door to her chamber opened, not quietly, as a servant might do in order to creep in and stoke the fire, but firmly, as the lord of the castle might do.

Sofia turned, and through the darkness saw a tall, broad figure standing in the door. A brief moment of confusion and panic passed as he turned to close the door, throwing the bolt, until she realized, by his blond hair, that it was Kayne.

He moved toward her in strong, steady strides, as if he meant to snatch her up, and she backed away a step, murmuring his name.

"Sofia," he said, reaching out to her as he came near. His movements were swift and sure, but his touch was gentle, and he drew her close.

"Kayne?" she repeated with confusion, but the next moment he was kissing her, tenderly and with great care, holding her face between his hands. His mouth moved over her lips, her skin, traveling in rapid, fervent caresses across the line of her cheek before finding her mouth once more.

"Kayne," she tried again, but he did not seem to hear her. There was an urgency to his gentle onslaught, a hunger in the movement of his hands and mouth. Sofia could do naught save give way to it.

In but moments she began to feel the same hunger, and lifted her arms to put them about his neck, pressing close against his half-clothed body. The action made him groan deeply, and his arms lashed about her waist to crush her tightly to himself.

Pain sliced across Sofia's back, and she stiffened and gasped. Kayne at once altered his grip.

"Sofia, forgive me," he pleaded, his breathing harsh

with desire. "Forgive my thoughtlessness. Are you all right, love?"

She had already recovered by the time he finished his apology, and drew in a long, easing breath and relaxed. "'Twas but a small spasm. It has passed." She touched his hair with her fingertips. "You're wet," she said foolishly, and then realized that she was now wet, too, from being pressed so near to him. "And you are all unclothed. Kayne...you have not been out in this weather?"

"Aye," he murmured.

"But why?"

"To find a measure of peace."

Sorrow knifed through her, far more painful than what her body had just experienced. "Oh, Kayne," she murmured sadly, stroking strands of wet hair from his face. "'Tis all my fault. I am so deeply ashamed and sorry."

He shook his head. "You are not the one to blame. It is my own sickness that makes me ill within. You are my only refuge from the misery of it. I need you, Sofia."

For a moment she did not understand what he meant, but he spread his hands carefully against her hips and drew her near once more, pressing her firmly against himself.

"I need you," he said again, whispering the words this time. "But if you tell me to leave, I will go at once. Indeed, I should go. I have no right to ask anything of you."

Sofia swallowed heavily. "I want you to stay, Kayne. But I am afraid...because I cannot stop thinking of Sir Griel and...everything he said and did."

He began to release her altogether, and his tone, when he spoke, was filled with remorse. "God's mercy, Sofia— I had not remembered, or thought—and now I have given you such grave insult as cannot be forgiven."

"Nay!" she insisted, clutching him with her small strength, not letting him pull away. "I only want you to take away the pain of such memories. If you do not, I must live with them forever. When Sir Griel did those...those things to me, I was so afraid. But the worst of it was thinking that he would be the first to know me, and not you, as I had always dreamed.''

Kayne's arms slid about her again, much more carefully now. He held her in a light, comforting clasp.

''Don't think of it, or of him,'' he said. ''I would not have you so tormented.''

''Then let us give each other peace this night,'' she murmured. ''Give me new memories to think upon, and I will strive to give you peace, as well, though you must be patient and show me how best to please you, for I know so little.''

In the dim firelight, he searched her face intently.

''Are you certain, Sofia?''

''Aye.'' She smiled. ''Is it not what you came for?''

He nodded. ''But the madness that possessed me has been tempered.'' His hands lifted to frame her face again, gently, his fingers soft against her skin. ''I would not bring you harm, Sofia. Ever. You are all in this world that matters to me now. All I have to love and care for.''

She slid her hands over his, gazing at him solemnly. ''Then love me, Kayne. Mayhap I am wanton and full sinful—but I have dreamt of you almost from the moment I knew you.''

''And I of you,'' he whispered, lowering his head to tenderly kiss her. ''So many nights, lying in my solitary bed.'' He kissed her again before adding, ''And so many days, working by the forge.'' His hands lowered to clasp her own, and pulling her along, he slowly backed toward the bed. ''Always, you were in my thoughts, even when I did not want you there.''

''I'm glad,'' she said, shivering with a mixture of antic-

ipation and fear as they reached their destination. Another
flash of lightning briefly lit the chamber, followed by a low
rumble of thunder. "I suffered for you as well."

"You're trembling," he said, his hands releasing her
own and sliding upward, slowly, until his fingers touched
the bare skin of her neck. His thumbs caressed the delicate
flesh beneath her ears.

"'Tis cold," Sofia murmured, striving to keep her eyes
from closing at the pleasure of his touch. "And you
are…we are…wet."

"Aye." His fingers moved lower, to the ties of her night
rail. Slowly, he pulled them free. "We must remedy this
as soon as we may."

Sofia did close her eyes then, as he undressed her. The
night rail slid from her shoulders and pooled about her feet,
and she stood before him, naked and intensely embarrassed.
She tried to control her heightened breathing, but to no
avail. He would know full well just how naive and foolish
she was.

Kayne's big hands, warm now, smoothed over her shoulders, and his fingers skimmed downward across the soft
skin of her arms, making Sofia shiver even more greatly.
He bent and kissed her mouth, then, very gently, the skin
beneath one ear. She could hear that he, too, was breathing
more harshly than before.

"You are more beautiful than all my dreams," he whispered into her ear. When he straightened, he pulled the
length of her unbound hair over her shoulders, and spent a
full minute or more running his fingers through the myriad
strands. Sofia, standing very still beneath this touching, at
last opened her eyes.

He was gazing down at her, his face lit only dimly by
the firelight, with equal measures of awe and desire. Seeing
that she had opened her eyes, he ceased his wondered play-

ing with her hair and smiled. Then he bent and, taking every care, lifted her in his arms and laid her upon the bed.

"Stay warm until I join you," he said, pulling the bedcovers up.

He sat in a nearby chair and removed his boots, tossing each of them aside to land upon the floor with a thud. Another flash of lightning filled the room, and Sofia saw that Kayne had stood, and was pulling off his wet leggings. Their eyes met in that brief flash, and the desire she saw in his made her draw in a breath and pull the bedcovers up more closely.

The next moment, the bed dipped as his weight came onto it, and the covers lifted as he slid beneath them and next to her.

His chest was warm and dry, his legs were yet cold and a bit damp. Sofia tried to scoot farther away to give him room, but Kayne only followed, sliding an arm about her waist to stop her from going further.

"Sofia, love," he murmured, leaning over her, seeming so much bigger and more solid of a sudden. "Don't be afraid." He took her hand and held it over his bare chest, where his heart beat in a firm, steady rhythm. "You hold every power over me, now and always. If you tell me to go, I will go at once, without a murmur of dissent. It will be thus each moment. If you begin to feel afraid, or to think of what happened before, tell me."

Sofia reached out to touch his well-loved face, then to stroke the length of his strong neck, down to his muscled and heavily scarred shoulders. He held himself very still as she made her tentative exploration, though she could feel, by the tautness of the muscles beneath her hands, and hear, by his rapid breath, that he did so only by great force of will.

How long had she dreamt of doing this? Of touching

him so intimately? Of becoming his in the way of a man and woman, with love making that perfect bond between them? Even if she never became his wife, she would have this one night to cherish, and to remember even when he had gone away from her. For a few precious hours she would know what it was to lie with the man she would love forever.

"I'm not afraid," she whispered, as yet another shock of lightning glimmered briefly in the room, revealing his eyes, filled with fierce desire and hope. "I love you, Kayne. Show me how to give you pleasure."

Kayne came awake to find Sofia's warm, naked body spooned comfortably against him, and for one confused moment strove to remind himself where he was and what had occurred. Memory rushed back as sweetly as the pleasure they had shared, and he closed his eyes and released a deep, relaxed breath.

Never had he known such joy with a woman before; never had he realized what satisfaction and completion might be attained in joining with the one who was, and would ever be to him, all beloved. He had selfishly thought to find a measure of peace in seeking Sofia out this night, and instead had discovered a truth that had shattered his very soul. Aye, she had given him peace, and a reprieve from his demons. But she had done far more, as well.

She had loved him. Not only in the physical sense, but with all of herself. It was as if he had finally realized the truth of it for the very first time. Sofia *loved* him.

Why she loved him or how such a miracle had occurred was beyond his understanding; whether he deserved it was a consideration he wouldn't let himself think of—certainly not now. But one thing Kayne did know: he would never take such love for granted. It was far too precious and rare a treasure.

Sofia stirred within his embrace, sighing in slumber, and resettled herself more comfortably. The slight movement caused her smooth buttocks to press against his manhood, and Kayne reacted accordingly. Within but moments he was fully aroused.

He tried to control himself, to keep from touching her or pushing his traitorous member searchingly against her, but his body refused to obey. Her skin was soft and warm beneath his callused hands, even softer beneath his lips. His fingers curled over the curves of her breasts, stroking until the nipples hardened at his touch, arousing him further. His mouth found the silky skin of her neck and shoulder, where he placed small, nipping kisses which he smoothed over with his tongue.

Sofia began to moan softly as she climbed out slumber, responding with sweet, sleepy murmuring to his caresses. But he knew the moment she came fully awake when she stiffened and drew in a sharp breath.

His manhood was pressed fully against her from behind, needy and seeking, and he could feel panic rigidly possessing every inch of her by increasing degrees.

"Sofia," he said gently, smoothing his hands soothingly over her flesh, "trust me, love. I'll never hurt you. Trust me."

Her breathing was heightened, and her body taut with fear, and Kayne resolutely set out to dispel the cruel memories that haunted her.

"This is but one of many ways that a man and woman may find pleasure together," he murmured, continuing to kiss and caress. "Let me love you this way, Sofia. Let me…"

Slowly she began to respond to his touch, her limbs taking on a different manner of tension, yet pliant to his coaxing. He pulled one of her legs to lie over his own, and moved nearer until she could feel the probing of his manhood and understand what he meant to do. He wetted the tip of himself inside her warm, slick passage, and heard her sharply indrawn breath.

"Aye, that is how we will be joined, love," he said, desire mounting as she pressed her hips against him, arching to receive more of him inside her. "But not yet, Sofia. Not yet."

"Kayne," she murmured, pleading.

"Soon," he promised, caressing the shell of her ear with his tongue and the warmth of his breath. "You must be full ready. I want to give you every pleasure."

His fingers slid downward to find the delicate place between her legs, and so very gently and carefully teased and fondled, drawing shivers and moans from her that delighted him utterly. She was wet with moisture and heated with passion before he at last gave way to her entreaties.

"Aye, my love," he whispered, pushing into her ready passage. "Now we will be one."

Sofia threw her head back as he came into her, making a low noise of pleasure and relief. Kayne responded with equal gratification as her heat and softness enfolded his rigid flesh. He pushed firmly, surely upward, filling her with all of himself, and she pressed down on him hard, demanding, and taking, even more.

They moved together, joined in an ageless, perfect rhythm, uttering wordless pleasure sounds until they came at last, together, to the crest. Kayne shuddered and poured himself into Sofia's trembling body, thrusting hard and fast and deep, answering her shaking cry with a loud, unbridled groan that was filled with the unutterable sensations he felt.

Long moments later, they lay together, spent and replete,

still joined in body. Kayne's hands moved in long, lazy strokes over Sofia's heat-dampened skin, caressing, soothing. He thought perhaps she slept, so still and relaxed did she lie, but at length she turned her head backward, toward him, to find his mouth. Their kisses were long and languorous, and spoke of the contented tranquillity they both felt.

Sofia turned a bit to slide one hand up his arm and rest upon his shoulder. When he lifted his head to gaze down at her she smiled and murmured, "I never would have imagined how 'twould be."

"Naught between a man and wife should be shamed or feared," he said. "Every pleasure is ours, Sofia. A gift from God."

"I do not think I shall ever again remember what Sir Griel did. This is what I will think of, instead."

"That is well," Kayne said, touching his nose to hers. "But if you ever should begin to think of those dark moments, you need only tell me. I will gladly make myself the remedy for all that distresses you. I am your most willing servant."

She laughed and grinned. "Then I am indeed the most fortunate woman on God's earth, my lord. And I will spend my days thinking upon every hurt and misfortune that has befallen me, if you will rid me of such memories in this delightful way."

"Most assuredly, my lady," he murmured. "With a very glad heart, I will do all your bidding."

Chapter Fourteen

"**I** do think of the smithy at times," Kayne admitted, ducking his fair head so as not to strike it upon a low branch, "and I believe I will miss it. But I will do as my lord, Sir Justin, has ever done at Talwar and set up a smithy for my own pleasure at Vellaux."

"But it will not be the same as the smithy you had built at Wirth," Sofia said, letting Kayne bring her to a stop near the trunk of a fallen tree. It was slightly damp from the several days of rain that had just passed, and Kayne unclasped the cloak about his shoulders and laid it upon the wood before helping Sofia to sit down. "And your beautiful dwelling, which I know you dearly love—you will miss that most of all, will you not?"

With a weary sigh, he propped one booted foot upon the trunk and gazed out into the hazy mist of the forest.

They had left Vellaux only the day before, when the morn had dawned clear after a week of rain, and were on their way back to Wirth with an army of hundreds of fighting men at their heels. Sir Senet and Sir Aric and Lord John had waited patiently for the journey to begin, for the rain had delayed their time at Vellaux and Sofia knew that they were eager to return to their own estates and more especially their wives and children. But such was the measure of their bond with Kayne that they never spoke of such matters, nor murmured among themselves. And in the face of Kayne's sullen and impatient behavior they had been unfailingly patient. Sofia wished that she could say the same for herself.

Each night in the past week, following their first night together, Kayne had come to her chamber and stayed with her. Sofia welcomed him with love and gladness, for in those precious hours he was himself again, leaving behind, as if shutting them away with the closing of her chamber door, his bitterness and unhappiness. It was almost as if they were back at Wirth, long before Sir Griel had brought such ruin to them, and at peace again. But come the morn, when he had returned to his own chamber, Kayne reclaimed the darkness that ever haunted him. Perhaps he was not so openly wretched as he had been before—indeed, she knew that he strove mightily not to give way to it—but there were still times, long hours, when he fell into the somber melancholy that refused to go away entirely.

This new journey had been far easier than the one they had made from Havencourt. Sofia's back, though yet sore, was much improved, and the mud and wet that remained from the now passed storm made travel slow. With so large an army, they were forced to stop far more often than they would have done if the roads had been in much better condition. Kayne was faithful to pull her down from the carriage at each rest and walk with her for a few moments. This, as he knew very well, greatly relieved the stiffness and pain in her body, and she was most thankful to him for it.

In but two days' time, they would be at Wirth once more, and it was Kayne's intention to confront Sir Griel and arrest him for the assault he had committed. As this would doubtless require a great deal of fighting—Sir Griel's army was small but fierce, and his castle as unassailable as Havencourt—some manner of war would take place, and with it, most likely, much bloodshed. Kayne had assured her that he would not kill Sir Griel unless he deemed it necessary, but she was very afraid that he only spoke in such a manner to allay her fears. He already believed that Sir Griel was worthy of death for the grave insult he had visited upon her, and who would be able to stop Kayne if he managed to get Sir Griel alone in the heat of battle, even for a few minutes?

Once Sir Griel was dealt with, one way or another, Kayne and Sofia would stand on the steps of the chapel at Ahlgren Manor before the priest and all the people of Wirth, with her father present and in full agreement, and recite vows of betrothal. Then Sir Malcolm would accompany them back to Vellaux, where one week later, according to the terms of the betrothal, Kayne would take Sofia as his wife.

Upon this course of action, Kayne was firmly set, and Sofia, who had tried, and miserably failed, to convince him that it was not too late to back away from such commitment, found herself counting a multitude of minutes as they slipped away, taking with them her chances of giving Kayne back the peace and happiness he had lost because of her.

"It does no good to speak of what I will or will not miss, Sofia," Kayne said after a short silence. "We will live at Vellaux once we are wed, and that is where our children will be born. The house and smithy in Wirth will be given to another. But you need have no worries, for I will find a skilled blacksmith in need of such work, who will serve the villagers well, and will set him up there. He may even have my cattle to keep as his own. So long as I have Tristan, I have little need of them. The horses," he added with some regret, "are fine steeds, but he will need some few to hire out, and they would cost him too dear to buy if he has naught."

"But if you would only speak to your father," Sofia pressed, "he would let us stay at Wirth for a time. He is much better now than when first we arrived at Vellaux, for all that he insists he is yet dying. I am not so skilled as Lady Katharine, but you must agree that he is greatly improved these past many days."

"Because he is half in love with his new daughter," Kayne said, glancing at her with a brief smile, "and because you made him drink your medicinal brew each morn and night. But despite all this, he would not agree to let his heir live as a mere blacksmith. I am once again a knight of the realm," he said, growing somber, as he ever did when he spoke of the knighthood, "and must live by the vows I have taken. I cannot bring dishonor to the knightly order."

"And is it dishonor for a knight to make his living as a blacksmith?" she asked. "Is it not more honorable than killing men?"

His expression was cold and blank. "To be obedient to one's master, to kill for him, if need be, is of all things held to be the most honorable. If the king, to whom I have pledged my liege, would order me to be a blacksmith, there would be honor in it. But he will not do so." His mouth flattened to a grim line. "He would send me back to France before giving me such leave."

For the first time since he'd taken her away from Wirth, following Sir Griel's attack, Sofia felt a physical sense of dread. She had been worried for Kayne, aye, for she knew how deeply unhappy he was, but this was far more frightening.

"If he sent you back to France, Kayne," she whispered, saying the words without thinking of what she did, "you would die." She knew it was true, and felt faint and ill all at once. "You hated it so very much. And you would not have your friends about you, as you did before. Oh, Kayne…"

He sat beside her at once, setting one arm about her waist to draw her near, while with the other he searched for one of her hands.

"Forgive me for speaking in so thoughtless a manner," he said. "The King will not send me to France, Sofia, for it is well and truly lost to England. 'Twas naught but fool-ishness for me to speak so heedlessly."

"Nay, 'twill not do," she said insistently, pushing from his grasp and standing. She strode a few paces, folding and unfolding her hands, feeling the bitter chill through to her bones, despite the heavy surcoat she wore. "I cannot let this be, Kayne. 'Tis all my fault that you are so wretched. You would never have taken on the knighthood again if I had not been so foolish—and if I had not prayed for it to happen."

She heard him standing and moving, step by step through the dry leaves, until he was right in back of her.

"Sofia," he said gently, setting his hands upon her shoulders. "'Tis not your fault, but mine."

She wrenched free once more, moving a few steps away and shaking her head, not able to look at him.

"You do not understand. When I thought you were but a common blacksmith, I made myself accept that we could not be wed, but when I knew that you had once been a great knight, and that you were of noble birth—I had it in my mind that I would find the way to make you accept these things, so that we could be married. But it was all foolishness, and so very wrong." She set the fingers of one hand against her face and shut her eyes tightly. "Oh, God, so very wrong. I thought—I was so foolish that I thought you would one day consent to being master of Ahlgren Manor, after my father had died, and before that we would live peaceably in your dwelling. But how foolish I was!" she cried, dropping her hand and opening her eyes, turning to look at him with all the agony she felt. "I prayed to God for my petitions to come true, but never did I *think* upon what it meant. How could you be made legitimate and take back the knighthood unless you took back all that you had so greatly abhorred? You strove so mightily to leave it behind, all that made you so fully wretched, but I, with my selfish desires, have made you take it all back."

"Sofia, you do not know what you say," he began, but she shook her head and would not listen.

"I *do* know, and it is the truth! But I will not let you do this thing, not even for all the fear I bear Sir Griel. I love you so, Kayne. How could I see you destroyed because of me?" She drew in a shaking breath, then said, "I will not be your wife."

It was as if Kayne had turned to stone. He stared at her wide-eyed, disbelieving, and said, "What?"

Sofia licked her lips and blinked, striving not to weep.

"I will not be your wife," she repeated. "I will not wed with you, Kayne. You must…tell your father that you…do not wish to have the knighthood. If it is not too late, though I know how it will grieve him. But that is my fault, as well, and not your own. You must never think that it is otherwise."

He took a step toward her, holding out one hand. Sofia shook her head and stepped away. On her cheek she felt, with distress, the wet streak of a silent tear.

"You are already my wife," he said in a low voice. "We have lain together as man and wife six full nights. I have planted my seed within you, and even now you may carry my child. We are as good as handfasted, and therefore man and wife.''

Sofia wiped her wet cheeks with the tips of her fingers. ''We are not handfasted,'' she declared. ''We made no vows. We said naught before lying together. I have only been your...your leman.''

The color that had drained from Kayne's face now filled quickly with red. He strode forward and grabbed her up with both hands in a furious hold.

''You are *not* my leman!'' he shouted angrily, giving her a shake. ''God's mercy! I would kill any man who dared to utter so foul a thing! You are my *wife,* Sofia, and every law in England, both of Church and Crown, will proclaim you as such. We have declared our intent to wed and having lain together sealed our word. We are well and truly hand-fasted, made as one.'' He gave her another shake, uncaring of the cry she gave. ''I will *never* let any other man claim you as such.''

''And I will not see you live the rest of your days in misery!'' she declared with equal heat, struggling until he at last released her. ''Not when I have been the cause of it.''

''You are not the cause of it,'' he said. ''I have told you that 'tis naught but my own folly. I will master it, in time.''

''You must put aside the knighthood once more.''

Kayne threw his hands up with a measure of disbelief. ''I cannot put it aside a second time! I have only just taken it back! What manner of man would I be if I did such a thing? And how should my honor withstand the shame? Do you not know what would be said of me, that my vows are worthless, and that I cannot cling to any determination I make longer than my own comfort allows?''

Sofia had not thought of that, but it was true. It would

seem strange, indeed, for him to put off the knighthood yet again. He would be made jest of in every corner of England.

"Sofia, there is no other way," he said more calmly. "We must both accept that, and cease such foolishness. Let us have no more talk of such matters."

She shook her head silently, thinking that there must be a way to set him free, but said nothing. Kayne moved nearer and set his hands upon her arms, soothing with gentle fingers whatever pain he had given her earlier. Sofia could not even look at him, so great was her guilt.

"We will be married," he told her, "and that is the end of it."

"If only we could live at the smithy with some measure of peace," she said. "Then at least you might be content. If only there was some way to manage it."

"Sofia, even if I was not a knight of the realm, and heir to Vellaux—if I was yet but a simple commoner—can you think that I would ever allow you, the gently born daughter of a landed knight, to live in such a place? Never, love. 'Tis far beneath your due."

Wretched, she pushed free of him once more and moved away, her back to him.

"Just as I am so far beneath you now, who will one day be Lord Renfrow, and master of Vellaux." She turned to look at him. "How are these things decided, Kayne?" she asked. "It seems as if it must all be set in stone, yet 'tis not at all." She lowered her gaze. "But three months past we knew who we were, yet now 'tis all a muddle. I would have married you then and lived happily at the smithy."

"Your father never would have allowed it," Kayne told her. "I was a commoner then."

She looked up at him. "You were Kayne," she said fiercely, "and I loved you as fully as I love you now. I would have given all I possessed to be the wife of Kayne the Unknown.''

''Your father would not allow it,'' he repeated, ''and I would not, either.''

Sofia set both hands to her head and made a sound of complete aggravation. When Kayne tried to take her in his arms she furiously pushed him away.

''God help me if I ever come to discern men!'' she shouted at him. ''Do you not understand what I am trying to tell you?''

Clearly bewildered, he shook his head and said, ''Nay,'' only enraging her the more.

''It does not matter to me where we live, or if we are truly wed, or if you are of the knighthood. Once, I thought those things all most important, but truly they are not.'' She lowered her hands slowly. ''I cannot bear to see you unhappy, Kayne. And 'tis far worse knowing that I am the cause of it. If you'd never known me, you would yet be at Wirth in your smithy, living in your pleasant dwelling, content with your life and at peace. Whatever it is now that you require for your happiness, I will agree to it, even if it means that we must run off and live as strangers to the world, in whatever manner you choose. Only tell me, Kayne, and I will gladly do your bidding. But do not be a knight or a lord for my sake alone. Can you not see how wretched we shall both be if you do? You will come to hate me—''

He took a step forward. ''Never, Sofia.''

''—and I will come to hate myself.''

''My lord!''

They turned as Gwillym came striding through the trees. He bowed first to Kayne, then to Sofia.

''Forgive me, my lord, but Sir Senet has requested your immediate attention. Some of Lord Renfrow's men have not yet arrived, and he fears that they may have lost their way upon the last turn toward the east.''

"Damn," Kayne muttered. "I should have taken better care of my father's men." He looked at Sofia, saying, "We will finish this later, mistress." To Gwillym he commanded, "Do not leave Mistress Sofia alone in the forest. Senet will want to leave this place in another half hour. Make certain she is back in the column and made comfortable in her carriage before that time."

Gwillym made another bow. "Aye, my lord."

Without another word or look, Kayne strode away, and Sofia watched until she could see him no more.

"Men," she said aloud, "are the most trying of all God's creatures."

Gwillym gave her a beguiling smile. "Of a certainty, my lady. Though I pray you will not find it amiss in me if I say that I have ever found women to be the more wearying among the two sexes. Even the most beautiful and delightful among them can be troubling."

Sofia sighed and shook her head, finally looking at him when it was no longer possible to see any sign of Kayne's blond head weaving through the forest trees.

"I think you must have little trouble at all in regard to women, Gwillym," she told him. "You are far too handsome to be much plagued."

"But I am," he countered. "Since I have gone to Lomas to serve Sir Senet, I have fallen in love with seven different maids—and each as pretty and charming as the next. Though none, I fear, can approach your loveliness, Mistress Sofia. You are without peer among every lady I have ever known."

Sofia was hard-pressed not to laugh at such false gallantry, but she had well learned, from the days she had spent in Gwillym's company, just how smooth tongued he could be. She did not pity the woman who finally won his heart, for he would lead her in a merry chase all the days of their lives.

"I feel very sorry for these maids," she told him chidingly, "for 'tis clear that you care for none of them, else you'd not so openly divide your affections among them."

His smile became angelic. "But, mistress, there is more than enough to satisfy them all. And I am diligent to divide equally, so that none is more—or less—satisfied than any other."

His words had the desired effect of making Sofia's cheeks heat with embarrassment, and at this, he laughed.

She pressed her lips together and looked at him with full reproof.

"You are no chivalrous man, Gwillym. I will write to your father in Wales and tell him the full of it, I vow."

This made him laugh the more. "He is the one who taught me how best to deal with women," he told her, grinning widely. "He would only receive such a missive with joy. But, come—" he held his hand out to her "—I will vex you no more, lest Sir Kayne hear of it and knock me senseless. Do you wish to walk a bit farther before we return? Or would it better please you to make our way back to the others, so that you may rest in the carriage?"

The idea of bumping along in the carriage upon such muddy roads for another fifteen miles before stopping made Sofia want to groan aloud, though she knew that every man in the column would give much to trade places with her, for at least she was warm and dry and comfortable within Lord and Lady Lomas's fine carriage.

"Please," she said, "let us walk apace for a few minutes more, if 'tis possible."

He set the hand she extended upon his arm, and said, "With every pleasure, mistress."

Sofia could not later remember how far they had walked, or what they had talked of. Gwillym was a pleasant, practiced, well-educated companion who conversed readily on almost every topic, and she seemed to recall that he had attempted to divert her thoughts from the heated words she had just finished sharing with Kayne. She did know that they had slowly moved in the opposite direction of Kayne and the others for several minutes, and could no longer hear the sounds of men or horses. And she remembered vividly that they had been in the midst of laughing over one of Gwillym's foolish jests when the arrow came whirring through the trees.

Neither of them saw it, and the warning sound it made was so brief before it struck that they could not have avoided it. One moment Sofia was laughing and preparing to make some tart comment in response to Gwillym's jest, and the next he had been jerked back, as if struck by a fist, his own laughter stopped with a grunt and a sharply uttered "oof." Sofia was jerked back, too, her hand yet grasping his arm, and it took a moment before she was able to collect herself and realize that Gwillym had fallen to the ground. His face was as shocked as she knew her own must be, and one hand groped blindly to touch the arrow that now protruded from his chest. Blood seeped in a rapidly growing circle beneath his tunic.

"Gwillym!" she cried, falling to her knees beside him.

His bloodied hand left the arrow and pushed at her, and his handsome face, already contorted with pain, filled with sudden, intense panic.

"Run!" he shouted furiously at the top of his lungs, shoving at her, unwittingly bloodying her surcoat. *"Run, Sofia!"*

She obeyed almost without thinking, jumping to her feet and racing back in the direction of the camp, ignoring the pain that shot through her body at the rapid movement. Behind her, she heard the unmistakable sounds of many booted feet growing rapidly nearer. Heart pounding, she strove to run at a faster pace, but she was clumsy and unsure of her direction. If she could but get close enough to Kayne, he would hear her and come running. God help her—how far away was the camp?

The booted feet came closer—so close that she could hear the harsh breathing of her pursuers. A strong hand closed over one of her arms, the fingers tightening in a cruel grasp. Sofia was jerked back against a hard body, and had only enough breath to emit a loud scream before another cruel hand closed over her mouth.

Chapter Fifteen

The chamber in which Sofia was imprisoned at Maltane had no windows, no proper bed, no tables and no chairs. Sir Griel suffered a small fire to burn in the small hearth during the cold night hours, and each morn a servant brought a fresh candle to keep Sofia company throughout the day. In one corner, a pallet of straw and two blankets provided a place for Sofia to sleep, and in the other was a bucket with which she could relieve herself when necessary. Near the door a tray was set each afternoon bearing a pitcher of sour wine and a single goblet, and to this was added, morning, noon, and night a small meal of bread, cheese and dried meats.

If Sofia did not eat the offered victuals quickly, half a dozen rats scurried brazenly out of their nests to snatch them from the tray and carry them off. These same rats spent much of the night hours annoying Sofia, and she had awakened from a deep slumber more than once in the past five days since she'd been imprisoned to find them gnawing at her unbound hair with the intention of padding their nests with the stolen strands. The result was that she got very little sleep at all. However, she wasn't entirely unthankful for her furry cell-mates. At least they did her the great favor of killing and eating the other assorted vermin that found their way into the chamber.

It had taken less than a day and a night of hard riding for the men who had kidnapped Sofia to reach Maltane, and all she had been able to think upon was that Kayne and his army would never be able to catch them. Two full days, he had told her, it would take so great an army to reach Wirth, and very little could be done to make their arrival any sooner.

Sofia and her captors had arrived at Maltane in the early morning hours, and despite her utter exhaustion and misery, she had readily seen that Maltane was preparing for a battle. The castle had ever been well fortified, but now she saw hundreds of soldiers with swords at their waists and crossbows slung across their backs lining the high walls, ready and waiting. Great black pots were also set at regular intervals on those same walls, which looked so unassailable, filled, Sofia had no doubt, with oil or water ready to be heated to a boiling pitch. Anyone who dared to attack Castle Maltane by scaling its walls would have a very unpleasant welcome awaiting them.

Four of Sir Griel's best and hardiest knights had been following Sofia since she and Kayne and the collected armies of Sir Justin, Sir Aric and Lord John had left Havencourt. They had kept watch in the woods at Vellaux, and followed behind when the assembled had left on their journey toward Wirth, waiting for their chance to kidnap Sofia. Their only regret, the leader of them told Sofia when they took one of their few, very brief rests during their frantic ride to Maltane, was that the arrow that had surely killed Gwillym had not instead found Kayne as its target. Sir Griel, the man explained, had promised a rich reward to the men not only for capturing Sofia and bringing her safely to Maltane, but an even greater prize of money for killing Kayne the Unknown.

"And so you see, mistress," the man had said, grinning at her in an openly leering manner, "we'd have done better to kill the blacksmith and leave you behind, save that Sir Griel promised we'd be the first to have you when he tires of bedding you. And once we've done with you, you're to be made a common whore among all the men. But never fear," he added with a wink, "the four of us won't finish having our pleasure of you for many months, at least."

"If we ever do," another put in, and they all laughed as if this were a fine jest.

When they arrived at Maltane she was carried directly into the castle and, upon Sir Griel's previous orders, taken straight to the chamber that had been prepared for her imprisonment. There had been neither candle nor fireplace then, and Sofia, finding herself in utter darkness, had felt her way about the damp, chilly room until she'd found the pile of straw. She sat down on it and waited, refusing to let herself sleep or think, until Sir Griel came. It was not a long wait. He arrived but half an hour later, having clearly been roused from his bed and informed of her arrival.

He was preceded into the room by two servants bearing torches, blazing with a light that briefly blinded Sofia. Sir Griel entered the chamber, looking almost as disheveled as Sofia was, his bushy hair and beard even more untamed than usual. He blinked at her for a few moments as if he could not truly believe she was there, and then bade the servants to set the torches upon two iron brackets set in the wall on either side of the door and leave the chamber.

"Your champion has not taken very good care of you, Sofia," he said when they were alone, "to let you be captured by my men."

"Your men," she said quietly, "vilely and in a cowardly

manner killed an innocent man who was protecting me. He was the son of a nobleman, and a knight of the realm.''

"Who, Gwillym?" he asked, giving a bark of laughter. "He was a traitorous dog who betrayed me and the vows of fealty he had given. His death is just punishment for such, and I will not grieve it a moment.''

Sofia gave him a look of complete disgust and said nothing. He seemed unsettled and uncertain, almost nervous. He stood in his place, rubbing his hands together lightly, casting his glance about the room, sometimes looking at her, then looking away.

"Sofia," he said after a silent moment, "when last we met, I…behaved wrongly. I admit that. You had angered me greatly, and I became maddened and did not think upon what I did. The fault is as much yours as mine, perhaps even moreso, but you are a woman, and I, being a man, should not have let you…make me so crazed.''

Sofia stared at him. Surely he was not trying to make apology for what he had done? 'Twould be far too strange—certainly not in the least like him, or what she knew of him—if he should be doing so.

"You were going to rape me," she told him tautly, each word slow and deliberate. "You abused me in a vile manner. You might even have killed me.''

He spread his hands out as if pleading with her.

"You pushed me too hard, Sofia," he said. "You should not do that—ever. You must learn never to push me." He set one hand to his forehead as if he suffered a terrible ache there. "Once I have become angered, I cannot stop myself. You have always driven me to every kind of passion. But even though you have been soiled by the blacksmith, I will yet take you as my wife, if you vow to obey me in all things and never give me cause for anger. This is the measure of the great love I bear you, Sofia, that I am yet willing to forgive and forget all your sins. This is how greatly I desire to have you as my wife and bedmate.''

Sofia gaped at him now, utterly shocked. The blow Kayne had struck upon Sir Griel's head must have altered his mind. This was not Sir Griel as she had ever known him. Indeed, she was amazed that he had not already drawn his dagger and slit her throat for the many insults that he perceived she had dealt him.

"Love?" she repeated with little-concealed anger. "You dare to speak that word in my presence? You meant to rape me in the cruelest manner, with your men about you to watch and later take part, and you *would* have done so if Kayne the Unknown had not saved me.''

"Sofia, listen to me," he said in a reasoning tone, "'twill all be different once we are wed, I vow. Let me bring your father to you tomorrow to convince you that what I say is right. I will give you my word of honor, in his presence, that I will never raise a hand to you again, if you will also vow never to drive me to do so. Then we will be married the day after, and all will be well. You will be the lady of Maltane.''

"Nay, I will not be," she told him firmly, shaking her head. "And as to my father, I pray you will leave him in peace, else you will suffer the more for it. You are not unaware, having now had the report of your men who brought me here, that a great army is even now on its way to see you taken in chains to London for your just punishment.''

"God curse you, Sofia!" he shouted, suddenly lunging forward to drag her up from her straw pallet. "You must wed me, else all will be lost! I will kill you otherwise! I vow it before God!''

"Then do so!" Sofia shouted in turn, into his hairy face. "For I would rather be dead than suffer your touch again!''

He was shaking with fury, scarcely able to contain it.

"You *will* wed me," he said in a trembling voice. "You will, Sofia. And then you will write a missive to the king, in your own hand, and tell him that you took your vows willingly. Once you have done so, all will be well."

"I will drive you to kill me first," she vowed. "I'll make you angry, as I have already done, and you will not be able to help yourself."

He seemed to realize how painful a grip he held her in, and released her at once, stepping back. He ran one shaking hand over his now sweating brow.

"Forgive me," he muttered. "Forgive me, Sofia. I will try not to harm you again, and certainly not once we are wed."

Sofia gazed at him in the torchlight, rubbing her arms in the places that burned from his ungentle handling. She began to realize the truth of what had changed. Sir Griel was afraid to harm her, though 'twas clear he would like nothing better. Something held him back. Something…but what?

Could it be only that Kayne and his powerful friends were coming soon with their combined armies? This would be something to be feared, indeed, but she couldn't imagine Sir Griel behaving in so nervous a manner only for that. In truth, it would most likely only cause him to react more cruelly and angrily. But he was making every effort not to harm her as he had so readily done before. Could her father have possibly been brave enough to inform the king of what Sir Griel had done? If that had been so, and if the king had written Sir Griel of his displeasure…aye, the chance that he might incur the king's wrath would truly be enough to strike a grave fear into him.

"We will never wed," she said. "Sir Kayne, the heir of Vellaux, is even now on his way to find me. Aye, I can see by your face that you have already discovered who he truly is—not a mere blacksmith, but the son of a great and powerful nobleman and a knight of the realm. He wants to kill you, and believes he has the right to do so, without fear of what the king or any other man might say. I've made him promise that he will give you no harm—but only so long as you are taken to London to stand trial.''

His expression became savage. ''It will seem very strange if I were to stand trial for attacking the woman who later became my wife—and willingly so. And once you write your missive to the king, telling him that all is well, naught will come of your lover's claims. If you do not readily agree to do as I ask, Sofia, then I will find the way to make you do so.''

He moved toward her threateningly, but Sofia stood her ground and met him eye to eye.

''If you harm me, Griel Wallace, Kayne will see you drawn and quartered.''

The words seemed to shock him in a stunning way. He fell back and stared at her as if horrified, his mouth moving wordlessly. His face had gone utterly white, and he looked suddenly old and feeble. When he at last began to speak, his voice shook badly.

''You…you *will* be my wife. It is the only way. A few days is all I need to convince you.''

He'd stumbled to the door and shouted for his men to let him out, and Sofia had been left alone once more in darkness, for they had taken the torches with them.

That had been five days ago. Sir Griel had come once each afternoon to pursue the matter, each day far more desperate than the last. He'd tried to starve her into submission first, but after three days had given way and decided that she should have a small measure of sustenance, lest she begin to sicken. It was this same consideration that had led to the fire during the nights and candles during the

days. He had not touched her once in all those days, and
had even been careful not to get very near to her. He'd
even attempted, when she had continually given him her
refusal, to control his temper, though at this he had been
somewhat less successful. He usually departed the chamber
in a rage, leaving Sofia with her ears aching from his loud
and furious shouting.

Sighing aloud from where she sat on her straw pallet,
Sofia cast her gaze slowly about the grim chamber, so
dimly lit by the day's lone sputtering candle. She was full
weary with having naught to do or anything to occupy her
mind, apart from her predicament. How long would her
imprisonment continue before Sir Griel gave way? Kayne
and his friends and their army must have been surrounding
Maltane for at least three full days now and, even if they
could not get inside, they would surely not go away. Maltane was well stocked, but winter was coming fast, and a
long siege would strain supplies of both food and coal.
Water would not be a problem, for she was certain Maltane
had several clean wells within its walls, but fighting men
who were hungry and cold would soon begin to lose their
desire to hold out against an enemy that was enjoying far
greater comforts.

She prayed it would not come to so lengthy a siege. Five
days living in this dark, foul chamber had been bad; she
didn't know if she could bear being locked away in it for
perhaps four, or mayhap even five, months. If Castle Maltane held out any longer than that, it would be a miracle.
She knew the truth of this, and was confident that both
Kayne and Sir Griel did, as well.

She wondered what Kayne was thinking now, how he
was, and whether he regretted, as she did, that they had left
their last conversation unfinished. There was so much more
that she had meant to tell him, to reassure him of her love.

She had meant what she'd said, that she would go wherever he wished and do whatever was necessary for him to find peace. Now that Sir Griel had taken matters out of their hands, she very much feared that it would be a long while before Kayne knew rest.

He would be terribly grieved over the death of Gwillym, Sofia knew, just as she was. And if it had not been for her, Gwillym would yet be alive. Indeed, if not for her, none of these men would be here, ready to fight and even kill on her behalf. Though she was not so foolish as to entirely take the blame upon herself—Sir Griel was far more at fault, and would justly pay for his sins.

A jangling of keys alerted Sofia that someone was coming, and she turned to watch as the heavy wooden door swung open on its rusted hinges. Torchlight temporarily blinded her, and Sofia knew at once that it was Sir Griel who had come. He alone was preceded by servants bearing light upon his visits.

He strode into the room and stopped in the midst, looking down at Sofia as she sat upon her pallet.

"How does the day find you, mistress?"

Sofia spread her hands out, indicating her surroundings. "I am still here, as you see."

She was a terrible sight, she knew. She'd not been allowed to bathe or even wash her face since coming to Maltane, and, having been raced across many miles of muddy roads by Sir Griel's men, had arrived at the castle in a filthy state. Her leggings and soft boots and the skirt of her surcoat were yet caked with dirt, and her fingers were crusty with streaks of dusty, dried mud. Her hair, unbound, was not only filthy, but crawling with whatever tiny, creeping creatures inhabited the straw pallet. But she didn't particularly care whether Sir Griel found her fully repulsive; indeed, she hoped he did.

"Aye," he said, "you are still here, and as stubborn and willful as when last I saw you. But I have come to make a measure of amends. Come, Sofia."

He held out a hand to her. Sofia stared at it, and didn't budge an inch.

Sir Griel gave a sound of exasperation. "Stubborn woman! I mean you no harm. Come, and I will take you to a proper chamber where maids await to tend you."

Slowly, Sofia rose from the pallet, gazing at him warily.

"Why? For what purpose?"

"Only for the purpose of your comfort. Do you not wish to leave this place?"

"I would leave Maltane altogether."

"That is not possible, but since your stay will be of great length, why should you not pass it in greater comfort? Sofia," he said, sounding very weary, "please, do not make me angered. I am pulled very tight now, and cannot answer for what I will do if you press me. Now...come."

Sofia considered his words, and considered, too, that she could scarce do worse than this chamber he'd already imprisoned her in. Lifting her head, she moved toward the open door, saying, as Sir Griel tried to take her elbow, "Do not touch me."

He made a low, growling noise, but dropped his hand and moved aside to let her pass.

From the depths of the castle they climbed upward, into a lighted passageway, and farther upward still, until they reached a stairwell lit by the sun itself. Bright daylight confused and blinded Sofia, and gave her dark-accustomed eyes such unexpected pain that she had no time to prepare herself for it. She turned into the nearest wall and set both hands against her face.

Sir Griel was instantly beside her, but she shrugged him aside.

"Will you not even let me guide you?" he said, exploding with impatient wrath. "Will you spite yourself only for the hatred you bear me, Sofia?"

"Whenever you touch me," she said, breathing harshly, "I think of that day in the forest. If you have forgotten what you did to me there, I have not, and never will." Tears filled her eyes, though from necessity rather than sorrow, and the fluid seemed to pour over her cheeks like waterfalls. She blinked rapidly, and wiped the moisture away. "I am better now," she said, much of the pain soothed away. "Lead on."

They continued their upward climb, moving slowly, as Sofia had to feel her way for much of the journey, until reaching a large winding hallway with many doors. One of these was already opened, and it was through this that Sir Griel led Sofia.

It was a beautiful chamber—as lovely as her prison had been awful. Large and airy, with a window in one wall allowing sunlight to pour forth and beautiful tapestries lining the remaining walls. Rich carpets covered the floor, and beautiful furniture filled the room, including a large and comfortable-looking bed, curtained with fine blue silk. A long hearth blazed with fire, filling the room with gentle warmth, and near this a wooden tub was set, only just now being filled by two serving maids with buckets of hot, steaming water.

"I hope you will not find it amiss in me to provide you with garments to wear during your stay. I had already ordered certain clothes to be made for you when we became betrothed—"

"We are not betrothed," Sofia said firmly, though without heat. She was staring fixedly at the tub and could scarce think of anything else save how lovely it would be to sink into it.

Sir Griel cleared his throat. "When I thought to become betrothed to you," he amended. "The clothes were to be wedding gifts, but you have greater need of them now. I have asked the maids to lay them out for you, here. Do you see?"

He pointed to an elegantly crafted clothing chest. Sofia managed to turn her gaze from the tub to look. Her eyes widened at what she saw. Several surcoats, all very beautiful and made of the finest cloth, had been carefully laid out, one slightly atop the other, on the closed lid of the chest.

"There are undergarments as well, everything in plenty," Sir Griel assured her. "And now, mistress, I will leave you to the ministrations of the maids. Once you have dressed, I will send a servant to escort you to the great hall, where we will partake of the evening meal."

Sofia opened her mouth to tell him that she'd not eat with him as if she were an honored guest, but stopped herself. Perhaps it would do her well to learn something of the castle. She might even find some weakness, some way of escape, that might prove helpful.

"Thank you," she murmured, letting herself stare at the tub again. One of the maids had unstopped a vial of perfume and was pouring a small measure into the steaming water. Almost at once, the smell of lilac filled the air. "I am most hungry."

"I will await your presence with great anticipation, mistress," he told her. "My cook has been instructed to prepare the finest meal possible, and we will enjoy my best wines."

Sofia did look at him then, wary and bewildered.

"I will not give myself to you for a bath and decent food," she told him. "If that is what you believe, you may take me back to my former chamber. Now."

He held up his hands, his expression all innocence. "I expect nothing from you, Sofia, save to bear me company. And mayhap I will even take you, afterward, to the walls, to see your lover's army. You would like that, would you not?"

"Aye," Sofia said so quickly that she feared she gave too much away.

Sir Griel merely bowed. "Then it shall be done. Enjoy your bath, mistress, and we will speak more once we have eaten."

Chapter Sixteen

It was going to rain again.

Kayne pulled his gaze from the massive walls of Maltane only long enough to look up at the ever darkening sky, which filled moment by moment with the oncoming storm. Then he looked back up at Maltane, the high, sheer, insurmountable walls lined along their tops with hundreds of well-armed soldiers. Occasionally one of them let fly an arrow in Kayne's direction, as more of a taunt or dare than any real attempt at striking him, for he stood too far away, and they always fell short. Kayne had no doubt, however, that any man who dared to move within their range would be shot at not merely by one or two archers, but that a hundred or more arrows would be let fly.

Though he longed to mount an attack—to do anything to get Sofia out of Maltane—Kayne knew the rashness and uselessness of such an act. He had confronted enough such castles to know that he must wait for the right moment, the right number of forces and kinds of weaponry, and the right information. But they had done nothing in the past five days since Kayne and his comrades had arrived with their assembled armies save sit and wait, and he had come to the end of his tether. He was full ready to scale the castle walls by himself the very moment darkness fell and take his chances.

It maddened him to think of what Sofia must be suffering at Sir Griel's hands. She must wonder, too, why he had not yet come to save her, when surely she knew that they were there, waiting outside the castle walls. God above, how it grieved him to think of her hoping and praying and looking for him to come every moment. Did she think he had abandoned her? Could she possibly believe such a thing?

He thought continually of the last words they'd had together, of how her sweet declaration had so nearly unmanned him. She had said that she would go anywhere, accept any condition, only for his happiness. If he had not already known that he loved her, he would have been overwhelmed by the almost painful sensation that had taken possession of his heart. And, more, he had realized, with sudden clarity, that he would do the very same for her— and must.

How selfish and foolish he had been to worry over his own pitiable reactions to what he'd gone through in France. Many had suffered. Even now Sofia was suffering God alone knew what miseries. How cowardly he was compared to her, compared to so many. But he would coddle himself no more, nor hide away, as he had striven to do at Wirth. Now, he would live, openly and without fear, and take every responsibility that had come his way with full acceptance. And he would do it with Sofia by his side, please God…if he could but get her safely away from Griel.

They had communicated with Maltane in the past five days through messengers running back and forth beneath a white flag of truce. Kayne had sent the first message, demanding Sofia's immediate release; Sir Griel had replied that he would not do so. Kayne responded that Maltane was now under siege, and would continue to be so until

Sofia was released, completely unmolested and unharmed.
Sir Griel had assured him that Sofia was as yet untouched,
but would only continue to be so if Kayne and his friends
removed their armies—at once. Kayne had sent back a message inviting Sir Griel to take himself off to hell, offering
to personally lend his aid in sending him on the journey.
He had included a great deal more, in detail, about what
he would do to the man, and how he would suffer if Sofia
was harmed in any way. A full day had passed before Sir
Griel gave his reply, far more amenable now, still insisting
that Sofia would not be released unless he, Sir Griel, had
some assurance of safety from the threats that he had received from Sir Alexander Baldwin, the lord of Gyer. This
had confused Kayne—for what did Sir Alexander Baldwin
have to do with any of this? John had finally given an
explanation.

While they were all still at Havencourt, John, unbe-
knownst to Kayne or the others, had written to their former
master, Sir Justin Baldwin, and informed him of their plans
to take an army to stand against Maltane. John, having been
formally adopted into the Baldwin family, now had the
right to request aid not only from Sir Justin, but from the
entire, and very formidable, Baldwin clan. The head of this
clan, Sir Alexander Baldwin, the lord of Gyer, was among
the most feared and powerful men in all of England, as was
his younger brother, Sir Hugh Baldwin, who was the earl
of Siere.

Sir Justin, upon receiving John's letter, had at once sent
missives to these two men, with the result that yesterday
all three of them had arrived with their armies. Sir Justin's
army consisted, much like Aric's, only of the boys he was
presently fostering, but these were such skilled and eager
youths that they were very welcome. The lord of Gyer, on
the other hand, and the earl of Siere, possessed armies that

dwarfed the combined forces that Senet and John had gathered together, with the result that there was now assembled against Maltane a massive organization of fighting men such as Kayne had never even seen in France.

But there was more.

Sir Alexander Baldwin, having received Sir Justin's missive, had taken it upon himself to write a missive to Sir Griel, informing him not only that he and his brothers were coming to Maltane with their men to aid Kayne in his taking of the castle, but that if Mistress Sofia suffered so much as another moment of grief because of Sir Griel, then Alexander Baldwin would personally see him not merely executed, but drawn and quartered in the gates of White Tower. And Sir Alexander Baldwin, as was commonly known, never made false threats. It was Kayne's only comfort now, praying that Sir Griel might be swayed enough by thoughts of such a dire fate befalling him to keep from setting a hand to Sofia.

The sound of boots crunching their way up the gravelly hillside pulled Kayne out of his fixed thoughts.

"Rain is on its way," Senet muttered, coming to stand beside him. "God help us, that's the last thing we need now." He looked back at the hundreds of tents and several larger pavilions dotting the valley below. "The tents will have a good soaking, and the men will grumble at the lack of fires."

"No more than we grumbled in France," Kayne replied, staring at Maltane once more. "He said he would bring her out tonight. Why does it take so long? 'Twill be pouring rain soon, and only a dog would make a woman come out in that. If he has harmed her—"

"The messenger he sent this afternoon saying that we might see Mistress Sofia on the wall swore he has not, and said that she is full well and being given every care. It will be another few minutes before he brings her out, and the rain will hold until then, most like. You must be patient, Kayne.''

"Nay, I cannot!" Kayne retorted, glaring at his friend. "Five days I have been patient, standing outside these damned walls, waiting—ever waiting—but doing naught! You saw by your own eyes how Griel abused her once before—like an animal. Can you doubt that he will do far worse now that he holds her captive?''

"Unless he is a great fool," another voice, far more calm and reasonable, said from behind them, "he will bring Mistress Sofia no harm."

Kayne turned to see his former master, Sir Justin Baldwin, taking the last few steps up the hill upon which they stood, with John and Aric following him. They had all come to see whether Sir Griel would bring Sofia to the wall or not.

"You know that my eldest brother, Alexander Baldwin, the lord of Gyer, sent a missive threatening to see Sir Griel not only dead, but drawn and quartered, if Mistress Sofia should make any complaint of abuse once she has been freed. 'Tis no false claim my brother makes. You have all met him, and know that he has the power to do as he says. What is more, Sir Griel knows it."

"Drawn and quartered," Aric said, giving a shudder. "Even the bravest man would be mad not to rightly fear such a death."

"And yet Sir Griel must be carefully dealt with," John said in his softly spoken, well-measured voice. "A man hard-pressed and without way of escape may take such matters into his own hands. If he believes that certain death awaits him, it may be that Sir Griel would rather choose his own preferred manner of dying."

"And if Sir Griel chooses his own death, then what value

would Sofia's life have?'' Kayne added, pacing and striking a gauntleted fist against his palm. ''Griel will kill her before taking his own life, you may be sure of that. We *must* get her out of Maltane soon.''

''We will, Kayne,'' Sir Justin assured him.

''When?'' Kayne demanded furiously, turning about to face him. ''You would never have waited so long to fetch your good lady wife, Lady Isabelle, out of her uncle's hand, when he had taken her prisoner. Indeed, you did *not* wait, even when your brothers bade you to do so.''

Sir Justin, who was as kind and gentle a man as Kayne had ever known, set a reassuring hand upon his shoulder. ''I know that you want your lady back, and we have come—all of us around you, all who are as brothers to you—to make certain she is retrieved in whole, perfectly safe. But this is not as the time when Isabelle was taken. You know that. That small keep was as a crumbling ruin compared to this great fortress. So many men would be killed here in the attempt to scale these walls that 'twould grieve your soul forever.''

Kayne closed his eyes. ''I care nothing for my soul now. I want Sofia away from that devil.''

''Aye, and so do we all, but even if we could master these walls, we could never do so in secret, and there is no assurance that Griel would not kill her before we had made our way into the inner bailey. Nay, Kayne, we must use our wits, and stealth and trickery. Alexander's missive has put fear into Sir Griel's heart. Let us play upon it as best we may, and make our plans accordingly. Can you be patient a little more, lad?''

What could he say to his master, whom he loved as a father? With resignation, Kayne nodded.

''I will be patient, my lord.''

Sir Justin smiled encouragingly and gave him a playful

shake. "'Twill not be much longer, I vow. We will meet
with Hugh and Alexander in another hour and decide what
is best to be done. But, look, fresh torches are being lit
upon the wall in great number. Is your lady being brought
out now so that we may see her?"

The evening meal was sumptuous. Sir Griel's cooks had
provided a thoroughly delicious array of dishes, with
courses of fish, meat, fowl, eggs, cheeses, vegetables and
sweets. Fine wines accompanied each of these, and the servants proved how excellently they were trained not only in
portioning each offering but also in placing and removing
dishes in almost complete silence. Sofia had only seen such
rich perfection in one other place—Vellaux. She never
would have thought that Sir Griel would possess either the
refinement or personal preference for such things. She had
always supposed that, being so animal in nature, he would
be animal in his surroundings, as well. But it was not so.

Maltane was another surprise. She had seen the outside
of it many times in her life, but had envisioned the interior
castle as being cold, dank and harsh. Nothing could have
been less true. Castle Maltane was a beautiful dwelling,
light and clean and airy, ornamented with fine carpets and
tapestries and furniture. If it was not quite of the same vast
elegance as Vellaux, it was certainly very near to it.

"You are very beautiful in that color," Sir Griel said,
lifting his wine goblet to her as he admired the elegant blue
surcoat one of the serving maids had chosen for her to
wear. "It matches the color of your eyes," he added before
sipping from the cup. "Makes you look like a bride."

Sofia said nothing, but drank from her own goblet,
slowly, watching him with some deliberation. She didn't
trust him—didn't dare do so, but she admitted that his present behavior bewildered her greatly. She had never thought

him capable of the least measure of kindness, under any circumstance, yet now he behaved as any other noble host might do, and Sofia his honored guest.

She would be a liar if she did not admit to being relieved at the change in her circumstances. The bath she had enjoyed in her new chamber earlier had been nothing short of sinfully pleasurable. The maids had washed her hair twice, completely scrubbing away the filth and vermin that had resided there for so many days. Her equally filthy skin had been cleansed as well, and then rubbed with soothing, sweet-smelling oils until it was soft and glowing. Then she had been dressed in a soft chemise of pure linen and set in a comfortable chair before the fire to have her hair combed and dried.

So pleasant this had been, with the glowing warmth and the steady stroke of the combs, that she had nearly fallen asleep. But all too soon it had been time to prepare for the coming meal she would share with Sir Griel, and the maids had helped her to dress in the silk surcoat she now wore, of a blue color so light that it gleamed almost white in the candleglow. Her long golden hair, still a bit damp, had been braided down the length of her back and crowned with a simple circlet of gold and pearls. New slippers had been provided for her to wear, though they were a little overlarge and Sofia had to walk with some care to keep them from falling off.

Following the manservant who had come to light her way to the great hall of Castle Maltane, Sofia had felt nearly herself again, and for that she could not be but grateful. In the back of her mind was the knowledge that this night she was going to sleep on that soft feather mattress in her new chamber—instead of a dirty straw pallet writhing with insects—with a decent blaze burning in the hearth to keep the room warm and comfortable. She was ashamed to discover how much this meant to her, but she realized, too, that she would be foolish to turn such suddenly offered comforts aside merely to anger Sir Griel. He would not care if she chose to stay in the damp, dark cellar with only rats for companions, and, in the end, she would truly only end up spiting herself.

Sir Griel had greeted her at the bottom of the castle's main stairway, which ended directly in the great hall, dressed in a fine and lordly manner. He offered his arm to escort her to the table where they alone would share a meal—for except the servants, there was no one else present—but Sofia had merely stared at him until he had dropped his arm.

The meal itself had proceeded in a casual, though very elegant fashion, with servants dressed in full livery undertaking their duties as if they were serving a king and queen. Sofia found it all rather foolish, considering that she was Sir Griel's prisoner, who only a few hours before had been held captive in one of his dungeon cells. But the food she could not ignore. She was full hungry, and for one horrible moment thought she might actually faint when the delicious smells from the first course of a wine-boiled salmon covered in mustard sauce was brought to the table. She tried so hard not to devour her food as it was placed before her, but feared that she failed miserably, at least until they had reached the vegetables. By then, her hunger had been, for the most part, sated, and she could at last attend to what was taking place about her.

Sir Griel strove to be a charming companion, though even the most generous spirit could not say that he was very good at it. Not that Sofia gave him any encouragement, for she most assuredly did not. He tried to make conversation, and if she replied at all it was with but one

or two words. For all that, he did not give way. He seemed
to enjoy their shared meal, despite Sofia's reserve.

"I have sent a missive to your father, also to Kayne the
Unknown—"

"Sir Kayne Sager," she corrected. "Son of Sir Ronan
Sager and the heir of Vellaux."

"Indeed." Sir Griel gave a nod of his shaggy head. "I
have also sent a missive to Sir Kayne, requesting that your
father be allowed to cross the siege lines and visit you here
on the morrow. Would you like that, Sofia?"

Sofia nearly dropped the knife she was holding. He had
said before that he would bring her father to speak to her,
but she had not truly believed that such a thing would be
possible in the midst of a siege. She had assumed that Sir
Griel had been baiting her in his previous offers, but now
she could see that he meant what he said.

"I...I would like to see my father," she said, very surprised at this generous and unexpected offer. "That would
be...most kind in you."

"I can be kind," he told her, "and will be, if you do
not press me otherwise. We could be happy here together,
at Maltane."

"Nay." She shook her head. "Never."

"If you would but give me a chance to prove myself,
Sofia," he said earnestly. "Only a chance."

Sofia set her knife down. "I wish you would not speak
of it. You have been too cruel, my lord. I can never forget.
You ask the impossible of me."

His face darkened, and she saw the inner struggle that
took place playing itself out on his features. But, at length,
he said, "You must speak to your father before making
such a final determination." He wiped his lips on a linen
cloth and, with the help of a servant, pushed back the heavy
chair in which he sat. "Now. Do you wish to see the army

outside of Maltane's walls, before darkness comes? You will like to have some fresh air, I think.''

"Aye," Sofia said, her heart beating faster with anticipation. She wondered if she would catch a glimpse of Kayne. Even a brief sight of him would fill her with joy. A servant was behind her at once, pulling her own chair back. She stood, and moved away from the table. "I should like that very well."

"Then come," he said, wisely not offering his arm this time. "The climb is high to the outer walls, but well worth the view."

"Steady," Sir Justin murmured, his hand on Kayne's shoulder, holding him back from surging toward the castle as more torches were lit. "Steady, lad."

Kayne drew in a deep breath and calmed himself. It was not yet dark, but the time had come for Sir Griel to bring Sofia out, and the additional torches marked the spot where she would be seen. He hoped for the best, that she would be perfectly well, but prepared for the worst. He had seen Sir Griel's handiwork before.

"There," Senet said, pointing. "There she is, Kayne, do you see?"

He did see, and pulled free of Sir Justin's restraining hand to take a few steps forward, gazing intently at the small, feminine figure that appeared on the wall like a magical fairy set amongst Sir Griel's armed soldiers.

"Sofia," he murmured, staring raptly at her. She was dressed in white—or blue, but that hardly mattered now—and was gazing all about in a confused manner, her head turning as she took in the sight before her, the hundreds of tents in the valley, the massive army spread out in siege of Castle Maltane. He could not be certain from this distance, but he thought—believed—that she appeared to be well and unharmed. He took another step forward, ignoring the warning calls of his friends, and lifted his voice, shouting, *"Sofia!"*

"She cannot hear you!" Senet told him. "Come back, Kayne! Don't risk your life!"

Oh, but she did hear him. Kayne saw her tilt her head in a quickened motion, listening.

He took another step forward. *"Sofia!"*

Her eyes riveted to him as if pulled by force, and then her entire body, so small and slender upon the wall, surged forward. He heard her voice, as soft as a distant bird's call, crying out his name.

She looked as if she would pitch right over the wall, so far did she lean over it, held back only by Sir Griel's hand upon her arm. She cried his name out again, and yet again.

Kayne found himself moving forward without thought, each step quicker than the last, until he was nearly running.

"I'll get you out!" he was shouting, uncaring of who heard, if only Sofia did. "I swear it by my life! I'll get you out, Sofia!"

"Damn you, Kayne!" It was Senet, tackling him from behind, pulling him down into the damp earth. "Don't be a fool! She's well, and you'll do her no good if you get killed only to see her more closely."

As if to prove his words, an arrow landed but a few feet away from them, and Sofia's loud scream filled the air. More arrows followed, before Sir Griel gave the sharp command to stop them, but Kayne and Senet did not wait for that. They picked themselves up and ran for the safety of the hill upon which the others stood. Aric reached out and physically dragged Kayne up the last few steps.

"You God forsaken fool!" he shouted, shaking him. "Has love driven you out of your senses?"

"Aye," Kayne said, breathing harshly and thrusting

Aric's hands away so that he could turn and look at Sofia again. She was yet leaning over the parapet, looking directly at him. A heavy drop of rain fell on his cheek, and within seconds another fell, and then another, thudding all about them, solidly striking the ground.

Sir Griel took Sofia's arm once more and began to pull her away, out of the coming storm. She struggled to free herself of his touch; the sight made Kayne's entire body clench with fury.

"By the Rood, I'll *kill* him!" He would have stepped forward again, but both Aric and Senet stopped him this time.

"Aye, aye," Senet said, "kill him, then, but don't get yourself killed as well in the doing. You were never such a fool as this before."

Sir Justin turned his gaze from the wall, where Sir Griel had just dragged Sofia out of view behind the line of soldiers. A few more arrows were let fly once the lord of the castle had gone, and the additional torches upon the wall were quenched.

"Your lady seems to be just as you described her to me, Kayne," he said. "Even from a distance, 'tis clear that she is very lovely."

"Aye," Kayne murmured, his breathing yet harsh, his eyes fixed upon the spot where Sofia had disappeared. He shook off Senet's and Aric's restraining hands. "She is all loveliness."

"And now you have seen her," Sir Justin said, clapping him reassuringly on the shoulder, "and know that she is well. Sir Griel has not yet dared to harm her, whether because of Alexander's threats or the size of the army arrayed against him. But whatever has stopped him, Mistress Sofia has benefited from it. Now, we must find the way to make certain that she remains well until we can get her out of

Maltane. Come,'' he said, ''the rain is falling harder now, and Alexander and Hugh will be waiting for us to arrive so that we may begin making plans.''

Sofia could feel Sir Griel's temper rising as he escorted her back to her chamber, half a dozen soldiers following behind them, their boots loud in each passageway they took. Sir Griel's stride was as angry as it was swift; Sofia, in her over large slippers, had difficulty keeping apace. Sir Griel at last put his hand on her elbow, his strong, hairy fingers squeezing hard, and dragged her along.

When they reached her chamber he threw the door open and thrust Sofia inside the room. She whirled about to face him.

''I told you never to touch me!'' she told him.

''And I warned you, Sofia, never to push me too hard,'' he returned just as hotly. He took a step into the room, his dark eyes flashing. ''I could have seen him killed, when he came so near to the castle. I could have sent hundreds of arrows flying toward him—and one surely would have struck its mark.''

Sofia knew he spoke the truth, and remembered the moment upon the wall with renewed terror. Kayne might have died—because of her—before her very eyes.

''But I did not do so,'' Griel went on, ''for your sake alone, Sofia. Remember that in days to come. And remember, as well, that his life is yet within my power, just as yours is. I have already given this instruction to all my men, that if the army laying siege against us should storm the castle walls, and if by some miracle they should manage to get into the castle proper, they are all, to a man, to dedicate themselves to one goal. Not to fighting the enemy or protecting their master, but to killing Kayne the Unknown.

Every man, each of my soldiers, Sofia, will make that his goal, and one will assuredly achieve it.''

Sofia shivered at the words and mutely shook her head.

Sir Griel smiled, the evil, cunning smile she knew too well.

"Aye," he said. "Think upon that as you find your dreams tonight, my dearest. If you wed me, Kayne the Unknown lives. If you do not, he will make the attempt to save you, and he will die.''

Chapter Seventeen

Sir Alexander Baldwin, the lord of Gyer, was an imposing and authoritative figure, a nobleman who rightly overtook the place of almost any other—short of the king. When he arrived at Maltane with his impressive army, that was exactly what he did—took over, without asking whether he should do so or not.

The first thing Sir Alexander did, apart from having his own large and comfortable pavilion set up, was to reorganize the men into proper companies, each led by his own master, but answering ultimately to him. After this he organized and separated living areas from cooking and eating areas, and made certain that the large number of horses present had separate enclosures for each company, with men to care for them. He also commanded that several especially large tents be set up to receive and portion out food and supplies as needed. About these tents he placed a constant guard, and threatened to see any man who tried to steal from them immediately hung.

In anticipation of wounded from the coming battle, pavilions had been raised and filled with waiting pallets, and were already manned by a variety of leeches, barbers and actual physicians. To make certain that they had a constant

delivery of supplies, Sir Alexander had his best men go out
to every village and farmer within a ten mile distance to
arrange for the daily delivery of ale, wine, bread, cheeses,
eggs, meats, oats, hay, firewood and most importantly,
clean water. Sir Hugh, who had fought in France many
years before Kayne and his comrades, had happily had the
forethought to include a number of skilled blacksmiths with
his army, and these men Sir Alexander had set up in their
own tents, so that they were already hard at work shoeing
horses, repairing armor, and sharpening swords.

In short, within less than a day of his arrival, Sir Alexander had taken a fairly well-organized assortment of fighting men and refined them into a completely organized,
well-supplied army ready and capable of carrying out a
long, hard siege.

Half an hour after seeing Sofia on the walls of Castle
Maltane, Kayne found himself comfortably ensconced in
Sir Alexander's luxurious pavilion, with servants pouring
him wine and filling a plate for him with choice cuts of
meats, a variety of fine cheeses and slices of both herbed
and sugared breads. Senet, Aric and John were likewise
being fed, along with Sir Justin, while Sir Alexander and
his brother, Hugh, the earl of Siere, sat indolently in their
chairs, having already eaten their fill, sipping wine and
watching their companions enjoy their repast.

Sitting cross-legged on a carpet in one far corner, silent
and sullen, sat one of Aric's lads, an empty plate in his lap.
He stared at the gathering of men with little expression, but
his eyes burned with a fervency that Kayne well remembered from his own youth. Impoverished boys, bastard-born
and scorned by both Crown and Church, had difficulty
quenching the inner fires of anger and resentment, even
when fortunate enough to find a benefactor so kind as
Kayne had once had in Sir Justin, and as this boy had in

Aric. But that same fervency, when applied to any task, served one well. This boy appeared ready at any moment to leap to his feet and do his master's bidding, to serve, to labor, to fight, even to die. It had been exactly the same with Kayne.

Rain furiously pounded overhead, filling the tent with its mottled sound, but the roof held fast and strong. Sir Alexander certainly didn't appear to be worried in the least of getting wet during the long night, despite the strength of the storm. But Kayne did not doubt that, even if the tent should collapse, dozens of Sir Alexander's servants would at once cover their master with their own bodies in order to shield him from every single raindrop. That was the manner of nobleman he was.

Kayne found it difficult to speak his thanks to such a man, though his gratitude knew no bounds. He was yet bewildered as to why both Sir Alexander and Sir Hugh should have come all this way, at much discomfort and cost to themselves and their armies, when they owed him naught. Perhaps it had been for John's sake, because he was now a member of the Baldwin family, or perhaps for Sir Justin's, because he had ever looked upon the lads whom he'd fostered as his own sons. But it could not have been for Kayne's.

He had met Sir Alexander and Sir Hugh several times when he was fostered at Talwar, when they had come to visit their youngest brother and his wife, and had ever been amazed at the vast differences between the two men.

Sir Alexander was the eldest, the revered leader of the powerful Baldwin clan, a handsome man now well past his fiftieth year but yet strong in body, mind and will. His manner and speech were elegant, solemn and aristocratic, always formidable and intelligent. His brother, Sir Hugh, was completely opposite. Bigger, taller and more muscular than his eldest brother, he appeared, outwardly, to be a common fighting man, rather than the earl of a vast and rich estate. Sir Hugh, though well past his fortieth year, was full handsome and agreeably charming, ever grinning and jesting, as sinful, lazy and pleasure seeking as any lusty tavern keeper might be. He'd become an earl only through his fortunate marriage to a wealthy heiress, Lady Rosaleen of Siere. He'd not wanted to become so great a nobleman—indeed, like Kayne, he'd not even desired the knighthood, though he had at last taken it on—but he *had* wanted Lady Rosaleen, enough to suffer anything to have her as his wife.

They had been married now for nearly twenty years, and Sir Hugh had gained almost as much fame at being an earl as he had done while being a soldier. In that regard, he was one of the bravest men that Kayne had ever had the honor of knowing. Sir Hugh Baldwin's famed exploits in France had been lauded in England long before Kayne and his friends had crossed the Channel to fight on French soil. Tales of his bravery were yet told among soldiering men, and he was held a great hero of England by one and all.

Sir Justin, the youngest brother of these two very different men, was a mixture of both. Being thus, Kayne could not but be thankful that Sir Justin was the one to whom he had been fostered, for a kinder, gentler, more steady man he could never have hoped to find elsewhere. Strange as it was, among the brothers, Sir Justin was the most muscular and powerful, his arms and shoulders mightily strengthened by years of partaking in smithing, the love of which he had passed to each of his lads, and most especially to Kayne.

"Now, we will have a right understanding of the matter," Sir Alexander announced once the meal had been cleared away and the wine goblets refilled. As if in agreement with Sir Alexander's steely tone, a loud clap of thunder suddenly broke overhead, rumbling slowly away in the space of several moments. Noisy rain continued to pour, and one of the servants hurried to more securely tie the pavilion's entry flaps in an effort to keep the cold, rising wind at bay. The sides of the elegant, striped tent fluttered and snapped regardless, while several small, warm fires set in independent grates at intervals along the length of the tent provided a warmth and comfort that belied the storm.

"My lord," Kayne said, standing and smoothing his hands over his damp tunic, wishing that his clothes were perfectly dry and his hair in better order, "before you speak, I beg that you will allow me to render my thanks for all that you and Sir Hugh and Sir Justin have done. I am not well-known to you, save for Sir Justin, and my betrothed wife is entirely a stranger. I had no hope that any of you should ever—"

"Kayne," Sir Justin interrupted kindly, smiling at him, "there is no need."

Sir Hugh laughed and said, in amused tones, "God save us, boy, sit down and don't trouble yourself. We are all as close to family as could ever be."

Sir Alexander looked down his long, noble, aquiline nose at Kayne with a haughty offense that made him sit in his chair again like an ill-behaved child who'd been roundly corrected.

"Justin holds you dearly as a son," he said, "and John, who is now our own brother, as dearly as a brother. If we did not come, we would have no claim to honor, and therefore you will not be allowed to shame us with words of thanks."

Kayne opened his mouth to say "Aye, my lord," but was silenced by the stern expression Sir Alexander directed at him.

"Now, we will determine what is best to be done," Sir

Alexander repeated. "I will send a missive to Maltane come the morn, demanding a meeting with Sir Griel."

"He will never agree to see you," Sir Hugh told him. "Not after the threats you sent."

"No, he will not," Sir Alexander agreed with a sage nod. "But, having been frightened by the demand, he *will* agree to see you, brother."

"Me?" Sir Hugh's eyebrows rose with surprise. "I don't want to speak to the man, or even set sight on him, by the Rood. Why should I be the one to go? Send Justin in there with a good sword to threaten the knave into obedience."

"That," said Sir Alexander "is the reason why. Justin would deal with the scoundrel with the sharp end of a blade, which would only get both him and Mistress Sofia killed the moment any of Griel's soldiers realized what had happened. But you, Hugh, have the devil's own tongue."

"Worse," Sir Justin put in, smiling, "you could charm the devil into doing your very bidding. Sir Griel should be but a simple matter by comparison."

Sir Hugh looked rather pleased at these wayward compliments, which were, as Kayne knew full well, perfectly true.

"I suppose that's so," Sir Hugh admitted, casually inspecting the fingernails of one hand, "but I gather there is more to your plan than this, my dear brother. My speaking to Sir Griel, whether I charm him senseless or not, will get us precisely nowhere in regaining Mistress Sofia."

"Nay, it will not," Sir Alexander agreed. "But that is not what I want you to do. I have already spoken with John and Aric about this, and, having gained their full agreement, will now disclose the rest to you all."

"To John?" Kayne murmured, looking from him to Aric. "And to Aric?" He began to feel a sense of unease.

Sir Alexander ignored him, and continued.

"John will accompany you, Hugh, dressed as a servant. Griel has never set sight on him before and will have no recognition of him. You will devise a way to send him away once you are safe inside the castle—mayhap on some errand that none of Sir Griel's servants can fulfill—and then you will keep Griel occupied with some of your mindless chatter while John does what he can to discover the castle's weaknesses. You will have other servants to attend you, so that if he must stay behind to complete this task, he will do so."

Kayne stood once more, all manner of humility gone.

"My lord, Sir Alexander, I must respectfully disagree. If any is to go, it must be me. Sofia is my bride, and 'tis not acceptable that John should risk his life in such a manner for her sake."

Sir Justin would have spoken again, but his eldest brother set out a hand and made him be silent.

"You would allow him to perish on the field of battle for her sake," he said. "You would allow all of us to do so."

Kayne flushed at the words, at what they implied. "Nay, my lord," he said, "'tis not the same. In battle, with his army about him, a man has a chance to defend and protect himself. But if Sir Griel should discover John within his walls, a spy, you know that he will kill him without moment."

"And yet," John said, "I will go, Kayne."

"But we will let Kayne decide what is right," Sir Alexander said in a tone that was both soft and frightening. "Do we charge the walls on the morrow at early light, sir, and let many die, as will surely be, or do we proceed with stealth, that few may die and many live? Most especially Mistress Sofia."

"We use stealth," Kayne replied at once. "But I must be the one to go. Sir Griel will not know me if I am dressed in rags and covered with dirt."

Sir Hugh laughed at this and Sir Alexander looked very grave.

"My good lad," said Sir Hugh, "you jest. Sir Griel would see the size of you, and those shoulders, which have known the blacksmith's tools, and he will know you at once."

"But more," said Sir Alexander, "Mistress Sofia will know you, and that is where the greatest danger lies."

"She will also know John!" Kayne countered.

"She does not love John," Sir Justin said more gently, sitting forward and holding Kayne's gaze. "Kayne, you must calm yourself and think without the love you bear this woman. John is the one to go. Did not your ten years in France with him teach you that he is by far the one most suited to such a task?"

"Aye," Senet put in, "it must be John. You know this is right, Kayne. You must accept it."

"God's mercy," Kayne muttered, rubbing one hand over his face in exasperation. He sat down in his chair once more. "If he dies because of me—"

"I will not die," John assured him, a touch of insult evident in his tone. "And assuredly not because of you, Kayne. You take too much upon yourself."

"Go then," Kayne said, throwing his hands up with defeat. "I readily admit that I can think of no better plan." Overhead, another rumble of thunder made the air shudder.

"As this is so," Sir Alexander said, "then bring forward the boy, Aric."

Kayne's head snapped up with renewed surprise as Aric lifted one hand to beckon forward the boy who'd been sitting in the corner.

"Domnal, come here."

The boy, dark-haired and dark-eyed, rose to his feet in a fluid, easy movement and moved forward. He was tall for a youth, and slender, and had the look of a beggar. His clothes were ragged and worn, and his hair, overlong and unkempt, tumbled past his shoulders and over his forehead. The boots on his feet had clearly seen a great deal of use. Taken all together, he looked like any ragged young urchin who might be found in any village, city—or castle.

But Kayne knew better than to mistake the lad for a mere boy. He had been trained by Aric, and would be well skilled in the ways of fighting, and even of war.

"Domnal will make one of the party that accompanies you inside Castle Maltane, Hugh," Sir Alexander said. "He will find a way to separate himself from the group and hide himself, and he will remain at Maltane once you have departed. Some of Aric's other lads will accompany you, as well, to make certain that the confusion is greater, and 'twill be far more difficult to see that one is missing."

"Nay, I like this even less than the thought of John remaining behind," Kayne said, shaking his head. The boy's eyes blazed at him, filled with daring and anger and bold, youthful confidence.

"I'm not afraid," he stated. "I can take care of myself."

"You will have to," Sir Alexander said sternly, "for you will be required to keep watch over Mistress Sofia and make certain that she is fully safe, most especially when the attack is made. You must keep Sir Griel from using her as a shield to save his own life."

The boy nodded, strands of his dark hair falling forward over his eyes. "I'll keep her safe," he vowed. With a rapid, well-practiced movement he swiped the hair out of his face and gazed at them all, one by one. "By my life, I will."

"Domnal means what he says," Aric stated proudly.

"He's one of my best lads, and knows how to defend himself."

A voice from outside the tent shouted loudly, seeking permission for a messenger to be allowed entrance, pulling their attention from the matter at hand. The two guards who stood inside the tent opened the flaps with weapons at the ready to see who stood outside in the pouring rain.

"My lord," one of them addressed Sir Alexander after a moment, "'tis a messenger from Maltane, come under the white flag, sent by Sir Griel to speak to you on an urgent matter."

Domnal immediately returned to his dark corner, staying well within the shadows, and John, moving at an equally rapid pace, rose and moved to the far side of the pavilion, where three of Sir Alexander's servants surrounded and hid him.

As the messenger, dripping wet from the thorough soaking his ride had given him, with his helmet held in his hands, was allowed entrance, every man in the pavilion save Sir Alexander and Sir Hugh rose. Sir Griel's soldier approached them and, bowing, said, "My lord has sent me with a message for you, Sir Alexander."

Sir Alexander tented his long, aristocratic fingers together and said, without expression, "Speak."

The man bowed again.

"My lord desires to inform you that he has sent a missive to Mistress Sofia Ahlgren's father, Sir Malcolm Ahlgren, inviting him to visit with his daughter at Maltane on the morrow. Sir Griel requests that Sir Malcolm be allowed to enter the castle beneath the white flag, my lord."

Kayne, hearing the words, stiffened. What purpose could Sir Griel have in sending for Sir Malcolm—for he would never do so merely because Sofia wished it, unless it suited his own purpose.

"He will take Sir Malcolm captive, my lord," Kayne said, ignoring the warning look Sir Justin set upon him. "This will strengthen his hand, and mayhap through her father he may force Sofia to wed him. If in this he succeeds, our cause will be lost."

"Sir Kayne speaks truly," Sir Alexander said, though he, too, cast a stern glance in Kayne's direction. "What proof can you give that this is not Sir Griel's intention?"

The man stared at Sir Alexander, fingering his helmet with nervous agitation.

"My lord, I can give you none," he said at last.

Sir Alexander clearly appreciated the man's honesty, and spoke to him more kindly.

"Then we will suggest a manner of such proof, which you may relay to your master once you have returned to Maltane. It is my wish to speak to Sir Griel face-to-face, beneath the white flag, with every honorable intention that this portends. To this end, several of my men and I will accompany Sir Malcolm on the morrow into Maltane and meet with him there. While Sir Malcolm visits his daughter, Sir Griel and I will speak terms."

The man's heavy brows lowered, and, struggling to conceal his dismay, he said, "But, my lord—"

"Nay." Sir Alexander held a staying hand into the air, silencing their visitor. "I realize full well that Sir Griel may not agree to receive me. You may tell him that I also would not receive a man who had threatened to have me drawn and quartered, most especially a man who means that threat, as I do."

A momentary silence, lending power to the statement, hung in the air, filled only by the never-ending rainfall. Then Sir Alexander continued on in the same pleasant tone.

"If Sir Griel does not wish to welcome me into Castle Maltane, mayhap he will receive my good brother, Sir

Hugh Baldwin, Earl of Siere. If he will do so, then we agree that Sir Malcolm may journey to Castle Maltane beneath the white flag on the morrow. Be pleased to tell your master, howbeit, that my brother will not come alone, but will, as is the accepted manner, be accompanied by a full complement of attendants, including a dozen of our finest soldiers.''

This was more than acceptable, and Sir Alexander's reasonable offer of sending another in his place could only be viewed as generous. The man bowed yet once more.

''I will deliver your message to Sir Griel, my lord, and with your permission return in but a few hours under the white flag to deliver his answer.''

Sir Alexander nodded. ''It is well, but do not come again tonight. Return in the morn, when at least the light of day will make your way more safe, even if the rain has not yet ceased. Apart from that, I am tired,'' Sir Alexander added with what Kayne knew was feigned delicacy, ''and will soon seek my bed. I will not receive you again this night even if you should brave the weather. Now, go.''

With a curt nod, the messenger put his helmet back on his head, turned and left, striding back into the wet, noisy storm.

''Now,'' Sir Alexander said, standing at last and looking directly at Kayne, ''are you closely acquainted with Sir Malcolm Ahlgren?''

''Well enough,'' he replied. ''He is a cowardly man, but in no way evil. And he loves Sofia, even if he does not watch over or take care of her as he should.''

''If you tell him that the matter is dire on the morrow, will he lend us his aid? Coward or no?''

Kayne had to think on that for a moment, but at last replied, ''For the sake of Sofia's life…aye, he will. But I cannot say whether he will do us well or ill. He is, in truth, a timorous man.''

"That is so much the better," Sir Alexander said with one of his rare smiles. "He will add the extra confusion that is needed for John and the boy to slip away unnoticed and hide themselves. And if he is allowed a private word with his daughter, he may be able to alert her to Domnal's presence, that she may look for the lad when he comes to make her safe on that day when we make our attack.''

"If she knows, she might unwittingly betray the boy," Sir Aric said, frowning deeply.

"Nay, she will not," Kayne told him at once. "She is not so foolish. 'Tis a good plan, and I will ride to Ahlgren Manor at once to speak with Sir Malcolm.''

"And I will go with you," Senet said with finality, draining his goblet and setting it aside.

"There is no need," Kayne told him. "The storm is fierce. I would not have you in it.''

Senet made a scoffing sound. "Do you think me a child, then? I have never shied from any storm, nor will I from this pitiful one.''

"I will go, as well," Aric said, but Kayne shook his head.

"Nay. Stay and ready the lad, for the morrow will ask much of him. John, you will need time with Domnal to make your plans.''

"Aye," John said with a single nod. Then he smiled and added, "'Tis a poor excuse for keeping out of the rain, i'faith, but one I will use. The time will be well spent, Kayne, never fear.''

For the first time since coming to Maltane, Kayne's spirits had risen to hopefulness.

"I fear naught," he told them, looking from one man to the other. "The plan is in all truth a good one, my lord,'' he said to Sir Alexander, "and I have no means to thank you properly, though you have said you want none, nor any of you." His gaze took in the men surrounding him, and Domnal as well. "But my thanks you have, with full heart."

"Only thank us once Mistress Sofia is safely out of Maltane," Sir Justin said, his expression somber. "We must act quickly and pray that Sir Griel is not too hard-pressed. One mistake on our part, and I fear that Mistress Sofia will pay dearly for it."

Chapter Eighteen

Sofia slept so deeply in the soft feather bed that she did not rise until well past noon on the day following her dinner with Sir Griel and their visit to the wall. Rain poured throughout the night, and thunder and lightning filled the sky, sending Sofia dreams of another night, very similar but far more wonderful, when she and Kayne had shared a bed together.

When she at last woke and pulled back one of the bed curtains, it was to find the two serving maids moving quietly about the room, one of them setting out a new surcoat and underclothes for her to wear, and the other stoking the fire with great care. The tapestry covering the window had been pulled back to reveal a sky that was partly blue, partly gray, with a little sunlight shining through to brighten the day. It was very much the same as a morning at Ahlgren Manor might have been, and, thinking of that, Sofia wondered if her father would truly come to visit her.

The moment the serving maids realized she was awake they turned all their attention to getting Sofia out of bed and dressed, with her hair combed and braided down her back. Then one of them left and returned a quarter of an hour later with two additional servants and a large tray bearing a great quantity of various foods for Sofia to break her fast with.

"You must hurry and eat your fill, mistress," one of the maids said as she poured Sofia a mug of hot, spicy-smelling cider, "for your father and several other men are to come soon, and Sir Griel desires that you be present to greet them."

"Several other men?" Sofia asked. "My father's men?"

"Nay, mistress, men come under the flag of truce to speak terms with Sir Griel."

Sofia's heart lurched painfully. "Do you know who it is?" Could it possibly be Kayne and his friends? Would Sir Griel allow them to come into Maltane?

The maid busily buttered a slice of sweet almond bread as she replied, "I overheard someone say that 'twas a great lord come to see the master. An earl, though I do not know for certain. 'Twould be strange, indeed, if 'twere true." She set the bread upon Sofia's plate with care, then smiled up at her. "There's never been so fine or noble a man as an *earl* come to Maltane before. We none of us knew you could claim acquaintance with the nobility, mistress, and 'tis certain the master did not know, either." She leaned forward and said, with great confidentiality, "Sir Griel has been overset since last night, when a messenger returned from the camp of those arrayed against us. He did not even seek his slumbers, but has remained awake and most unhappy."

An earl? Sofia thought with confusion. Surely the girl was mistaken. She could make no claim to such an acquaintance, unless Kayne's father, Lord Renfrow, had written to the king for aid. But if Sir Griel was upset at the idea of such a man coming to see him, then Sofia knew that she must be more especially on her guard. It would not do to make him angered before such a guest.

She broke her fast as quickly as she could, though she was far too nervous to feel hunger. Just as she was finished, two of Sir Griel's knights, dressed in their master's colors, black and red, arrived to escort her belowstairs.

Sir Griel was waiting for her at the bottom of the stairs in the great hall. He, too, was dressed in the castle colors, most certainly the finest and most expensive clothes she'd ever seen him in.

He was sweating and very pale. He took one of Sofia's hands in both of his as she came to the bottom step and squeezed so tightly that she could not help but make a sound of distress. He softened his grip at once, but she was yet repelled by how wet and slippery his flesh was, and longed to pull away from him completely. By a great force of will, however, she did not, and listened to him intently as he began to speak.

"Sofia, your father has come to visit with you, just as I promised you that he should, but with him are a number of men from those who stand against us. You must make them know that all is well, and that you have been treated kindly."

Sofia looked at him with a measure of disbelief. Had he forgotten the foul chamber she'd been imprisoned in for five days, at his command? Or that he had tried to starve her into submission? She suddenly realized why he had undergone a change in heart regarding her treatment at Maltane. It was not because he cared for her comfort, but because he so greatly feared the charges that she might lay against him in the face of someone powerful enough to retaliate.

"Who has come with my father?" she asked.

Sir Griel's features hardened, and his black eyes filled with anger.

"'Tis no concern of yours, for they've come against *me*,

and not for your sake alone. But you must send them away
well-pleased, and give them no reason for concern. Look,''
he said, stepping back and gazing at her from head to toe,
giving a curt nod, ''you are dressed in fine clothing, clean
and gently cared for. 'Tis plain that you have suffered no
abuse at my hands. 'Twould be clear to any and all who
saw you. There can be no complaint, and you must give
them none.'' He pulled one of his hands away and, in a
swift movement, drew a long, sharp dagger from its sheath
at his belt. He held it up into the air, near her face. ''Do
you see this, Sofia?''

Saying nothing, she nodded. The dagger was brought
nearer, until her eyes nearly crossed from looking at it. The
blade was very thin and needlelike.

''I will keep you beside me while they are here,'' he
vowed, ''and if you should make one word of complaint—
only one, Sofia—I swear before God that I will slit your
throat before the assembled. And afterward I will make
certain to kill your father, if I can but reach him before I
am stopped. I will assuredly make every attempt to do so.''

''Then you will die for it,'' she told him as calmly as
she could.

He made a scoffing sound and slid the dagger back home
again. ''That is what I am trying to avoid,'' he told her.
Taking her arm in a steely grip, he began to lead her farther
into the hall. His men clattered along behind them, and
Sofia saw dozens of other servants in their finest clothes
lining the hall itself, awaiting the arrival of their visitors.

''Today,'' Sir Griel went on as they strode forward,
''you must act as my lady—as the lady of Maltane, which
you will soon be, in truth. You must make them all know
that you are not displeased to be here, and that 'tis a great
foolishness for them to set their armies against me. Understand me well, Sofia. I will die before letting them take me

to London to stand trial for an act that is, by all rights, your fault rather than mine. And if I die, you will surely go before me, and your lover as well, as I have already promised you.''

"I will not act a lie for your sake," Sofia told him, holding her chin high. "But I will not distress my father, or shame him before another. If you do not desire that I speak to any other man who comes to wait on you, then keep him from me. 'Tis as simple as that. But if you do not release me and allow me to walk without aid," she threatened, "I will let you kill me now. I cannot bear your touch, as I have told you time and again. How much more must I do so before you begin to believe me?"

Sir Griel released a taut breath and brought them to a stop. He removed the grip he held on her and touched his dagger once more. "Be very sure of yourself, Sofia," he warned, "for I mean what I say."

"As do I," she returned.

"Then we understand each other. Come," he said, and motioned for her to walk ahead of him, "let us meet them together, and see what comes of the day."

Sir Hugh Baldwin, the earl of Siere, came riding through the gates of Maltane Castle as if he were a royal prince, surrounded on all sides by knights wearing gleaming armor, each carrying upon his horse the fluttering standard of Siere. Servants, also on horses and clothed in their master's colors, followed behind, and running after these were several serving boys of various ages and sizes, ready to take care of the horses when those who rode them dismounted. Sofia scanned the face and form of each man, looking for Kayne, but to no avail. She would have known him at once, even if he had been disguised, but he was not among the others.

Riding directly beside Sir Hugh on a familiar steed was Sofia's father, Sir Malcolm. Standing next to Sir Griel on the steps of Maltane Castle, she could see the uneasiness on her father's pale face, while Sir Hugh, smiling broadly from side to side at all those in the inner bailey, looked as pleased as a foreign potentate amongst his worshipping minions. He made it all seem a grand, festive affair, which had nothing to do with a castle siege.

The visitors—Sofia could scarce count them, there were so many knights and attendants—drew their horses to one side of the bailey and began to dismount. The serving boys who'd come with them ran up to take hold of each horse's reins, and for several long moments all was a mass of confusion and noise. Sir Hugh, with her father yet at his side, was the first to emerge from the crowd of men and horses, and the confusion smoothly melted into order as his knights and servants followed behind him.

The ground was yet wet and muddy, but Sir Hugh, handsome in both face and form, strode forward as if he were walking across a silk carpet. He was a tall, muscular man, with golden hair touched by faint streaks of gray that alone bespoke the fact that he was no longer a youth. In all other ways he seemed very young, especially in his smiling, jovial manner.

"Ah, Sir Griel," he said without preamble as he came to the stairs where they stood, not even waiting to be formally introduced. "Well met. I am Hugh Baldwin, sent to you by my brother, Sir Alexander Baldwin, the lord of Gyer. I believe you are already well-known by Sir Malcolm Ahlgren?" He swept a hand toward Sofia's father, who had met Sofia's gaze and held it. "And this, I can only believe," he went on, stepping forward, and holding out a hand, "is Mistress Sofia Ahlgren, on whose behalf we have all come together in this happy place. Mistress," he said grandly, taking her hand in his own and bowing over it, "your betrothed husband, Sir Kayne, spoke of your beauty, but he did not tell the half." He kissed her hand, then straightened and smiled down at her in a lusty, appreciative manner that took Sofia by surprise. "But you will wish to greet your father," he said, gently tugging her toward that man.

Sofia was indeed glad to see her father, who looked so relieved at the sight of her that tears had filled his eyes. They embraced and she murmured that she was well, and the next moment Sir Hugh had taken charge again and suggested that they all go indoors, as he was in need of a glass of wine and hoped Sir Griel had a goodly supply.

Sir Griel seemed to have become speechless and powerless in the face of Sir Hugh's brilliant energy, and allowed himself to be guided into his own castle as if he were the one who had come from elsewhere. Behind them, the loud clattering of Sir Hugh's many knights as they followed their master made a deafening noise.

For the first hour Sir Griel was as stiff and guarded as he'd been earlier, but after several goblets of wine shared with his loud, cheerful guest he began to relax.

The entire hall was ringing with the laughter spawned by Sir Hugh's constant humorous remarks. Sofia, silent, sat in the place where her captor had put her, very aware that Sir Griel often had his eye on her, as did her father, sitting opposite her, who clearly desired to speak to her privately. Sir Hugh, having seated himself in the midst of one and all, neither addressed Sofia nor spoke to Sir Griel of her imprisonment. Indeed, he did nothing more than laugh and drink and tell merry tales, as if he were in a tavern, surrounded by his closest comrades. Only once did he depart from this behavior, when, after the first half hour had passed, he suddenly seemed to realize that he'd forgotten to bring from his saddlebags the missive that had been written out for Sir Griel by Sir Alexander.

Straightening in his chair, he swore in a loud, fulsome, and quite shocking manner, finally looking about at his servants, who had immediately jumped to the ready, and shouting, "Damned fools! Don't you see I want that missive? Go on, the lot of you, and fetch it back to me at once! Hurry!"

The servants, at least a dozen or more, all identically dressed in green-and-gold tunics with feathered, green velvet caps covering their heads, raced off as one, flying out of the great hall on soft-booted feet.

Sir Hugh, much displeased by this oversight, turned back to Sir Griel and said, with all the confidentiality that friends might share, "Servants, bah! God save me if they're not more trouble than they're worth—and God alone knows what they cost to feed and clothe!"

Sir Griel agreed with this wholeheartedly, and the two men toasted each other with their goblets, commiserating on the great misfortune they suffered in being responsible for so many vassals.

Sofia, for her part, noticed that her father had grown even paler, and sat in his chair more stiffly. He repeatedly refused the wine that was offered to him—which was certainly unlike him—and looked as if he were utterly wretched.

Several minutes later, the servants all returned, just as they had left, a surging crowd of gold and green. One of them strode triumphantly ahead of the others, a tightly rolled parchment in his hands, and, kneeling, offered it to his lord.

Sir Hugh snatched it up and impatiently told the man to go away. When Sir Griel sat forward to receive this missive, which had been meant for him, Sir Hugh tucked it into the folds of his tunic and waved Sir Griel's hands away.

"Nay, let us have another draught of wine before we begin to speak of such unpleasant matters. I cannot think Mistress Sofia will mind. Here, Sir Malcolm, have you not yet had a moment to speak to your daughter in private, as my brother promised you? Go now and have a turn about the hall."

Both Sofia and her father froze, staring at each other before turning to look at Sir Griel. She could see by the indecision on his hairy face that he was not comfortable in allowing them such privacy, and opened his mouth with what she knew was a denial, but Sir Hugh blustered ahead before he could make a sound.

"Go on, go on, go on," Sir Hugh ordered with a measure of aggravation, waving at them with such fervency that they felt compelled to stand. "Don't be so foolish," he chided, still waving them away, as if they were naughty children to delay so long. "Sir Griel and I will discuss nothing of import until you return, have no fear. Go and have your walk and we will speak of such dull things soon enough." He turned to Sir Griel with a bark of sudden laughter, saying, "By the Rood! Do they think we need watching, as if we were infants?" The thought made him laugh the harder. "But, come," he said invitingly, leaning forward to speak more directly to his host as their goblets were refilled, "tell me of the hunting here at Maltane. Do you use birds? I vow, you must come one day to try the birds at Siere, for you have never seen the like. Now, my own falcons—for I train them myself, and my sons along with me—are among the fiercest creatures you have ever…"

Sofia, taking her father's arm, had gratefully walked too far away to hear any more. Sir Hugh Baldwin might be a powerful nobleman, but he was the greatest fool she'd ever

beheld! She longed for Kayne with all her heart, a man
possessed of both sense and intelligence. Why in the name
of all that was holy had the forces allied against Sir Griel
sent this lackwit to speak for them? Why, he was ready to
invite Sir Griel to visit at Siere and go hunting!

Beneath her hand, she could feel how tense and nervous
her father was.

"Father," she murmured as they moved toward one long
wall—though not too close, for there were servants attending each fire, "you tremble. Please, calm yourself. There
is no need to be so distressed."

She heard him gulp loudly, in the same moment as he
glanced behind them to see what Sir Griel was doing.

"I feel as if I've a hot coal burning its way through my
flesh," he told her as he began to fumble in a pocket within
the cloak he yet wore. "God save me…Sofia, take this."

She felt a sharp poke in her arm, and looked down, seeing that he was pressing a tiny, folded bit of parchment
against her.

"Take it!" he whispered more urgently. "Quickly, before any see! And hide it well!"

Sofia did as he said, taking the tiny parcel and putting it
in the first spot she could think of—her bosom—for she
had no other pockets. A glance at Sir Griel showed her that
neither he nor anyone else had seen the exchange.

Her father almost fainted with relief, and Sofia was
obliged to set an arm about his shoulders to support his
heavy weight as she guided him about one turn.

"I have been in such turmoil since you disappeared," he
told her wretchedly. "If Sir Kayne had not been so good
as to send word of what had become of you, I surely would
have perished from the fear I suffered o'er your absence.
Sofia," he said more urgently, grasping one of her hands
and squeezing tightly, "you must get out of this place and

find the way to wed Sir Kayne. He is the heir to such power and wealth as I never would have dreamed of for you—aye, even despite all your beauty. Sir Griel has nothing to him. You will be the lady of Vellaux! Only think of that, and set your mind to it.''

''I am not at Maltane of my own choice, Father,'' she told him angrily. ''I am a prisoner here, else I'd certainly have returned to Ahlgren Manor many days past. Now—'' she gave him a slight, gentle shake to make him attend her ''—please, Father, tell me what is in the missive you just gave me. Is it from Kayne?''

He groaned and shook his head. ''I do not know, Sofia—I swear that to you. Please, I pray you, do you press me. Sir Hugh gave it me as we came, and bade me give it to you. It's for Sir Griel to discover and see, that's all I know of it.''

''Ah,'' Sofia said, ''then 'tis a deep game we are playing.'' She glanced at Sir Griel as they made another turn, but he was raptly attending whatever Sir Hugh was saying. ''Then I will make certain that he happens upon it later, and fight for it well. And I shall tell him, when he asks, that Sir Hugh sneaked it to me earlier, when he kissed my hand. He would ride to Ahlgren Manor and kill you if he thought you'd dared such a thing, but he'll not be able to touch Sir Hugh once he's safely back in his encampment. What else did Sir Hugh say? Was there any message from Kayne?''

''Nay, nothing,'' Sir Malcolm said miserably. ''There was only a riddle of sorts—Kayne gave it to me last night, when he dragged me from my slumbers in the midst of the night.''

Sofia brought him to a halt, turning to face him.

''Kayne came to you last night?'' she whispered furiously. "What did he say, Father? You must tell me every word!"

"I was half-asleep, Sofia," he said pleadingly, "and full weary from all my worrying over you. I was to tell you something about a man named John sneaking into the castle in disguise—but God save me if I can remember a word of it!"

Sofia straightened and blinked. John...it could be none other than Kayne's dear friend, Lord John. She looked at Sir Griel once more, this time to find him ignoring Sir Hugh and watching her intently.

"That only means," Sofia said slowly, speaking to her father but holding Sir Griel's steady gaze, "that a man named John will be among the first to make the attack, when it comes. That is all, Father. Nothing else."

"But there was more," her father insisted. "There's a boy who's to come, as well, to hide among the common castle folk and seek you out when the attack comes...."

"Hush!" she said urgently, yet looking at Sir Griel, who had stood. "Speak of it no more, unless you want us both to die!"

Sir Griel began to walk toward them, first slowly, then with a more rapid stride, his face clearing of the dull contentment that Sir Hugh had set upon him and filling with increasing awareness.

Sofia lurched forward, tossing her arms about her father and hugging him tightly.

"Weep!" she whispered fiercely into his ear. "Weep to make him think you're full overset!"

Amazingly enough, her father began to weep, almost as if he'd been waiting for permission. He bawled like a baby, loudly and with great emotion, so that by the time Sir Griel had reached them Sofia had busied herself with calming her wretched parent.

''Please don't worry, Father!'' she pleaded aloud, lovingly stroking his back. ''I'm certain all will soon be well.''

''What are you speaking of?'' Sir Griel demanded. ''What has he been saying to you, and you to him?''

''Naught, I vow,'' Sofia told him, still soothing her father. ''My father is but overset at my imprisonment, that is all. I have told him that I am well and completely unharmed. Is that not so, Father? You can see that Sir Griel has treated me with only kindness and respect. Come, let us return to the others and rest.''

Setting one arm about her father's shoulders, Sofia guided him back toward where Sir Hugh and the others waited and watched. She passed Sir Griel without looking at him, but could feel his gaze hard upon her. She prayed that he would let the matter—and his suspicions—pass for now. If he had the least idea that her father had been telling her information—or knew that he had been the one to give her the note—he would surely do whatever he must to discover what that information was. Sofia did not care so much for herself, but could her father be kept safe from such a man? Sir Griel might find the way to send men to Ahlgren Manor to ferret out what had been said, and she knew full well that even torture might be used to encourage her father to disclose the truth. Why had Kayne ever trusted her father with such a message? He knew how cowardly a man he was.

Sir Hugh and his many knights stood as they approached.

''We have stayed too long,'' Sir Hugh said, the rolled missive from his brother held in one hand. ''Sir Malcolm, you are not well, I perceive, and the visit has distressed you, as it surely would any man who saw his daughter held prisoner. Sir Griel—'' he handed that man the missive ''—if you will be so good as to read this now, we will speak terms and then I will leave Maltane in peace.''

As Sir Griel broke the seal upon the document and unrolled it, Sir Hugh approached Sofia, taking her hand in his again and smiling down at her with a warmth and charm that made him even more handsome than ever.

"I have a message for you, mistress, from your betrothed husband. Sir Kayne wished me to tell you that he is sorry for having been so great a fool when last you spoke to each other, that he concedes the argument to you and that he will gratefully accept the generous offer you made." Sir Hugh gave a laugh and added, "I pray you understand what it means, mistress, for it makes no sense to me."

"Oh, aye, my lord," Sofia said, filled with gladness, her smile trembling, "I understand full well. Thank you. Please, will you tell Kayne, when next you see him, that I will gladly keep my word to him. Most gladly."

"Fortunate man," Sir Hugh said, a lazy, seductive admiration glowing in his eyes. "If I were not so happily married to the most wonderful woman who ever graced God's earth, I believe I would steal you away from him."

Bending, he kissed her hand. Then he turned to Sir Griel, whose face had grown red as he finished the missive Sir Alexander had sent.

"He but repeats the foul threats he made in the missive he sent me earlier!" Sir Griel said furiously. "This insult is too grave to bear! You see for yourself that Mistress Sofia has been untouched and unharmed."

"Aye, and that is how she had best remain," Sir Hugh said, moving to stand before Sir Griel, over whom, being so much taller, he towered. "I should tell you that my brother is a man of small patience and great influence. If you should continue on in this fruitless cause, I can in no way promise that he will not have you chained to four steeds and torn apart before you've yet perished from being drawn." He gave a shudder. "For my part, I think it a terrible way to die. Mistress Sofia is beautiful, but no woman is worth that measure of torment.''

''I will not give way until I am promised that I will be left in peace,'' Sir Griel insisted angrily, tossing the document to the ground. ''I will not go to London to face trial for a crime that is in no way my fault! Mistress Sofia is my betrothed wife,'' he stated, ''and a man may do as he pleases—whatever he pleases—to his wife without fear of reprisal.''

''Mistress Sofia is not your wife,'' Sir Hugh countered gravely, his former genial manner completely gone, as if it had never existed, ''but a gently born maiden who is betrothed to another. The man who is to be her husband has every right to kill you himself for the insult you visited upon her.''

''Mistress Sofia will be *my* wife!'' Sir Griel shouted furiously. ''*Mine!* Just as she was *ever* meant to be. Kayne the Unknown is the one who has done the stealing!''

Sir Hugh leaned closer and spoke very softly.

''You have the missive written to you by my brother, and I confirm every word of it. If you do not release Mistress Sofia, Maltane will be taken, and you and your people will be lost. I believe you will die whatever the outcome, but your *only* chance for mercy is to give way now and allow my brother and me to take you to London. If you plead your case well enough, the king may grant you your life.''

''There is a far better way to make certain of that,'' Sir Griel told him. ''Mistress Sofia will become my wife, and then even the king himself cannot gainsay what I have done—if any man could rightly gainsay what a man will do when driven to it by a woman. She is the one at fault— not me!''

A look of pure disgust crossed Sir Hugh's handsome features.

"Only a craven coward would say such a thing," he muttered, shaking his head. "I told Alexander I did not wish to come, but he bade me charm and please you and strive to speak to you with all reason. Well, that is done, and 'tis clear you have no desire to reason. Now I am free to speak as I wish." He brought his face very near to Sir Griel's, and spoke with such menace that it made Sofia tremble. "If you should force yourself upon Mistress Sofia in any manner—even to make her accompany you to the altar, which she clearly does not wish to do—I vow by God above that I will chain you to the horses myself, limb by limb, and give the signal to send them running to tear you apart. But only after you've been drawn to the full, and your innards pulled out of your living body and burned with hot coals while you lie both awake and aware, knowing every moment of that torment. Think on that in the coming days and nights, knave, and believe that it will happen—if you should survive the assault that will fall upon the castle."

Sir Griel was pale and sweating again, and Sofia feared the moment when Sir Hugh and her father and all the men with them would depart, leaving her alone to face his wrath.

"She is well and unharmed," Sir Griel said, shaking visibly now, "'tis clear that naught had been done to her, and she will attest to it herself. Ask her," he urged, waving a hand at Sofia, who stood with one arm yet about her quavering father. "Ask her. She will tell you."

"Do you think me a fool, or that I should ever subject Mistress Sofia to such an unpleasant farce?" Sir Hugh asked. "No captive will gainsay his captor in that same man's presence, for fear of reprisal. But hear me well, Sir Griel. Take every care with Mistress Sofia, for she will indeed be asked of her treatment when once she has been taken safely out of here. Treat her as if she were my daughter, and the daughter of Sir Alexander Baldwin, and of Sir Justin Baldwin. You cannot begin to know what agonies would befall you for daring to touch the child of any of them. Before we had done with you and you had drawn your last breath, you would *plead* to be drawn and quartered, instead. On this, Sir Griel,'' he said threateningly, ''I make my solemn vow.''

Chapter Nineteen

Sir Griel was near the end of his tether now. Sofia was truly afraid of him. He'd sent her to her chamber under escort immediately upon Sir Hugh's departure, and she had waited there, alone, for the space of three hours before he finally came.

He entered the chamber alone, breathing harshly, holding a green-and-gold tunic in one hand. Sofia, who had been sitting in a chair near the fire when he came in, stood at once and began to move away as he strode forcefully toward her.

"Deceiver!" he shouted, thrusting the expensive garment before her eyes, crushed in his fist. "Do you see what that is, Sofia?"

Dumb, Sofia shook her head.

"Do you not?" he demanded. "But three hours past Maltane was writhing with green and gold! Green and gold! Sir Hugh's men!"

Lord John, Sofia thought with dismay, praying that her face gave away none of what she felt. He must have come with the servants, dressed as one of them, and hidden himself away somewhere in the castle. He would have removed the tunic, but been unable to destroy it, and somehow Sir

Griel or one of his minions had happened upon it. And now Lord John's life was in danger, for he was trapped, as she was, behind Maltane's walls. Sir Griel would have no mercy for him at all, should he be discovered.

"I—I did not…"

She did not know what to say. She thought of the note that her father had given her, which she had laid so carefully upon a nearby table in order that Sir Griel might "accidentally" discover it. That, at least, she had planned out—but what could she answer to Sir Griel's fury? He clearly thought she had played a part in bringing a spy into Maltane.

"Did you not, Sofia?" he said, his face dark with rage as he stepped closer, wringing the tunic in his fist. "Will you stand there and tell me you knew nothing of it!"

She glanced at the note, edging nearer to the table.

"Mayhap I did," she said, her breath coming faster, her heart pounding loudly in her ears. "But we are enemies, and I would be a fool not to lend aid to those who would rescue me."

"Who is he?" Sir Griel demanded, closing the distance between them. "*Where* is he?"

Sofia cried out as he grabbed her by the arm, bringing her retreat to a stop.

"I do not know!" she told him, which only made him shake her violently. Sofia set her teeth against the pain and shouted, "Sir Hugh warned you!"

He released her immediately, and glared at her with pure hatred, his chest heaving with each breath he drew.

"Vile *bitch!* I wish that I had killed you when I had the chance. God knows how I wish it."

Sofia began to inch toward the table once more, saying, "I did not know until Sir Hugh had nearly gone that he'd left a spy behind. Surely you did not expect me to tell you such a thing.''

''How did he tell you?'' Sir Griel asked angrily, throwing the tunic across the room as if it were what he wished to do to Sofia, instead. ''The sly bastard—to coddle and cosset me and make me think him a friend. But he had no time with you alone, no chance to speak to you—what is that you have, Sofia? *What is it?*''

She'd nearly thought he'd miss altogether the manner in which she set one hand behind her back and swept the note up. Now, feigning terror, she leapt away and ran for the fire—not too quickly, for he was not so quick to react as she'd expected. When he caught her she did not fight very hard, for he would strike her if she gave him too much trouble, and she had no wish to feel his fist upon her again.

He tumbled her to the ground, took her fisted hand in his, and forced her fingers open.

Taking the note, he stood, staring at it.

''My God!'' he murmured. ''My God! He gave you this when he took your hand—as I was reading the missive from his God-cursed brother. He knew how distracted I should be. Treacherous, deceiving swine!''

Sofia was relieved that he had made the assumption she'd desired. She could never have swayed him from the truth if he'd realized her father had been the one to give her the note.

She watched as he unfolded the tiny bit of parchment and read what she had already read beforehand.

''There is a man at Maltane now. Watch for him. Three days from now, the time will come. Be ready.''

Sir Griel's face drained of color as he lowered the note.

''In three days, they will attack. Three days.''

Sofia watched him in silence. He looked hunted, terrified. He was trapped and knew it, with no way of escape. She prayed that Kayne and the others had not played the game with too fine an edge. Sir Griel's eyes were beginning to possess a look of wildness and madness.

"I meant to give you time to make your choice, Sofia, but now it has been taken away from you. From both of us. But I told you once, did I not, that you would be my wife before you reached the age of twenty?"

It took Sofia a moment to realize what he meant, and to her dismay, she realized that she had forgotten—or that events had made her forget—that she would attain the age of twenty in but a week's time.

"We will be wed on the morrow," he stated, then thought on the matter a moment before revising the decision. "Nay, it cannot be tomorrow, but must be the day after. The priest will need time to write out the necessary documents, and you will need time to write those missives which will be sent to both Sir Alexander and the king, saying that you have agreed of your own accord to be my wife. Once they have them, they will not be able to attack Maltane. They will have to go away and leave me in peace."

Sofia shook her head. "I have told you that I will not wed you. I'll write no missives."

He looked weary, suddenly, and absent of emotion. Sofia knew that his mind had at last fixed upon an unwavering course.

"You will write them," he said calmly, "or you will die."

He meant it this time. Utterly and completely. Sofia had no doubt that he would do as he said. Afterward, he would most likely end his own life, as well, to keep from being taken during the attack on Maltane.

"You have the night to think upon it," he told her. "Guards will be set at your door without ceasing, and none will enter that have not been given permission. This man who has come to spy upon us will not be able to speak to you or save you, Sofia, and you would do well not to hope in that direction. I will have his head thrown over the wall only moments after he is discovered."

He spoke so quietly now, so steadily. It was as if he had accepted that his death was near, and nothing else mattered or had value, certainly not Sofia's life or the life of a spy.

"I bid you good eve," he said, making her a slight, formal bow, as if they were not enemies pitted against each other in so fatal a manner.

He left the chamber, and Sofia heard the bolt at the door being slid shut. On the floor, crumpled near the fire, lay the tunic of gold and green, forgotten and of no import now that Sir Griel had made his decision. Sofia prayed that whoever it had belonged to would find a way to keep safe. Sir Gwillym had already lost his life because of her; she could not bear for another to do so.

"You've checked your men's horses twice today. There is no need to do so again."

Kayne glanced at Senet, who strode beside him, but did not slow his pace as he made his way toward the enclosure where his own troop's mounts were kept apart from the others.

"In two days we attack," he replied. "I will have all perfect."

"I do not know why I try to stop you," Senet said with a sigh. "You were ever thus in France."

"As were you," Kayne replied. "And Aric worse than the two of us together."

"Aye, aye," Senet admitted, "but our men and horses were ever tired and scarred from so much battle, and thus required more constant inspection. You know full well that each man here is well-rested and ready to fight, and each horse fed and coddled like those in the king's own stable.''

"I cannot be easy until 'tis all over and Sofia safely out of Maltane," Kayne told him. "Sir Hugh said—"

"Aye, Sir Hugh said that Mistress Sofia is well, and that Griel is terrified, just as Sir Alexander intended that he be, and that his visit accomplished all that it was supposed to."

They reached the enclosure and Kayne nodded to one of the caretakers to open the gate. He and Senet strode inside and Kayne shouted for another man to bring the horses to him one by one for inspection. Then he turned back to Senet.

"'Tis a relief that Sir Hugh's visit went so well, but I can have no confidence in what remains of Sir Alexander's plan until John has returned with his report. If he is able to return," he added grimly. "He should have come out of Maltane by now."

"Aye," Senet said with a sigh, "'tis troublesome that he has not yet returned, but John is far too skilled to be caught—especially by a man such as Sir Griel. He'll come out of Maltane when he's satisfied that he has all he needs to know. And then he will be sorely aggrieved to know that we worried o'er him as if he were naught but a babe."

"I only pray that he comes to no harm, even if he should be angered by such concern," Kayne said, "and even more do I hope that he is successful in his undertaking."

Senet helped him to examine the horses, carefully checking their hooves and mouths and making certain that they were ready for battle. That evening, before dark fell, Kayne and some of his soldiers would inspect weapons and supplies, and the morrow would bring a full day of inspection for each man in the assembled army.

"This one is fine," Kayne told the man holding the head

of the horse he'd been checking. "Take him back and bring another."

"Aye, my lord," the man replied, then looked up and nodded northward. "Sir Aric is coming, my lord."

Kayne and Senet turned to see Aric riding toward them on a mottled brown steed.

"What news?" Senet shouted.

"John's just come!" Aric jerked his head back in the direction of the large pavilions. "Sir Alexander wants us. Hurry!"

They were already striding out of the enclosure before he could finish speaking.

They found John sitting in Sir Alexander's luxurious tent, drinking wine and laughing and wiping his grimy face with a damp cloth. Sir Justin and Sir Hugh were on either side of him, and Sir Alexander sat in the comfortable chair which was his alone.

"John!" Kayne uttered as he pushed his way past the tent flaps. "Praise God you are safe out of Maltane. What news?"

John grinned up at him.

"All is well, Kayne. Never fear. Mistress Sofia was locked in her chamber after Sir Hugh left, but she is well and being watched o'er by some of the serving maids. Domnal is well placed. The tunic was left where it could easily be discovered, and if he had the note—which her father gave to Mistress Sofia—then they will surely search for a man and not a boy. He will do well until the attack comes."

"But there is better news than this," Sir Justin said, smiling up at Kayne.

Kayne waited impatiently until his recently returned friend had finished another drink of his wine.

John wiped his mouth with the back of one hand before speaking.

"There is great discontent among Sir Griel's servants and some of his men, for he is known to beat and even murder them for small offenses. As well, the soldiers within believe that Gwillym was killed when Mistress Sofia was kidnapped, and many of them are full angered, for he was their comrade. Some of them have come together in secret and decided to escape Maltane before the fighting begins. They mean to throw themselves on Sir Alexander's mercy and beg to be allowed to fight for him against Griel."

"I do not suffer such lack of loyalty among soldiering men," Sir Alexander said, "but any who leave Maltane will be allowed to stay behind the lines and wait until the fighting is done. Afterward, they may take their things and go. Those who stay within Maltane's walls and lend us aid, however, will afterward be allowed to make me their pledge of fealty, if they desire it, and serve me at Gyer."

This was indeed a great boon to any fighting man. It was no small honor to be allowed to serve the lord of Gyer.

"You took the chance of speaking to some of them, John?" Kayne said, suddenly realizing what a risk his friend had taken. "You revealed yourself?"

"Aye, but with every care, I promise you," John replied. He seemed almost giddy with happiness at his success. "I did not know of a certainty what Sir Alexander would promise any man who threw his lot in with us, but was close enough in what I ventured to tell them. The outcome is that at least twenty of the soldiers will lend us their aid from within Maltane. They will see that Domnal is able to get into Mistress Sofia's chamber to speak to her, and they will make certain that the gates are opened to us when the attack comes."

"Most important of all," Sir Hugh said, "they will keep

the whispers and rumors that have been plaguing Sir Griel flying about Maltane, and thereby create even greater confusion than he has dealt with thus far.''

Kayne looked gravely at John.

"Do you trust that they will do as they've said? Is it not possible that they will instead reveal the truth to Sir Griel, in the hope of gaining reward from him?''

John smiled and shook his head.

"They would have taken me to him at once if that were so, and received a far greater boon. Nay, these are not cowardly wretches, Kayne, but seasoned fighting men. Many of them served in France, and two were even known to me as men who'd fought beneath Senet's command. They despise serving a master such as Griel, and want no part of bringing harm to a gently bred lady. And, as I have said, they are full angered at what they believe is Gwillym's murder.''

"But he is alive.''

John's smile widened. "I fear I was amiss in telling them so. It seemed a better plan to use their anger to our benefit.''

Kayne drew in a slow breath, thinking of all this, almost afraid to let himself believe all could be so easy and simple. Wars did not proceed in such a happy manner. But, mayhap…mayhap this time, all would go well. He did not want many to die because he had been so foolish in letting Sofia be taken, and he did not want Sofia living with so bitter a knowledge, either.

"God is on our side, it seems,'' he said at last. "And He could scarce ask for a better helpmate than John Baldwin. You have all my thanks, my friend.'' He offered his hand and John clasped it.

"Now,'' Aric said, "we must pray that Domnal does his work well, and is able to see Mistress Sofia very soon. But have no fears, Kayne." His eyes lit with pride. "If any can manage the task, 'tis Domnal. He's the cleverest lad ever born, and by far the most cunning."

Sofia was standing by the chamber's lone window, gazing out at the preparations taking place in the inner bailey below, when one of the two serving maids who were now constantly with her moved to open the chamber door. She'd not heard the scratching that had summoned the maid, but turned as the door opened and saw the girl speaking to one of the guards outside, whispering in turn and nodding her head. At last, she stepped back and opened the door wide enough to allow a serving boy bearing a bucket filled with coal into the chamber.

With a sigh, Sofia turned back to gaze out the window. It was dark now, but so many torches were lit upon the walls and in the bailey that she could readily see the figures of men moving rapidly in every direction, preparing the castle for the coming attack—if it should come. One of the maids had told Sofia that Sir Griel required her presence in the great hall early in the morn, and that the priest would be there before her. Sofia realized what Griel intended. She was to write the missive he would recite to her, and thereafter sign it. The priest would serve as witness, and afterward write out the documents required for the marriage service. It would be far more binding according to the law of the land than the betrothed marriage that Kayne insisted existed between him and her; and unless she was already with child by Kayne, 'twould be a difficult thing, indeed, to prove which of the marriages had come first.

But Sir Griel did not understand how it was. He thought that such a document would keep him safe, but it would not. Kayne would yet come for her. Nothing would stop him.

"Mistress."

Sofia turned and saw the serving boy standing before her, dirty and ragged, his dark eyes very intent.

"I am Domnal, sent by my master, Sir Aric of Havencourt, at the command of his lord, Sir Justin Baldwin, and of his brother, Sir Alexander of Gyer."

Sofia gave a start, suddenly remembering that her father had spoken of a boy. She looked at the maids, afraid that they were listening and would discover the lad, but they were already watching him.

"Have no fear," Domnal said in a calm, serious manner, "they know, and are willing to help us. Without their aid and that of some of Sir Griel's soldiers, I could not have come to you this easily."

Sofia stared at him, uncomprehending. "What do you mean?" she demanded. "What are you saying? They're *helping* you?"

He nodded. "We have been fortunate to discover friends within the castle. Sir Griel has not been a master to command loyalty."

"Nay, he is not," she agreed at once. "But what of Lord John? Is he safe?"

"He is well," the boy replied, "and escaped from Maltane. He will be back at camp by now, making his report to Sir Alexander and the others, Sir Kayne among them."

He was the most solemn boy that Sofia had ever beheld. He looked as if a smile had never touched his lips in all his life.

"Kayne is well?" she asked. At his curt nod she said, "Thank a merciful God. I have lived in dread, since they killed Sir Gwillym...."

Domnal's brows lowered. "Sir Gwillym is not dead, but merely wounded."

"Not dead," Sofia murmured. "Are you certain? I saw him felled."

"He is alive, returned to Vellaux, to which place his parents and brothers have been fetched."

Tears of relief stung Sofia's eyes. "Oh, thank God," she said. "Thank God."

She reached out and tried to take Domnal's hands, a gesture of simple thanksgiving, but he stiffened and pulled free.

"We do not have much time," he told her. "Only one of the guards at your door is with us, and the other will become suspicious if I do not come out soon. You must listen to all I have to say, mistress, and listen well. On the morrow you play your part, and on the day after, you must be ready for all that is to come. First, we will speak of your marriage to Sir Griel."

Chapter Twenty

The attack came in two days, rather than three, in the very midst of Sofia's marriage ceremony.

Though perhaps it could not truly be called a marriage ceremony. Sir Griel had forcibly dragged Sofia all the way from her chamber, dressed in naught but her chemise, into Maltane's small chapel and thrown her to her knees before the priest, who stood at the altar, hastily dressed in all his finery, so pale and frightened and trembling that Sofia thought he would faint at any moment. Sir Griel, too, was trembling, as he stood over Sofia holding his long, sharp dagger. The fist in which the knife was clutched swayed back and forth, back and forth, ready—perhaps even wanting—to strike.

She had spent all of the previous day with the same deadly blade held over her head, her constant companion as she labored on the two missives that Sir Griel had instructed her to write. Opposite her, sitting at another table, the priest had served as witness to the act, wisely agreeing with Sir Griel that Sofia had written the documents of her own free will.

Both inside and outside the castle on that day, preparations for war had continued, loud in Sofia's ears as she'd

carefully scratched out with quill and ink each word Sir
Griel spoke. There had been neither rest nor sustenance
until she had finished the exacting, time-consuming task,
and it was quite late when all was done to Sir Griel's satisfaction. He snatched the documents aside and instructed
his soldiers to return Sofia to her chamber, reminding her
that they would be wed early on the following morn, and
that she was to be ready to receive him, fully clothed in
the elegant surcoat he had chosen for her to wear. His intention, she knew, was that the ceremony be as grand as
possible, even in the midst of a siege, with all his castlefolk
in attendance, as well as his most favored soldiers. They
would serve as witnesses, in future, should there be any
question of the propriety of the ceremony and the willingness of the bride.

But Sir Griel had not considered that the attack might
come not only a day early, but while 'twas still early morn
and very dark. Domnal and the two maids had arrived in
Sofia's chamber with the object of secreting her to a safe
place, but Sir Griel had been alerted to the sudden attack
much sooner than anyone had suspected he would be, and
had burst into Sofia's chamber knife in hand, utterly ignoring the others as if he didn't see them at all. His eyes
alive with fear and desperation, he strode forward and took
hold of Sofia, dragging her out of the chamber, her long
hair streaming behind her as she stumbled along in order
to keep pace with the frantic madman.

Loud shouts of confusion and the clattering of boots running in every direction penetrated the thick castle walls, but
the fighting would be confined to the outer and inner bailey
for a time. Gaining entrance to the castle itself, which was
guarded by Sir Griel's most trusted soldiers, would be a far
more difficult matter.

The small chapel was not separate from the castle itself,

as was oftentimes the case, but located in a wing off the great hall and reached through a short, wide passageway. The only doors were two ornate and elegant, deep-red velvet curtains which had been parted to allow admittance, and then, as soon as all were present, tightly shut once more. The chapel itself was grimly lit by the light of a single torch, fixed near the altar to show the priest, who had been summoned but a few minutes earlier.

As Sir Griel dragged Sofia forward down the center of the cold stone chamber, she saw that the chapel walls were lined by some of Sir Griel's men, their faces shadowed in darkness, but small flickers of light gleaming from the armor they wore. They were dressed for battle, ready and waiting.

Now, kneeling before the priest in the place where Sir Griel had thrown her, her hands pressed flat against the smooth, icy floor, Sofia strove to slow both her heightened breathing and the rapid pace of her heart. She was frightened, but, strangely, not trembling. Kayne was coming for her. He might even now be inside the castle walls, fighting his way toward her. And Domnal had vowed that he would not desert her even if the fighting came lapping at their very feet. Now, Sofia knew that she herself must stay calm and think clearly. This was the only advantage she held over Sir Griel, who was breathing so harshly and was so clearly unnerved that his voice shook badly even as he shouted at the priest to begin the ceremony.

The priest began to recite something in Latin, mumbling his way through the words, while outside in the great hall the sounds of confusion and terror grew ever louder. Sofia could hear tables being knocked over and dragged across the rushes laid out on the floor. A woman screamed and a man shouted back at her just as loudly. Through it all, the priest strove to speak.

"Faster!" Sir Griel shouted at him. "Wed us!" The knife in his hand began to move at a more rapid pace, gleaming in the torchlight. Sofia dared to lift her head enough to glance upward and saw it there, rocking back and forth like a pendulum, the tip of the needlelike blade pointed downward, aimed directly at her.

"Wh-what is your intention t-toward this w-woman?" the priest asked in a shaking voice.

"I will have her as my wife," Sir Griel replied bluntly.

"What is your intention—" the priest turned his gaze upon Sofia, kneeling yet on the ground, and swallowed loudly "—your intention toward this man?"

Sofia knew what Griel wanted her to say—knew that she had to say the words to save her life—but she could not. She opened her mouth to utter the lie, knowing fully that no man present could swear before God that she had done so willingly, but her tongue was frozen. How could she speak aloud that she wanted Sir Griel for her husband? She despised him beyond all knowing.

"Say it," Sir Griel said, his voice filled with the madness that had now possessed him. All about them the battle noises raged more loudly. Above Sofia's head, the knife in Sir Griel's hand swung dangerously closer. *"Say it!"*

"Father, I beg your forgiveness!"

The words came from the velvet curtains, which were fumblingly pulled aside to admit a boy who was dressed in white robes similar to those the priest wore. He rushed in, nearly tripping over the robe's long skirts, running his fingers desperately through his long, dark hair to straighten it. Everyone had turned at the intrusion, and each soldier had set his hand upon his sword, but at seeing that it was merely an altar boy late in coming to serve the priest in the marriage rites, they relaxed and laughed among themselves. Sir Griel growled with acute fury as the boy stumbled up to the altar, yet muttering apologies for being so late in coming to tend his duties.

"Forgive me," Domnal said, moving about the small dais on which the holy elements were kept, "forgive me." He kept moving and talking, rushing about to fulfill the duties of an altar boy, while Sofia stared in amazement. No one else seemed to realize that the clothes the boy wore didn't fit him at all. No one realized that his hair was untrimmed and his face filthy—as surely no altar boy's would be.

Domnal kept moving, his back turned to them now and hands busy rearranging religious objects which Sofia was certain he knew nothing about. He had just picked up a large, spiky candlestick and walked it to the other side of the dais when Sir Griel roared, "No more foolishness! Make your vows, Sofia! *Now!*"

Sofia felt every gaze save Domnal's held upon her; her own gaze was held fast on him. He moved so swiftly that she didn't understand what he'd done until it was nearly over. Picking up the candlestick once more he swung about and, without a moment's hesitation, stabbed Sir Griel directly in the stomach with it. Giving a grunt of pain, her captor fell backward toward the ground. In the same fluid movement, Domnal dropped the candlestick and bent to pull Sofia up from where she knelt.

She stumbled to the dais with the roar of angry voices rising up from Sir Griel's men loud in her ears. The next moment two things happened at precisely the same time. The priest fainted dead away, slithering to a heap upon the dais, and Domnal reached up, snatched the torch from its place on the wall, and doused it in the baptismal, throwing the chapel into darkness and utter confusion.

"Come!" Domnal shouted, the long, lean fingers of one hand clasped tightly about her wrist. "This way!"

They ran not to the velvet curtains, which Sofia heard some of Sir Griel's men clattering toward with the intent of barring their way, but in the opposite direction, farther up the dais. The rest of Sir Griel's men—though some surely must have gone to aid their fallen master—were fast finding their way up to the altar, throwing aside everything that got in their way.

Domnal came to an abrupt halt, slapping his hand along one wall with such force that Sofia heard it clearly. At last, uttering a sound of triumph, he found what he was looking for, and pushed wide a door that Sofia had not earlier seen there. Pulling her through into yet more darkness, he quickly slammed the door shut once more and threw the bolt that was on their side—and just in time, for the next second one of Sir Griel's men pushed at the heavy wooden portal with such violence that it shook.

"They'll be through soon," Domnal stated. "Hurry."

He took her hand and pulled Sofia along.

"Where are we?" she whispered.

"It leads to the priest's private quarters. But Griel's men will realize that soon and hurry around the other way to meet us through the main door. We must be quick."

"Has Kayne come into the castle?"

"I've had no time to discover it, if he has," the boy replied. "I've been too busy trying to get you away from Griel to do anything else. I've no doubt my own master, Sir Aric, is here. He's ever the first in a battle." He spoke with obvious pride.

"Did you kill Sir Griel?"

He uttered an unholy laugh. "Nay, but I wish I had. 'Twould have been far better for us. Look. The priest's quarters."

There was a door ajar at the end of the short tunnel, and light spilled in through the darkness. Behind them, Sofia heard a heavy, single thump at the door of the chapel, and the sound of wood cracking. Voices were shouting in every direction, but she could not tell whether they were friend or foe.

They came to the open door and she could see Domnal's grimy face at last, intent and determined, a finger set to his lips, warning her to be quiet as he peered slowly around the opening to see if it was safe to enter. A tug at her hand pulled her along and into the bright glow of what she thought, at a cursory glance, must be a study. Huddled near the room's main door were several of the castle servants, including her own two maids, who gave a momentary start of gladness at seeing her safe, only to fall immediately into fear once more.

"Where is Sir Griel?" one of them asked Domnal. "You swore to keep us safe!"

Domnal, still holding Sofia's hand, replied very matter-of-factly, "This is not the place. He is fast on our heels, and many of his men. When they come, send them after us and speak the truth to save your lives, else come with us now and take your chances, as we shall do. Once you are out of the castle, find any man wearing the blue and gold of Havencourt and declare that by Domnal's word you have thrown yourself upon the mercy of my master, Sir Aric of Havencourt. You will be taken safely out."

Without waiting for an answer, he moved across the chamber toward another door, dragging Sofia after him, and for the first time she took note of just how tall he was— some inches taller than she was, in fact—and how long his legs were. She stumbled in her chemise, striving to keep pace with his greater strides.

He seemed to know the castle as if he'd lived there all his life. The first door led them to another short hallway, into an elegant bedchamber, and a similar door led to a private praying chamber. Here there was a small, but very beautiful, stained glass window which came nearly down to the floor, depicting Christ upon the cross.

"Stand by the wall and cover your face with your hands," Domnal commanded, releasing at last the grasp he'd held on Sofia. She did as he bade, then watched as he calmly bent to take up a heavy wooden chair from the floor and throw it mightily into the window, covering his head with one arm as the glass shattered into thousands of pieces about them.

Sunlight, which had only just begun to fill the inner bailey, streamed into the small chamber. The absent glass revealed an herb garden outside, and several men in armor already fighting there, trampling the innocent plants. They all stopped but briefly to take note of the strange happening, but seemed not to care at all that Domnal, standing so near the now missing window, stared back at them, and shortly returned to their fights. With a candlestick, Domnal knocked out the few remaining shards that clung to the window frame, and then motioned for Sofia to come forward.

"Hurry." He helped her to make the short leap from the room out into the garden. She wore only soft slippers, but miraculously didn't cut herself even as she landed in the soft mixture of glass and mud below. Domnal leapt after her. As he gained his balance, he took her elbow in one hand and nodded back at the window.

"Look."

She did, and saw the servants who'd been hidden in the chamber leaping out behind them.

"Find the blue and gold of Havencourt!" Domnal shouted in reminder, even as he pulled Sofia toward a nearby outer stairway. The servants ran toward the garden gate, one by one as they gained their feet, right into the midst of battle and what seemed to Sofia a sea of fighting men. Struggling against Domnal's insistent grip, she sought to see Kayne's blond head among them—though they were all helmeted, and she knew it to be a useless attempt.

"Where are we going?" she asked with aggravation as they began to climb the stairs. "I want to find Kayne!"

"Sir Griel's men have orders to kill you, should they see that you've escaped, and we're fortunate that these in the priest's garden have been kept so busy, else they'd have surely made the attempt by now." He pulled her upward, hardly waiting for her to gather up the skirt of her chemise to keep from tripping upon it. "There will be some fighting on the roof, but 'twill be far safer than in the castle or baileys. I know of a place where we can hide 'til the fighting is done. Hurry!"

The place to hide turned out to be a low wall that ran just behind the stairs as they emptied out onto the roof, providing a small space between that wall and the parapet that ran the length of the castle's rooftop. For fifteen minutes or more, Domnal pressed Sofia into this small area, placing himself on the outside to protect her. They crouched together, listening to the fighting as it took place all around them, and even watching it, a time or two, as soldiers ran by and engaged in battle mere feet away from them. Anyone who looked behind the stairwell, however, only saw Domnal crouched there. He made certain of that, much to Sofia's discomfort. But as the fighting began to dim, he allowed her to peek over the parapet and view the activity that was taking place in the bailey below.

Sofia had never seen such a sight. Everything was trampled in the bailey, utterly ruined. It was a mass of mud and blood and many bodies lying about. Sofia didn't know how many were dead, or if any could be saved. She looked at them and felt a hot, searing guilt. How could she ever be forgiven for causing so many to be harmed, even to die, for her sake?

"The main fighting is done now," Domnal told her as they both peered over the ledge. "I must go to find my master. Stay here and keep your head down."

Sofia grabbed his sleeve. "I want to go with you!" she said fiercely. "Kayne will be looking for me."

Domnal's expression gave nothing away as he pried her fingers loose. "I'll send him to you," he said, "but until Griel is captured, you must not show your face."

He disappeared down the stairs, still wearing the altar boy's robes and looking ridiculous.

Sofia sat back into the dark safety of their hiding place and closed her eyes. Soon, it would all be over. She would be with Kayne again, and safe from Sir Griel forever.

There was still a great deal of noise and activity below, but the sounds were far different than those of the fighting that had earlier taken place. Now there were shouts striving to bring the men back under some measure of command, to organize and confine whatever prisoners had been taken, to carry the wounded back to the camp, to capture horses that were running loose and tie them up. Among the shouts, Sofia thought she heard Kayne, and pushed back up to her knees to peer over the parapet once more.

Silently, she searched the large courtyard below, filled with men, women and activity, but saw no sign of Kayne.

Where could he be? Domnal had been gone for far longer than she'd have thought necessary. Something must be wrong. The idea had Sofia rising to her feet and turning— just in time to keep from being grabbed by the hand that Sir Griel had put out toward her.

With a shriek both of fear and surprise, Sofia dodged away, scraping her back along the low parapet wall. She dashed headlong, managing to evade Sir Griel's clumsy attempts to catch her. At last, standing in the midst of the roof, he gave way and fell still.

Sofia put a goodly distance between them before turning, her back against the opposite parapet wall now, and stared at him.

He looked half-dead already, swaying upon his feet, the slender knife yet clutched in the same hand that it had been held in an hour before. The early-morning sun revealed the exhaustion upon his dark face, in his dark eyes. His tunic, in the place where Domnal had struck him with the candlestick, was matted with blood. His breathing was an audible thing, gasping and clearly labored.

"I've come," he said, struggling as if the words were hard to speak, "to throw myself from the rooftop. All is lost."

Sofia watched him closely, ready to run away again if he came too near. She prayed Kayne would come soon.

"I've never," he said, panting as he spoke, "favored death by fire or the blade." He took one unsteady step toward her, striving to maintain his balance. "But I will have the death of my own choosing. Come, Sofia." He held a trembling hand out to her. "You will go with me. My bride. My wife. In life and death. Come."

Slowly, she shook her head and moved farther away along the length of the wall. There were no stairs in this direction, but she dared not go forward and bring herself closer to Griel. He appeared to be very weak, but there was strength in him yet.

The knife in his hand began to swing back and forth again, as it had done in the chapel, and his lips twisted upward into a sickening grin.

"Come, now," he said, moving toward her, swaying from side to side like a drunken man. "Come, Sofia." He began to laugh as he neared her, utterly maddened.

Sofia kept moving backward, stumbling, holding her gaze on Sir Griel and not seeing where she went. He laughed the louder and began to move more quickly, saying, over and again, "Come! Come, Sofia!"

"Sofia! Stop!"

Domnal's fierce cry arrested Sofia's retreat. She spun about to find herself only two steps from the roof's ledge, in an open space where there was no half wall to stop her from tumbling over. Now there was nowhere to run.

She whirled about to find Sir Griel still coming toward her, laughing and swinging the knife. Behind him a blur of figures were shouting and running, Domnal ahead of them all. The boy leapt at Griel, bringing him down to the rooftop, rolling over and over as the burly man struggled to be free. Sofia stared in horror as Griel came to the top and lifted his hand, holding the knife high. It was her own scream she heard as the shining blade was brought down into Domnal's arm, which the boy had flung up to ward off the killing blow.

Sir Senet's hard fingers closed over Sofia's shoulder, pulling her back from the danger of the ledge with a shout of words that she couldn't decipher, and at the same moment Sir Aric plucked Sir Griel off Domnal and physically tossed him through the air. He landed heavily on the rooftop, several feet away. While Sir Aric knelt to tend Domnal, Lord John unsheathed his sword and approached Sir Griel with the clear intention of killing him.

"John! Wait!" Sir Senet was dragging Sofia across the rooftop, toward the stairs. "I'll not have Mistress Sofia see it." He took her to the first step, saying, "Kayne is searching for you below. Go and find him."

"But," Sofia said, and sobbed, suddenly realizing that she was weeping, "Domnal..."

"He's not dead, by God," Sir Senet told her with im-

patience. "And he's not going to die. Aric will see to that."
He was covered with blood and sweat and grime, and
looked as if he'd be just as glad to throw her down the
stairs as let her go on her own. "Go to Kayne," he told
her, making it a command, "and if you love him keep him
below. He means to kill Griel himself. Do you understand
me?"

Trembling, Sofia nodded.

"Then *go*," he said in a voice that allowed no disobe-
dience.

Sofia took note, and turned about, fleeing down the stairwell.

Chapter Twenty-One

Kayne had known fear before, and panic and terror and every kind of overwhelming and unpleasant emotion. But he had never before felt what he was feeling now, standing in the midst of the great hall at Maltane, unable to find either Sofia or Sir Griel.

He'd chosen his best men to scour the castle, searching every chamber, every closet, every nook where a body might hide. He'd questioned servants and as many of Sir Griel's vanquished knights as could still reasonably speak, but each of them knew either too little or nothing at all. He'd been taken to the filthy pit that Sofia had been held prisoner in for five days, and the fine chamber where Griel had decided to put her in following the arrival of Sir Alexander and his army, but these gave no clue as to where she might be.

Now he stood in the hall, filled with dread, unable to stop visions of Sir Griel committing murder, and waiting for Senet, John and Aric to report what they and their men had found following their search of the outer castle, the walls and rooftops. Somehow he managed to continue on as the captain of his men, more from force of habit than anything else. He shouted out commands regarding the care of those who were too wounded to be sent back to the camp, and directed those servants who had remained to set up pallets along one wall and fetch water and linen cloths.

Physicians from the camp would be coming soon, hopefully before many more died. Almost all of the wounded were Sir Griel's men. Very few from the assembled armies who'd come for Sofia had been harmed, and fewer killed. For that, Kayne was very thankful. God had indeed been merciful in the taking of the castle, in more ways than Kayne could number.

But where was Sofia? Why was there no sign of her?

"My lord?"

He turned to see two of his men leading a man in white robes toward him—a priest, pale and shaking and unsteady on his feet.

"What is it?"

"My lord, this is Father Harold. We found him in the chapel, fainted amidst a great disarray. He says that Sir Griel sought to force Mistress Sofia to wed with him early this morn, even as the attack on the castle took place."

Kayne thought of the missive Sir Alexander had received from Sir Griel the night before, written in Sofia's own hand and stating that she had willingly agreed to become Sir Griel's wife. Sir Alexander had let Kayne and the others read it before he had ripped it to small pieces and thrown it into the fire. His only statement had been that Sir Griel would pay dearly for forcing a lady to write such disgusting lies, and that he hoped Griel believed the false note that had been left for him. If he did, he would be making wedding preparations rather than preparations for war, and that was exactly what Sir Alexander desired.

Kayne reached out to grasp the older man's shoulder, for he looked as if he might faint again, asking, "What happened to Mistress Sofia? Where did Sir Griel take her?"

The priest shook his head. "A boy," he said in a trembling voice. "An altar boy…I never saw him before, for he is not one of the lads who helps me. I never saw him…I swear it before God…"

"A boy?" Kayne shook him lightly. "Dark-haired? He came to Mistress Sofia's aid?"

The priest's eyes grew wide with remembrance. "He struck Sir Griel down and put the torch out…in the baptismal." He looked at Kayne with horror. "God's mercy. The *baptismal*. How could he have done such a thing? I saw it there with my own eyes just now. It's a sacrilege."

"You, stay with him," Kayne instructed one of the soldiers. "Give him some wine and find a comfortable place for him to lie down. You—" he nodded to the other man "—take me to the chapel where you found him."

It took but moments for Kayne to realize and admire Domnal's scheme. He followed the path from the broken door at the back of the chapel down the short hallway and into the priest's quarters. From there it was a simple matter of making their way into the prayer chamber, and finding the broken window.

"Clever lad," he murmured as he leapt down to the garden below, landing amidst the glass and now trampled plants. He looked about, wondering which direction the boy would go.

There was blood on the ground, evidence that fighting had taken place. It was unlikely that Domnal would take Sofia out into the battle.

Kayne turned and saw the outer stairway, and knew at once that this had been their course. He began to run up the winding steps, one hand on his sword, intent upon reaching the rooftop as quickly as he could. The last thing he expected was to turn a corner and find himself running headlong into a soft, slender body encased in a cloud of white cloth with long golden hair falling all about her.

"Oh!" Sofia cried, striking Kayne full length and falling back against his greater height and bulk.

"Sofia!" His hands flew out to grasp her before she might fall upon the stairs, only just managing to take hold of her fingers and pull her up to him. "Sofia! My God! What do you do here?"

He gave her no chance to answer, but crushed her hard against himself. Her arms lashed tightly about his armor and she pressed even nearer.

"Kayne, thank God I've found you!"

"I've searched everywhere…. Are you well? Let me look at you." He took her face in his hands and tilted it upward, gazing at her searchingly. "He gave you no harm?"

"Nay." She shook her head. "He was too afraid of Sir Alexander's threats to touch me."

"Thank God," he murmured fervently. "Thank a merciful God. I saw the pit he kept you in, Sofia, but hoped he had visited no greater harm upon you. I vow, I can hardly think, holding you now." He felt as if he might laugh and weep all at the same moment. "I prayed only for this moment, to have you safe again. I've lived in torment knowing you were here and beneath his hand."

He lowered his mouth and kissed her, long and fully, uncaring of where they were or what was taking place around them. Then he pulled away and smiled and stroked the hair from her face, and then kissed her again and again. They laughed like two children, touching each other's faces with gentle fingertips, kissing, smiling and weeping with joy and relief. It was the strangest and most wonderful happiness Kayne had ever known.

"I knew you would come for me," she told him, giddy and light headed. "I never doubted it."

"You're my wife," he said, touching her nose with his own, "my love, my joy. I would not have left you, not even for the sake of my own life. I will no longer wait until we reach Vellaux to be fully wed. On the morrow, we will be married at the chapel door, for one and all to see, and after that, I care not where we go or how we live, whether it be in a smithy in Wirth or the estate of Vellaux. So long as you are with me, Sofia, all sorrows are put away."

"We will live in whatever place will make you happy, Kayne," she said, "just as I told you before."

"Then it does not matter to either of us," he said, and laughed and hugged her. "I hold all that I care for in my arms, and will not let her go again."

"Kayne, are there many wounded?" she asked, looking up at him, her eyes filling with the seriousness of all that had occurred. "I must go and tend all those who may benefit from my small skills. I do not have my medicines, but mayhap someone could ride to Ahlgren Manor and fetch them?"

He nodded. "It will be done. But first, I must deal with Sir Griel. Where is he?" He glanced at the rooftop from where she had come. "And where is Domnal? He hid you above?"

"Aye, and very well," she assured him. "But as to Sir Griel, he is dead."

Kayne stared at her. "Dead?"

She nodded.

"But how can you know? Is he…" His gaze lifted to the rooftop, and he took Sofia's arm with the intention of leading her back upstairs.

But she resisted his gentle pulling, and put herself in front of him to stop him.

"Nay, Kayne, do not. He is dead. You must believe what I say."

"How so?" he demanded, suspicion filling his thoughts. "I must see it for myself."

"You do not trust your lady wife, then?" came Senet's voice. He was descending the stairs, but not yet visible to them. "That is not a good manner in which to begin a marriage. I advise you by my own experience, Kayne, to believe every word she says and never argue."

He stepped around the corner, looking weary and hot. His sword, which he held in his hand, was covered with blood.

"Where's Griel?" Kayne demanded.

Senet looked at him levelly. "On the rooftop. He's dead."

"You killed him?"

John came into view, stopping just in back of Senet. His sword, too, was red with blood.

"It matters not, Kayne," John said. "Griel is dead, and Mistress Sofia has been fully avenged, as is right and just."

"But his death was to be *mine*," Kayne told them angrily. "Such vengeance was my right to claim."

Sofia set a hand on his arm and said, softly, "Nay, Kayne."

"He is dead," Senet said, "and we cannot truly say by whose hand, for the three of us had our share. If you must have a part in more death, then go above and destroy what is left of him. For now, we must move quickly. Aric is bringing Domnal, who is bleeding grievously."

At those words, they did move quickly. Kayne led the way into the great hall, shouting orders for a pallet to be made ready, and Sofia rushed to find whatever she could to clean and bind the boy's wound with. Sir Aric, looking very grim, carried Domnal across the hall to the place

Kayne had prepared for him, and laid him gently upon the waiting pallet.

He was very pale, Sofia saw as she knelt beside him, and his mouth set in a grim, stubborn line.

"I'm no babe to be coddled!" he said angrily as she cut his garments away with the dagger Kayne had given her.

"I am very glad to know this," Sofia told him as she inspected the gash in his arm. It was deep and bleeding copiously. She pressed hard upon it to slow the bleeding, knowing full well it could not be stopped in this manner. "Then you will not mind my sewing your flesh together to stop this blood flow."

He grew even paler, and the fingers of his well arm curled more tightly about Sir Aric's hand, which held him. But he licked his lips and said, as if daring her to do it, "Nay, I'll not!"

She had already threaded the needle for the work, and began to wash the wound as thoroughly as she could to better see what needed to be sewn.

"You are braver than many men, Domnal," she told him as she took the needle up. "I have known many to faint dead away at the very thought. You may weep, if you like, without shame. I have seen famed knights do so. I have no doubt Sir Aric has shed tears o'er such pain."

"That I have," he admitted, gazing down at the boy. "Hold tight to me now, Domnal, and cry out if you must, but lie still. I will make you insensible, if you wish it."

Domnal shut his eyes and squeezed his master's hand so tightly that both their fingers turned white.

"Nay," he said. "I will be still."

He did as he promised, though Sofia knew the boy suffered great pain at her hands. When it was done, she wrapped his arm in clean linen, wiped his sweat-soaked face with a cool, damp cloth and gave him a drink of water.

"Now, sleep," she told him, and gathered her things to move on to the next wounded man.

Kayne took her place. Domnal looked up at him through weary eyes, half closed. He yet clutched Aric's hand for comfort.

"You have done well," he told the boy, "and I owe you a debt of gratitude. When you have finished your training at Havencourt, come to me and I will make you captain over my armies at Vellaux."

Domnal's eyes began to drift shut. "I will come," he murmured, then added, yawning, "Will you have a daughter? With Mistress Sofia?"

Kayne exchanged amused glances with Aric. The boy had become foolish with pain and exhaustion.

"Many, I pray."

"Will she look like Mistress Sofia?"

"Most likely."

Domnal let out a long, sleepy, sighing breath.

"Then I will come, my lord, and serve you well."

The next moment, he was fast asleep, and did not hear the laughter that his master and Kayne shared.

Chapter Twenty-Two

Sofia rose early, much refreshed from the long sleep she'd had, and quietly slipped from bed. The smooth wooden boards beneath her bare feet were cool, but pleasantly so. The room itself was warm from the fire in the hearth, much at odds with the chilly rain that fell outside. Sofia moved to stand beside one of the thickly plated windows, watching as the steady droplets streamed down the glass, making the view even more indistinguishable than before.

Soon it would be winter, and these would be snowflakes rather than raindrops. The journey to Vellaux would be a miserable one, most likely, but it would be undertaken, nonetheless. Lord Renfrow was eager to see his son again, and Kayne desired the return, as well. He had lost his dislike of becoming a nobleman in the past many days. Now, he wanted only to spend what time his father had remaining in learning all that he must in order to be a good and competent lord. Sofia had no doubt that he would be both, but it would mean a great deal to both Lord Renfrow and Kayne to have that time together, to know each other and learn from each other. And if Sofia had her way, she would seek Lady Katharine Gaillard's advice on Lord Renfrow's state of health and discover a way of prolonging his life.

She wanted her children to know their grandfather, but more, she wanted Kayne and Lord Renfrow to reclaim the years that had been lost to them.

So much had changed in the past few days. Sofia had changed. She was twenty years of age now, and had received her mother's inheritance, including a small estate of her own in the northern part of England. She did not know if she would ever even set sight upon the place, but it was good to have something of her own—her very own, which no one could take from her and which she could give to her children.

More than that had changed. She was now a married woman, truly married, blessed in union before a priest and many onlookers, with her father standing beside her. Sir Justin Baldwin had stood with Kayne, and behind him all of Kayne's dear friends, Sir Senet, Sir Aric and Lord John. There had been a fine and merry feast at Ahlgren Manor afterward, greatly honored by the attendance of Sir Alexander and his brother, Sir Hugh, who had not only grabbed Sofia up and kissed her full on the lips, but also claimed her for several dances.

Sofia had tried to tender her thanks to her rescuers, but they had all refused to hear them, most especially Sir Alexander, whose face took on such a look of affront as she'd bumbled through her speech that Sofia had finally stopped speaking and given up. He'd relented, as well, and kindly patted her shoulder and reassured her that gratitude was not necessary. Then he invited her to dance, and proved to be much less wild and carefree in that undertaking than Sir Hugh had been.

Sound coming from the bed caused Sofia to glance back and see Kayne sitting up, yawning and stretching. The covers fell down to reveal his scarred, muscular body, and she gazed at him with appreciation. His physical scars he would carry forever; Sofia had traced each one with her fingertips over the past few days, time and again, and knew where each one lay. How strange that she should find such evidence of war so enticing, but perhaps that was because he had received those wounds and yet come away alive. They were proof of his courage and skill, and of his will to survive. None of them had held the power to take him from her.

Kayne saw her standing by the window and, naked, slid out of bed to join her. His warm arms enfolded her from behind, cradling her in his embrace. Sofia leaned back against the heat of his chest and felt his cheek nestle against the top of her hair.

"I have become slothful since wedding you, Sofia," he said. "I should have been up this past hour and more, I vow. The cattle will need caring for, and there is yet work to do in the smithy. I must have everything done before we leave."

They had come, after the wedding, to Kayne's house in the village, and here they had lived. The two men whom Sir Aric had sent to care for the dwelling and for Kayne's animals had done well, but they had possessed no smithing skills, and the work which Kayne had left unfinished yet remained. Now, after so long an absence, he was striving to finish the custom he had so unhappily abandoned, and to make the smithy ready for a new blacksmith to take his place. Sir Justin had promised to send a young man from among his fostered lads who had proven to be far more skilled at smithing than in the ways of war, and Kayne had agreed to not only give him the smithy and dwelling and all his cattle—save Tristan—but also enough funds to make a start.

The young man was to arrive within a week's time, and Kayne and Sofia spent much of their days in preparation of this. It would be, most likely, the only time during their married lives when they would live so simply and peacefully. Once they were at Vellaux, Sofia would take up again the many tasks of managing a large household and many servants, also of overseeing the well-being of all of Kayne's people, and Kayne would find himself immersed in first learning all that he required, and then in being master of Vellaux. Sofia was not dismayed at what must be, but she knew that these few short days spent with Kayne in this simple dwelling would be among the most precious she would ever know.

"I used to imagine being here with you," she told him, sliding one hand gently across the arms about her waist. "I used to wonder what it would be like to share that bed with you, to lie next to you and awake beside you each morn."

She felt him smile against the top of her head. "Did you? What lustful, wicked thoughts, Mistress Sofia. The priest would lecture you most heartily should he ever know you entertained such imaginings. But, I confess, I was far more wicked. I thought of you lying with me—and of all else that we would do in that bed."

Sofia chuckled. "I pray that reality has not disappointed you, Master Kayne."

"Nay," he said, bending to kiss her ear, "far from it. It has been much better than anything I ever dreamt or imagined."

"For me, as well," she murmured, closing her eyes as his lips caressed her ear, her cheek, and moved lower to her neck. "I have never known such happiness. I wish we might remain here forever."

Kayne lifted his head. "We will, if you desire it."

"Nay, we will go to Vellaux, as we have planned. 'Tis what we both wish. And 'tis what is right."

With a sigh, he settled his cheek against the top of her

head again. "You speak truly. Sir Justin said a great deal to me about duty and honor while we waited to make our attack on Maltane. If I had not already known how foolish I had been, he would have made me understand it."

"What did he say to you?"

"Much that he had taught me before, when I was fostered with him. To my shame, I had forgotten it—or pushed it from my memory. But 'tis all true. He said that a man may do as he likes for his own sake, but that when the lives of others are involved, he must act only according to what is right and just. I had taken a vow never to kill again, and so long as my own life was concerned, that was well and fine. But to stand aside and let evil men bring harm to others, when I might stop it—that is equally evil." He sighed. "I do not desire to kill again. It grieves my soul even to think of it, but there are times when it is right and just to do so."

"Then you must vow only to act when 'tis right and just," she said, "and for no other cause, not even at the king's command."

"That is what Sir Justin bade me do, and advised me to write the king's regents and explain how it will be. If it is not acceptable, then I must pay dearly for the privilege of retaining my vow of fealty to the crown." He shrugged. "It is but gold, and worth the payment, if need be."

"Indeed, it is." Sofia's fingers ran up the sides of his arms, caressing, stroking. "I am glad that you had naught to do with Sir Griel's death."

"As am I. I admit that I was full angered with my friends for taking the duty from me, but now I am but grateful. They did not let me kill any man that day. Did I tell you of that?"

Sofia tilted her head to the side to look at him. "Nay, you did not."

He smiled. "They had decided upon it between themselves long before the siege even began. I vow they must have found the task burdensome indeed, for I was intent upon battle. But each man whom I approached with my sword was either taken from me by one of my friends, or I was pushed aside before the killing stroke was delivered. My sword was not bloodied once during the fight. 'Twas most foolish of them—for I had long since left aside my determinations—but it proved the manner of friendship we bear. When I think of it now, that they strove so mightily to keep me from knowing grief, I am near overcome. I have been greatly blessed to claim such friends. Indeed, Sofia, though I cannot know why, God has richly blessed me in many ways—by my friends, by my father and, most of all, by you. I do not deserve any of it, but I am thankful beyond measure."

Sofia turned in his arms and reached up on her toes to kiss him.

"I do not know whether any of us deserve so many good things," she murmured, "for I have done nothing in my life to receive so great a boon as becoming your wife. It was my greatest wish almost from the moment I knew you, Kayne. I loved you beyond all reason, but never believed God would heed my prayers. But he has, and I vow I will not let a day go by without being thankful."

"Nor I," he said, his hands warm on her waist, drawing her closer. "My beautiful bride, who was stolen from me and then by God's mercy and the love of my friends returned to me. Nay, I will never cease being thankful. I will spend what remains of my life cherishing you, Sofia, no matter where we may be." He lowered his head to kiss her. "Starting now."

"Your work awaits, Master Kayne," Sofia reminded,

murmuring against his lips, though she slid her arms about his neck to encourage him the more.

"It can wait, Mistress Sofia," he said. "First I must cherish my wife, well and fully, so that she knows how much I love her."

The rain continued to pour outside, the fire glowed gently in the hearth, and Sofia, content to be the object of such ardent convincing, gave no argument.

* * * * *

You're not going to believe this offer!

In October and November 2000, buy any two Harlequin or Silhouette books and save $10.00 off future purchases, or buy any three and save $20.00 off future purchases!

Just fill out this form and attach 2 proofs of purchase (cash register receipts) from October and November 2000 books and Harlequin will send you a coupon booklet worth a total savings of $10.00 off future purchases of Harlequin and Silhouette books in 2001. Send us 3 proofs of purchase and we will send you a coupon booklet worth a total savings of $20.00 off future purchases.

Saving money has never been this easy.

I accept your offer! Please send me a coupon booklet:

Name: _____

Address: _____ City: _____

State/Prov.: _____ Zip/Postal Code: _____

Optional Survey!

In a typical month, how many Harlequin or Silhouette books would you buy <u>new</u> at retail stores?

☐ Less than 1 ☐ 1 ☐ 2 ☐ 3 to 4 ☐ 5+

Which of the following statements best describes how you <u>buy</u> Harlequin or Silhouette books? Choose one answer only that <u>best</u> describes you.

☐ I am a regular buyer and reader
☐ I am a regular reader but buy only occasionally
☐ I only buy and read for specific times of the year, e.g. vacations
☐ I subscribe through Reader Service but also buy at retail stores
☐ I mainly borrow and buy only occasionally
☐ I am an occasional buyer and reader

Which of the following statements best describes how you <u>choose</u> the Harlequin and Silhouette series books you buy <u>new</u> at retail stores? By "series," we mean books within a particular line, such as *Harlequin PRESENTS* or *Silhouette SPECIAL EDITION*. Choose one answer only that <u>best</u> describes you.

☐ I only buy books from my favorite series
☐ I generally buy books from my favorite series but also buy
  books from other series on occasion
☐ I buy some books from my favorite series but also buy from
  many other series regularly
☐ I buy all types of books depending on my mood and what
  I find interesting and have no favorite series

Please send this form, along with your cash register receipts as proofs of purchase, to:
In the U.S.: Harlequin Books, P.O. Box 9057, Buffalo, NY 14269
In Canada: Harlequin Books, P.O. Box 622, Fort Erie, Ontario L2A 5X3

(Allow 4-6 weeks for delivery) Offer expires December 31, 2000.

PHQ4002

If you enjoyed what you just read,
then we've got an offer you can't resist!

Take 2 bestselling love stories FREE!

Plus get a FREE surprise gift!

SUSAN SPENCER PAUL

who also writes as Mary Spencer, lives in Monrovia, California, with her husband, Paul, an R.N., and their three daughters, Carolyn, Kelly and Katharine. She is the author of twelve historical novels set in a variety of time periods, and especially loves writing about the medieval and Regency eras.